THE
FORGER'S
INK

Also by Jo Mazelis

Diving Girls
Circle Games
Significance
Ritual, 1969
Blister & Other Stories

Photography

The Democratic Elvis

THE
FORGER'S
INK

JO MAZELIS

SEREN

Seren is the book imprint of
Poetry Wales Press Ltd
Suite 6, 4 Derwen Road, Bridgend,
Wales, CF31 1LH

www.serenbooks.com
Follow us on social media @SerenBooks

ISBN: 978-1-78172-432-3
Ebook: 978-1-78172-433-0

A CIP record for this title is available from the British Library.

The publisher acknowledges the financial assistance of the
Books Council of Wales.

EU GPSR Authorised Representative
Logos Europe, 9 rue Nicolas Poussin, 17000,
La Rochelle, France
E-mail: Contact@logoseurope.eu

Printed by CMP UK Ltd.

Map and illustrations © Jo Mazelis 2025.

Cover design: Jamie Hill 2025.

To Swansea and all who sail in her;
past, present and future.

SWANSEA

RIVER TAWE

to Penllergare

Hafod Copperworks

Ferrymans Cottage — White Rock

Cambrian Pottery

to Sketty

Wind St

SWANSEA BAY

PART ONE

1967-1971

'Now more than ever seems it rich to die,
To cease upon the midnight with no pain.'

From 'Ode to a Nightingale' by John Keats

FERRYMAN'S COTTAGE

1968

Judith Hopkins did not believe in ghosts.

Her life had been too full of real monsters to consider other, unseen forces. Her mother was long gone and she'd finally left her father to whatever demons possessed him – most, she was certain, came from the bottle, but as she had never known him sober how could she tell?

She changed her name, shortening it to Jude and that was a rebirth, a liberation.

She became Jude from the Beatles' song. Never Judy as in Punch and Judy the powerless object of unbridled rage.

As names went, Jude was best.

Hey Jude.

She had inherited a house. A ramshackle place with a jerry-built, glassed-in extension and a wild garden that ran down to the river. Her mother's father was born there and lived there until he and the house were both crippled nearly beyond redemption. Grandpa Powell had left his home and died at the hospital two days after being admitted. She never really knew him; had only a vague memory of a visit and someone (it must have been her mother) loudly weeping.

After leaving the solicitor's office on Walter Road, she'd walked through the grounds of the church opposite and into St James' Park where it was leafy and cool. She sat on a freshly painted wooden bench and stared at everything around her, unable to grasp what had just happened. The key to the house grew so warm in her hand that she could no longer feel it. She had to look to see if it was real.

She moved into Ferryman's Cottage the next day, certain her father would drag her back, certain a mistake had been made and the house was not hers. She remained as nervous as a rabbit in a hutch, only secure when nothing came to disturb her, but skittish whenever anyone, friend or foe came near.

She took to silence. A profound silence that grew deep inside the thick walls of the old cottage. She liked to imagine herself in another century. She made her little journeys into the modern world only to buy the necessities of life, the small loaves of bread, the tins of salmon and soup, the tiny jars of bloater paste, the jolly packets of Typhoo tea. Her clothes came from jumble sales.

On her sallies into world, she sat on benches wherever she found them, in parks and on the promenade or outside the old hospital, and from those places, with a book held open on her lap, she surveyed all she saw and began to notice how codes of dress marked people out. Particularly young people. Young men's hair grew longer, women's skirts got shorter and shorter, then just as abruptly dropped to floor length.

Women over a certain age still had their hair cut short and wore it permed in a crown of black or brown or yellow-blonde. Then when they were older their hair turned an honest grey, or naked white, or was rinsed in shades of blue, mauve or palest pink. Spectacles were either clunky black or tortoiseshell, or they grew wings. Children's National Health glasses were round and surgical pink or blue depending if for a boy or girl. Schoolboys wore shorts to school until they were fairly bristling with testosterone and stubble, while girls' growing bosoms were imprisoned in old-fashioned gymslips and shapeless blazers. Nurses wore navy wool capes with a scarlet lining, the bus conductor his cap. Nuns sailed by in clouds of black.

If anyone caught her eye or tried to speak to her, Jude lowered her head and read furiously, until they gave up and went away.

The old house, the ferryman's cottage, had been built in the seventeenth century and all its ghosts, or so she'd heard, were the drowned dead and they came squelching and dripping, fish-nibbled and green with slimy weeds out of the river. At night, strange sounds like lapping water or the cries of animals terrified her, but by daybreak these noises were once again made mute or banal. The water noise was just traffic on the nearby road or it was wind in the trees; what had sounded like the jangle and creak of oars was the milkman rattling his crates, the screams were seagulls calling. That was all.

The unearthly chill, the creeping damp, all had their rational sources, Jude told herself, but she felt helpless and did nothing to remedy them. One awful winter, a bout of flu turned into a chest infection and she lay for nearly a fortnight in her damp bed with her lungs clogged and rattling, certain she would die there alone. When, finally, a little of her strength returned, she went out. She was like a walking corpse, gasping for air, weak as a newborn kitten. One step, another step, another. She had to get to the shop, had to get bread and milk. Get sausages, get a slab of greasy cheese. A banana that she could eat immediately.

Her eyes were sunk in her face and the black shadows beneath them gave her the aspect of a prisoner in a concentration camp. Her hair was a mass of knots and tangles. Not that she'd looked in the mirror. She was still running a temperature, still half-mad with a fever.

On towards the shops she trudged. Outside the greengrocer's two prams were parked, a baby inside each. The sun was out, the sky blue with huge white clouds hanging in them. She drew level with the first of the prams, all black canvas and silvery suspension parts, with the hood turned up to protect its tiny passenger from the sun. Jude had been feeling giddy all the way, but moved forward, letting the momentum carry her. She stopped a moment to catch her breath before she entered the shop.

Once inside, while the assistant glared at her, she manged to say 'banana', then 'please.' No good, not saying please, even if she was dying. A whole bunch of bananas were placed on the scale and her request for just one was, after a moment's hesitation, disdainfully obeyed. The room was kaleidescoping around her and grew black at the edges. She paid and lurched out of the shop, misjudged the depth of the doorstep, reeled unsteadily. She was a sailor setting foot on dry land after months at sea. She was a girl again, stepping out of the carriage on the waltzers at the funfair after she'd been spun around and around, with the flashing lights above her and the pounding music blaring, her legs all gone to jelly. To stop herself from falling, she grabbed at the nearest solid thing, which was the black pram. No sooner had she touched it than a cry went up from inside the shop and Jude, letting go as if stung, fell to the ground, leaving the pram lurching and rocking above her on its springs.

When they realised she wasn't a baby-snatcher and neither drunk nor drugged, an ambulance was called. She was taken to hospital, where after nearly three weeks of sleep, food and antibiotics, she recovered.

'Forty years ago, you'd have been a goner!' the porter cheerfully told her. He was young and in between his other duties he made it his business to talk to everyone. 'If it wasn't for the miracle of penicillin, you'd be kaput, pushing up the daisies, six feet under, toast! You poor dab.'

'Shut up Eddie,' said a nurse. 'We don't talk about that, do we?'

'Nah, better not, eh? Touch wood.' He tapped his head. 'Back home today then, Miss. But don't forget, a 'undred years ago you'd be the dearly departed.'

Back at the cottage she took account of her life. It was true – she might have died of pneumonia. Or simply starved to death, if she hadn't found the strength to go out. A hundred years ago, two hundred years ago, nothing could have saved her. And what had she done with her life? Nothing, came the dire answer.

She remembered the sensation of her choked lungs as they filled with fluid. It must be like drowning, she thought. Like those ghosts who drifted up from the river at twilight. Her lungs opened for air and found only liquid. Her fever sent her wild, vivid dreams and these seemed to cling to her still. They came back in brief moments, very alive and nearly tangible.

She wanted to remember this. To remember how close she'd come to dying. She also wanted to be remembered. To not die alone with nothing to show for her miserable life. The only way of doing this was to leave a record. She would write everything down, but write it as if it had all been a hundred years ago. One hundred and fifty years ago.

THE STORYTELLER

She began one evening with a blue biro and a cheap reporter's note-pad. The pen produced nasty gobbets of ink that, if touched, smeared. It made what she wrote ugly and the pen dried up grad-ually too, so that parts of what she wrote grew fainter and fainter until there were only the traces of indentation from the tip. She searched the house and the first pen she found had green ink. She used that, then when that ran out, a red pen and finally a pencil. Five hours produced twenty pages of such utter ugliness that she almost wept. The next day, in despair and on the brink of throwing the pages away, she reread her words. It was hard to ignore the handwriting, the blue, green and red ink, the blurry pencil marks, the narrow blue lines on the paper, the smudges, but somehow rising from the ruins like a phoenix, she saw that her words had power.

Somehow in the scratch and scribble, the niggling frustration with the various pens (which was all she really remembered of the day before) something had emerged which, as words are wont to do, spoke to her. But the most remarkable thing was that she had the sense, the very strong sense, that the sentences, the ideas, the syntax belonged to a presence other than herself.

Yes, she had been the one scribbling the words. Yet it had been, she thought, with a mingled sensation of fear and joy, as if she had been taking dictation from another wiser being. A being who did not belong in the twentieth century with its oil spills, its transistor radios, its rumbling articulated trucks, its factories, its plastic every-thing, its pollution and nuclear reactors and atomic bombs. It was a voice from a purer age, nearly but not quite entirely innocent.

Jude looked up from the page, her gaze travelling over the room as if the author of these words might step forward at any moment and introduce herself. This author, or rather 'authoress', for Jude was in no doubt that the voice was a woman's, seemed, as all ghosts are said to be, an unhappy, restless spirit with unfinished business to settle.

Jude picked up the pencil and, turning to a fresh page, sat waiting for more words to come. She listened, straining at the silence in the room and inside her head. For half the morning it seemed, she sat with the pencil poised over the paper. She tried closing her eyes. Nothing. She opened them, sharpened the pencil and again waited. But still, the voice or the dream or whatever it was, evaded her.

What had happened yesterday? she wondered. What was different? It had been later in the day; by the time she had begun to write the sun was already low in the sky. As she'd worked, the light had faded until the paper seemed to turn grey, and even the red ink was drained of its colour. Then, when she'd got up to switch on the overhead light, the bulb had popped and so, lacking a replacement, she'd lit the candles in the old cast iron candelabra and set it on the table, where its warm yellow glow cast flickering shadows.

It was easy to imagine that something, some ancient unseen entity, had caused the electric light bulb to fail, forcing Jude to write by the source of illumination it was familiar with. Or was it simply a matter of atmosphere? The candlelight of romance and witchcraft and psychics and séances. Easy to think that something malevolent or otherwise had crept into the house and wrapped its wraith-like form around her in order to guide her hand. She almost saw it in her imagination, a vague form like a mist that, when she inhaled, was drawn like a trail of thin smoke into her nose and her mouth, and from there circulated to every part of her body, to her lungs, bloodstream, heart and brain.

She remembered all too well the difficulty with the pens and the light bulb, yet her thoughts as she wrote, her plan or ideas or inspiration, were now a blank. It was as if she had been in a trance.

She was still feverish, her head when she touched it with the back of her hand felt hot, but the exhaustion had passed. It was eleven o'clock, the day ahead seemed to wait for her, the sun was out and there was no wind. She would walk to town and besides the necessity of some money from the Post Office and some food, she determined to go to the reference library on Alexandra Road and see if she could discover anything about hauntings and possession.

Before that day, she had never dared to enter the reference library; now she stepped into the huge circular room and was awestruck by it. The central well was filled with long tables at which various scholars sat amid piles of books, some merely reading, others busy making notes. None looked up, or if they did it was only the near-blind momentary glance of someone whose mind was elsewhere. The curving walls were dense with shelves of books, and an upper level was reached by an ornate metal balcony. High above was a great domed ceiling that let in some light, though evidently not enough, as there was also electric lighting.

To her left was an information desk with a small office behind it. Noticing Jude, who had stepped only a few paces into the library, a man behind the thickly varnished wooden counter asked, in a voice that was not quite a whisper, 'Can I help you?'

She hesitated. Her impulse was to turn on her heels and run, but something, some new strength or trust in strangers, perhaps due to her recent hospital stay, or maybe it was this other being who had possessed her, made her say with unruffled confidence, 'Yes, I want to see any books you have on the supernatural.'

'Did you want something on local paranormal sightings?'

'Maybe.'

'I have a file here for just that – newspaper clippings, photostats, some handwritten notes. The haunted rectory at Rhossili, the ghost of Swansea Castle, the white lady of Oystermouth: suicide, sorrow, suspicion, all the usual palaver.'

He sat her at a table near the desk and brought her a manila folder filled with a jumble of papers. She had been unprepared for this, bringing neither a pen or paper to make notes. So, uncertain what she was doing, she looked through the material, glancing over the news story about the 'melancholy discovery' of an unknown woman and an apparent suicide note. In the margin someone had written 'is the reported ghost in Wind Street?' Jude's interest was wavering and self-conscious. She was reading while also pretending to read, aware of the other people in the room whom she assumed to be 'real' scholars, not scarecrow students like her.

Later, she bought her other bits and pieces – bacon from the market, a meat pie and a small Hovis from Eynon's, a new fountain pen and a bottle of Quink ink from WH Smith's as well as unlined writing paper. Walking through town, she caught sight of herself in shop windows. Her face had the appearance of a skull, gaunt with dark eyeless sockets, bone-white skin. No wonder the man in the library had stared at her.

Her appetite had, at last, come back. She went into Woolworth's on the High Street and headed upstairs to its vast cafeteria. She ordered sausage, egg and chips along with two pieces of bread and butter. The chips were pale and soggy but she ate ravenously without a hint of the self-consciousness that usually plagued her. She washed it all down with a good strong cup of tea in a white Pyrex cup.

Before leaving the shop, she bought a pack of household candles and some light bulbs. Her mind, or so it seemed, was already entering the trance-like state she remembered from the day before. The fact that it was probably just tiredness and the dwindling effects of her illness or the natural effects of eating a greasy, stodgy meal did not occur to her. She hurried for the bus, stared blankly at the cheery bus conductor when he tried to chat about the weather, her eyes going out of focus, then tearing up with weariness. She was shaky by the time she'd reached the cottage, her hands visibly trembling. After drawing the curtains, she lit the candle and filled the new pen with ink. Its weight was sacrosanct. She sensed it in the palm of her hand for a moment, then forgot about it as she began to scratch out a story.

The threads of her tale seemed to arise unbidden; she began to frighten herself as the story spooled out. Everything frightened her, although she'd never have admitted it. She was a coiled spring ready to run at the merest hint of danger.

She gathered up the pages, lit the gas ring, and one by one burned them, dropping them into the white enamel sink where they turned into brittle black flakes.

PART TWO

1967-1971

'Then up I rose,
And dragged to earth both branch and bough, with crash
And merciless ravage: and the shady nook
Of hazels, and the green and mossy bower,
Deformed and sullied, patiently gave up
Their quiet being'

From 'Nutting' by William Wordsworth

THE MUSHROOM GATHERER

Of course, people watched her.

They stood behind their privet hedges, their net curtains, their shop counters, and followed her with their eyes. Jude gave the impression of being oblivious, but she felt like Moses parting the Red Sea, a tide of turning heads following in her wake.

Today, with a red plastic shopping basket, Jude ducked into a copse of trees in search of shaggy inkcaps. The secret with these was to cook them within an hour or so of picking them. She planned to fry them in bacon fat along with a bit of stale bread. There was a piece of rough ground, a very secret place close to an abandoned industrial site, where they always grew. Once the mushrooms were gathered, the route back would provide handfuls of ramsons that she would throw into the sizzling pan near the end of cooking.

Anticipating the feast to come, Jude strode forward until a noise up ahead stopped her. Voices and a crashing, thrashing sound. Laughter. The hoarse, rogue voices of boys on the brink of manhood. Their talk so peppered with foul language there was hardly any normal word or meaning left. It was a school day, too. If they were as young as she suspected, they must be mitching. And if they were mitching off school, they'd be bored; bored to the point of trouble and until that trouble found you, you never knew the measure of it. The boys wouldn't know either. Not until it was too late and there was blood on their hands.

Jude turned, going stealthily at first, then faster, and went back the way she had come. Nothing, not even wild mushrooms, was worth entanglement with feral boys. She decided to make her apparent retreat into a planned and necessary trip of exploration. She made her way to the abandoned grounds of a big house; there was a silted-over pond, the broken-down walls of ruined cottages, fruit trees, greenhouses without a bit of intact glass remaining, stables and the remains of an arboretum. The stately home had long been razed to the ground, its carriageways and paths swallowed up by alien species that Victorian collectors of rhododendron, bamboo and Himalayan Balsam had planted.

After hours of fruitless wandering, alongside a meadow and a shallow stream, she found what she was looking for. The inkcaps were standing in the undergrowth like a meeting of be-wigged lawyers with white and ruffled heads. Some had passed their best; others, with their skirts not yet flaring open, were perfect. Yet she hesitated before cutting them. How long before they melted away to black slush? How long would it take her to get home? While she pondered this, she failed to notice the approach of an old man.

'They aren't poisonous, you know,' he informed her, barely breaking his stride.

'I know,' she called after him, her tone indignant. If he heard her, he showed no sign, but carried on along the side of the stream and went out of sight. Stubbornly, as if to prove a point, she cut five of the mushrooms low down on their stems and laid them in two rows in her basket like corpses. She carried on, following the remains of a lane. The route opened into the broad expanse of an overgrown meadow and at the furthest edge was an ancient oak tree with some stout branches low enough to climb. She quickened her pace in the direction of the tree, set her basket down and climbed easily onto the first low branch; she was looking for her next footing when she realised she was not alone.

It was the agitation of the furthest branches that alerted her; a rustling and a less than bird-like tugging. She followed the sound with her eyes and spotted a pair of sturdy boots and grey flannel trousers tucked into thick green knee-high socks. She got a glimpse of an arm, and hands reaching, pulling, picking something. Acorns?

Bobbing about, she saw the person's head: snow-white hair, deeply-lined skin, eyebrows gone mad as well as grey. Certainly, if he was the same old codger as before (and alone) he was no threat, so feeling piratical she jumped down from her perch and landed awkwardly.

'Good gracious!' the old man said, mildly. 'You really should have shouted "timber!" or something.'

'Sorry,' Jude said, 'I didn't see you.'

'Oh, I think you did.'

He managed to say this both knowingly and with enough warmth to make Jude blush. He had an accent, she noticed – a rising and falling in the pattern of his words.

'Okay. Well, sorry again,' she said.

'Apology accepted.'

'What are you doing?' she asked. 'Are those nuts?'

'I could ask the same in reference to the contents of your basket.'

'Mushrooms, that's all. There's no law against it.'

'Are you sure? They used to hang boys for scrumping apples.'

'No, they didn't.'

'Is that so? What are you going to do with them, make ink?'

'No, I'm going to eat them.'

'Before they deliquesce, I suppose. But you could make ink with them; did you know that?'

Jude was silent. She knew they were called Ink Caps but hadn't imagined they could be turned into ink. She didn't have a clue what deliquesce meant, but she wouldn't ask; he'd only laugh at her. She guessed it was a word for how the mushrooms turned to mush.

'Sort of,' she said. 'Anyway, what are those you've collected? Do you cook them?'

'These?' he said, holding out what looked like a handful of dull brown marbles. 'Take one.'

She did as she was told; the nut, or whatever it was, turned out to be far lighter than she expected.

'See that tiny pinprick?'

'Yes.'

'One would imagine something bored its way inside, wouldn't one.'

Jude was tempted to reply sarcastically with, 'One would.' Or call him a poncey old twat. But she liked him, so, by way of reply, she merely nodded.

'What happens is rather more interesting. An insect called an Oak Marble Gall Wasp, or *Andricus kollari* to give it its scientific name, grows from a larva and that is what creates these galls. The tiny hole is where the wasp emerged. When I say 'wasp', please don't imagine those pesky yellow-and-black creatures that sometimes make a nuisance of themselves and give a nasty sting.' He paused to study her face, 'You must tell me if I'm delaying you. My wife tells me I talk too much.'

'Oh.' Jude didn't quite know how to respond to that.

'And speaking of my wife,' he glanced at his wristwatch, 'she'll have my guts for garters. She's waiting for me in the car and I said I'd only be half an hour. Must dash.'

'But…' Jude said.

'Walk with me and I'll explain the science and uses of galls.'

What could possibly go wrong, Jude wondered, and fell into step alongside him.

THE PROFESSOR

'Now the gall, you see, is caused by the wasp, but made by the tree. It's like a pearl in a shell – the organism gets a growth from an irritant; with the oyster it's a grain of sand. Oh, look, a heron! Don't they look ungainly flying? Where was I?'

'Galls,' Jude said.

'Oh, yes. Now my wife will tell you that not only do I talk too much, I'm inclined to go off at a tangent. Galls, and these particular ones,' he said, tapping the pocket of his tweed jacket which was bulging with them, 'are excellent for making ink.'

'Really?'

'Yes, so naturally when I saw you gathering the Shaggy Ink Caps, that was my first thought. I looked at you and thought, art student, she'll be making pigments. But then again more likely a gourmand. Certainly someone who walks unblinkered, who is unafraid of wild food. Was I right?'

'I suppose so, but how do you make ink from those things?'

'Well, it's fairly simple. You need some large flasks and ferrous sulphate, and gum arabic. And water. And oak galls. I used to do it in the university's laboratory, but now I use the garden shed. The smell, you see, is slightly unpleasant.'

'Oh.'

'But the odour is nothing compared to that of the Durian fruit, which I had the dubious honour of trying when I was stationed in Burma during the war. Not that Durian was the worst thing about that time and place. There was of course, the Death Railway.'

To Jude that sounded like a fairground ride; the ghost train, the wall of death, the death railway. 'So the ink,' she said, attempting to rein in his tangent. 'Do you write with it?'

'The ink? Oh, yes. Write with it, paint with it, draw with it. Just as with any other ink. Now in the eighteenth, nineteenth centuries, for someone who was literate and wanted to write a letter, the ink was no problem, very easily made, as were quills made from feathers. No, the expensive bit was the paper. People were economical with that.'

As they came to a particularly overgrown part of the old path, where shrubs with pretty pink flowers loomed ten feet high on either side of them, he said, 'Ah, Himalayan Balsam, it's an invasive species but…'

Jude was forced to fall into step behind him, so while he continued to talk, it was impossible to hear what he said. By the time the path opened up again, he was on another topic entirely. She didn't feel she could interrupt, so he talked on, oblivious.

'… the industrialists, for all their money and power, couldn't escape the stench of the copper smelting, particularly on the east side of the river Tawe, so they abandoned their great houses and moved west. Ah, here we are!'

They had popped, almost miraculously, from the undergrowth onto a gravel road, where a battered-looking black car was pulled up on a grass verge. A fair-haired woman was sitting in the passenger seat, or seemed to be, until she honked the horn in a double greeting and put both hands on the steering wheel.

'Thar she blows!' he said, gleefully waving with the full sweep of his arm. 'Our trusty Saab. She does look like a whale, I think, don't you? Come and say hello to my wife; she'll never forgive me otherwise.'

Before Jude had a chance to bolt, the woman was out of the car and striding towards them. And smiling with such warmth that Jude was hardly able to think.

The couple threw their arms around each other and kissed quickly on the mouth, before turning their attention to Jude.

'What have we here?' the woman said to her husband, then turned to Jude. 'I do hope he hasn't hypnotised you with his words, dear. He's an unstoppable force once he gets going. Anyway, nice to meet you. I'm Sigrid, but you can me Sigi.' She grabbed Jude's hand and gripped it in a strong handshake. She was tall and strongly-built with a swimmer's shoulders, but, despite her age, very beautiful.

'Goodness gracious,' he said, 'I don't even know this young lady's name.'

'Jude,' said Jude wondering if she could also say, I'm Judith, but you can call me Jude.

'Nice to meet you, Jude. This fool, in case he forgot to introduce himself, is Olof.'

'My wife likes to remind me now and then that Olof is an anagram of fool,' he said, chuckling and taking his wife's hand.

'Ah,' Jude replied, and stood awkwardly transfixed by this pair, who might have been aliens from another planet, so different were they from anyone she'd ever known.

'I caught her picking mushrooms,' Olof said, 'and she caught me picking oak galls!'

'Well, well, a fellow forager! What did you find? May I see?'

It was then that Jude and Olof realised that the mushrooms, basket and all, had been left under the tree.

'Oh,' Jude said, 'I'll have to go back.'

'No,' Sigrid said. 'It's going to be dark soon.'

'But my basket...my...'

'But this is silly, you can come back for that tomorrow. Now, do you have far to go? A car?'

'No,' Jude said, miserably; oddly for her, tears pricked at her eyes.

'Oh, *helvete*! See what you've done, Oli! We will, of course, give you a lift home. I may have to stop off on the way, but we're not far.'

Sigrid opened the passenger side door, pulled the seat forward and Olof folded himself into the back.

'Hop in,' she said to Jude, in such a way as to brook no argument.

Jude obeyed, casting a glance at Olof, who was sitting with his long legs folded sideways.

Sigrid drove fast, overtaking cars and gunning the engine, until she suddenly swerved off the road and up a long, tree-lined drive. She came to a halt in front of a large detached house, then pulled up the handbrake fiercely.

'Come on, you may as well come in for a coffee while I make my call. Then I'll take you wherever it is you want to go… as long as it's not Hammerfest!'

Sigrid hurried into the house leaving Jude to tip up her seat and allow Olof out of the car.

'She rings her mother in Sweden every evening at the same time. You mustn't take offence. It's important.'

He went through the open door. 'Do you take coffee?' he asked. 'Or something stronger, perhaps?'

Jude followed him though a dim hallway. The tiled floor had a geometric pattern of black, white, terracotta and blue. On the wall was a large abstract painting that seemed to throb with colour; splashes and broad strokes of orange, yellow, sky blue and red. As she passed by, looking through an open door into another room, she saw an upright piano and another abstract painting; in yet another room, there were floor to ceiling shelves of books.

'Come through,' Olof said. 'Make yourself at home.'

Oh, how she would have loved to do exactly that! But instead, she entered the enormous kitchen and stood awkwardly by the big pine table, not daring to touch one of the many chairs, let alone sit on it. Olof was fussing with various cupboards and pots, arranging brown bread on a board, jars of pickles and mustard, knives large and small. From the monster fridge with a silver decal reading 'Kelvinator', he took a brown-glazed crock, and numerous mysterious items of different sizes wrapped in greaseproof paper. Tempting aromas of cheese and cold cuts began to drift towards her. Within her reach there was already a bowl of fruit: grapes, apples, oranges and bananas. She weighed up her chances of taking just one thing on the sly, eating it and not getting caught. She thought about poor Tantalus punished by the gods, never able to reach the fruit that hung above his head.

'Oh, Olof, tell the poor girl to sit, why don't you?' said Sigrid, sweeping into the room. 'Please, sit, eat. I simply must have something before I drop you home – is that all right?'

Gratefully, as if finally forgiven by the gods she'd offended, Jude sat and ate, and drank a tiny glass of a strong, clear spirit they said was called Aquavit. Before she left, Olof asked her to come to their lumber room, where, tumbled in a corner, were several willow baskets of different shapes and sizes. He dug one out and said she'd be doing him a favour if she'd take it away. When she protested, he insisted, saying it was entirely his fault that she'd left her own bag behind.

After Sigrid dropped her back at the cottage, Jude allowed herself to weep for all she'd lost and all she'd never had. 'If wishes were horses beggars would ride,' she remembered her grandmother saying bitterly, nearly every time she saw her. She didn't understand the proverb when she was little and as she got older, she ceased to really hear it; now it came back to her with clarity and she found herself wanting to scream at the old woman, 'So what? Stuff your horses and your beggars and just shut up!'

OLOF THE FOOL

Jude was woken at six the next morning by a loud hammering on her door. Her first thought was that it must be her father, wild and still drunk from the night before. Next, she wondered if it must be the police or the Welfare people come to drag her away.

As she crept down the stairs, her letterbox clattered open and a woman's voice cooed, 'Hel-loo-oo! Ju-ude, it's Sigi. Rise and shine!'

Jude wrenched the door open, 'What's wrong?' she asked, imagining terrible things.

Yet there was Sigrid smiling broadly. 'Wrong?' she echoed. 'Nothing's wrong. Are you not even dressed? Did you forget?'

'Forget?'

'Yes, Olof asked you for breakfast, didn't he?'

'No… at least I don't think so.'

'But he asked you to join us for the day? He was so looking forward to it. He could talk about nothing else last night.'

'I must have forgotten,' Jude lied.

'He misses teaching so much. Now what did he call you… ah, yes, an apt pupil.'

'I…'

'Oh, no,' Sigrid said. 'He didn't ask you, did he? He has been imagining our day out and what he planned to show you and tell you so much that it's become real in his mind before even that first simple step of inviting you. He will be so cast down. Can you come? Will you come? Or do you have plans for the day?'

'No. Or rather yes, I can come. I have no plans.'

'Wonderful! I'll wait in the car.'

Jude dressed as quickly as she could, fearing any delay would mean the invitation was snatched away. She would have liked to dress with more care, choosing something special or failing that something clean, but yesterday's clothes were there already, thrown over a chair. She splashed her face with cold water, pulled a comb carelessly through her hair and brushed her teeth. Downstairs she pushed her feet into her shoes without unlacing them.

'Ready?' Sigrid asked brightly as Jude got into the seat beside her. Without waiting for a reply she set off, driving once more at high speed through the still-empty streets. In scarcely any time, Jude found herself once more approaching the door of the lovely old house and passing through the hall and into the warm kitchen where Olof stood by the enormous table, wearing a butcher's striped apron amidst clouds of flour.

'My dear girl!' he said, seeing her. 'I won't kiss you as I've doughy hands.' He held up both hands to show her; flags and tatters of stretchy dough adorned his fingers.

'Here she is!' cried Sigrid, coming into the room behind her. 'Your apt pupil, all ready for the day!'

'Indeed! And what a day we have planned. But first, breakfast!'

They sat together to eat. Just like a real family, Jude thought. Politely she ate yogurt for the first time, first dipping the furthest tip of her tongue into the dollop on her spoon.

All the time Sigrid was watching her with concern, but each time Jude returned her gaze, she smiled brightly to divert her.

Olof went to fetch the newspapers from the hall: *The Times*, *The Guardian*.

'Your magazine came,' he said.

'Oh, good,' Sigrid said, 'pass it over.'

Jude expected it to be *Nova* or *She* or any one of those women's glossy magazines, but it was *The New Scientist*. She tried not to show her surprise, but evidently failed.

'How rude of us,' Sigrid said. 'Sorry, Jude, would you like a paper to read? How's that bread doing, Oli?'

'Nearly ready for the oven,' said Olof from behind the open wingspan of *The Times*.

'We have a guest, Olof. Why don't you show her your latest experiment instead of lurking behind the newspaper like a true Englishman?'

As if struck by lightning, Olof leapt up and threw the paper onto the table.

'What?' he roared, his face distorted, terrible.

Jude shrank into herself. It had happened, what she had expected all along – the anger, the unstoppable rage over nothing. A wrong word, a wrong look, an object left out of place by a fraction of an inch, an official letter in the post, a stubbed toe…

Then Sigrid laughed.

Olof laughed.

Jude was frozen by an old fear; she sat rigidly, eyes wide, heart pounding.

Olof turned to Jude, smiling, but the smile fell away. 'Dear girl, what's wrong?'

Sigrid rushed to her side, put a hand on Jude's forehead. 'Are you unwell? Here, sip some water. Olof get the brandy!'

He hurried away to another room.

'I thought… I thought he was going to hit you,' Jude whispered.

'No. NO! He would never… that was just playacting. Just fun.'

Olof returned and with trembling fingers Jude took the glass he offered her.

'Olof! This poor child thought you were really cross, that you were going to hurt me. Say sorry.'

'I am sorry. From the bottom of my heart. I would never, never… It is a game we play.'

'For a time we were in a small theatre company. Just amateur, you understand, in Stockholm. Our friends know our japes and nonsense, but you… Will you be okay? Shall I drive you home?'

Jude shook her head so vigorously there could be no doubt about her answer.

'Good. Very good. We'd be disappointed if it spoiled our day. We were going to drive out to the Gower, but perhaps you would rather go somewhere else? Somewhere you haven't been?'

Jude had not been to the Gower very much, despite the peninsula being 'on the doorstep', as people said. Just once on a nature trip with the school, and a few times on the bus. The sad truth was, it might have been the moon, so out of reach was it for someone like her.

'The Gower would be lovely,' she managed to say, 'but I forgot to bring any money.'

'Money? What do you want money for? There are no shops, you know.'

'No, I know, but...'

'Really. You're our guest. It will be a pleasure to have your company, won't it, Olof?'

Olof was clattering about with the oven. Pulling the loaf from it and tapping the bottom of the bread tin. 'Perfect,' he declared. 'Have you done the coffee for the thermos yet?'

Jude insisted on sitting in the back of the car, saying she'd more comfortable.

Sigrid drove at her usual high speed, but as they approached Fairwood Common, she slowed down considerably. Jude gazed out of the window taking it all in. The wild ponies, the sheep, the far-off vistas, the blue sky so big all of a sudden.

'I'm sorry,' she burst out, surprising even herself.

'What's that?'

'I'm sorry that I got upset. It was just...'

'You mustn't apologise. We understand.'

How could they understand, Jude thought. No-one could.

AN APT PUPIL

Stepping out of the car at Rhossili they found a cold wind blowing in from the sea.

'Will you be warm enough?' Sigrid asked, opening the boot of the car. She dug around until she found what she was looking for. 'Here,' she said, 'put this on. It is from Iceland.'

Jude took the heavy jumper from her. It was white with a sort of black houndstooth pattern.

'Very traditional. Now you look like a proper *bondflicka!*'

'What's that?' Jude asked, loving the sound of the word in Sigrid's voice.

'*Bondflicka?* Oh, a strong working girl.'

'Oh.'

'It's a compliment.'

'Ah,' Jude said uncertainly.

They walked along the broad cliff path, Jude marvelling at the sheep grazing calmly at the perilous edges, then beyond them the wide sweep of the sands so far below. Ahead of them lay the Worm's Head and the old coastguard hut.

'We won't go over the causeway to the island today. The tide's just in by the look of it.'

'Jude has been many times, I daresay,' said Olof.

Jude didn't contradict him. It seemed embarrassing to admit she'd never even been this far. A failure of imagination, or just stupidity or laziness.

'The Red Lady of Paviland was buried here with great

ceremony during the Ice Age. Of course, "she" turned out to be a man. What's it – thirty thousand years ago? They found mammoth bones too. Hard to imagine. Perhaps he was your ancestor, Jude.'

'Or yours,' added Sigrid.

'True, true. Because, of course, as you know, Jude, those early tribes spread out across the globe. I have a book you might like to see, *The Bog People* by Peter Glob. A much later period, that's true. It's a study of the nearly perfectly preserved men put in peat bogs during the Iron Age.'

'And women.'

'Yes, yes, men and women. Sacrificed, most probably, but much is unknown. When we get home, I will show you the book.'

'Only if Jude is interested. Not everyone shares your passion for the ancient past.'

'I'd love to see it,' Jude said, concentrating more on the word 'home'; with them she would have agreed to an evening poring over the telephone book.

'We went to a lecture Peter gave in Copenhagen, and met him at the drinks reception afterwards. A charming man, handsome too.'

'Apart from that smelly pipe he was constantly smoking.'

'Oh, yes, I'd forgotten that.'

They passed very few people, but called 'Good morning! Beautiful day!' to all. Jude walked silently beside them, noticing how people responded warmly to them.

At the coastguard hut, Sigrid produced a camera and a tripod.

Leaning close to Jude, Olof said, 'Don't imagine she'll take a nice snapshot of us. Or indeed the Worm; it's that hut she wants. The splendid isolation of it. Let's look at this drystone wall instead.'

What Jude thought was sarcasm, turned out to be a simple statement. Olof stared at the wall, going closer at times, but mostly scanning it from a few feet away. Jude also looked, but she was stumped as to the reason.

'See anything out of the ordinary?' he asked, after fifteen or so minutes.

'I don't think so.'

'Me neither,' he concluded. 'My theory, you see, is that with so much evidence of prehistoric activity nearby, it could be that old stones were reused by farmers. As you know, the famous bluestones of Stonehenge came from west Wales, so I'm always on the lookout for stones that don't belong.'

Sigrid joined them. 'There's a fisherman's shed down the cliff, too, but I'll save that for another time. I think the weather's on the turn.'

'We should get around to Goat Hole sometime, too, see the Red "Lady's" cave.'

'Can you see her… him?' Jude asked.

'Oh no, not here. Not in situ. He was whisked off to Oxford.'

'Oh,' Jude said.

'It's desecration, plain and simple,' Sigrid said. 'Typical Western arrogance. A lack of respect that's excused by progress and science. Anyway, I'm in need of coffee; let's get going.'

They marched briskly back; the wind was gathering force, whistling in Jude's ears and making conversation impossible. A huge thundercloud seemed to appear from nowhere and cold rain spattered down just as they got to the car.

The windows of the car steamed up while they sipped their coffee, so between that and the driving rain it seemed as if the ordinary world had gone away and they were on an alien planet. Jude herself felt like an alien. An outsider, never fitting in, never finding her place. She had no doubt that Sigrid and Olof had seen her loneliness, her awkwardness, her frowning intensity too, and taken pity on her. She did not dare to ask them anything about themselves, such as what had brought them to Wales. She assumed they must have something to do with the university.

'Where now?' Sigrid said, and it seemed as if the words were a question that had escaped from Jude's mind. 'I hoped the rain would have cleared by now. I'm not sure it's the best for exploring the Salt House.'

'Have you been there?' Olof inquired pleasantly, peering at Jude from between the front seats.

'I don't think so. Is it a pub?'

Olof laughed as if Jude had made a witty remark.

'No,' Sigrid said, 'it's the ruins of a house where salt was dried and stored.'

'Salt was valuable, wasn't it?' Jude said. 'That's where the word salary comes from.'

'Did you study Latin at school?'

'No, not really. Our English teacher used to talk about words, where they came from and all that.'

'Ah, the tangle of language! Etymology is a fascinating subject.'

Jude thought etymology was the study of insects, but held her tongue.

'Perhaps we should just go home,' Sigrid said.

'I can show you how I make ink!'

'Only if you'd be interested, Jude. Oli thinks the world is as passionate about these obscurities as he is.'

'I would like to see how it's done,' Jude said.

'Excellent. Then the day won't be wasted,' Sigrid said.

'No day with you is ever wasted, *älskling*.'

'Fool,' said Sigrid and she leaned over and kissed Olof, smack-bang on the mouth. 'Off we go then; say if you're cold in the back.' She rolled her window down an inch and started the car. The windshield wipers began with a steady, squeaking rhythm. The cool air was refreshing, the green landscape flashed by as blurry as a watercolour painting.

CURIOUS PEOPLE

'Do you keep a diary, Jude?' Olof asked.

'I used to. Then someone read it.'

Sigrid had disappeared to her darkroom, while Jude watched Olof slicing red onions.

'This will be for *Picklad rödlök.*'

'Pickled onions?'

'Precisely. But how did you know that someone read your diary?'

'Because he told me.'

'He?'

'He was furious. He yelled at me and tore it to shreds.'

'I see. A boyfriend, was it? But what had you written? Tales of an illicit love affair?'

'No!'

'Will you pass me that glass jar, please.'

'This one?'

'Yes. That must have been upsetting, to have one's private thoughts invaded. Then for him to destroy them. Such a vile betrayal of trust. I can't imagine.'

'But I...'

'What? You deserved it? No, no. Now I'm going to boil the cider vinegar with sugar and water. In Sweden we have vinegar called *ättika*, but this will do. So was it your father, Jude?'

'Yes. I hated him.'

'I'm sorry. Is he gone now?'

Jude nodded cautiously; her father was gone and never gone, too.

'We will pour this over the onions. Always cool it a little and put a spoon in first, to conduct the heat from the glass. Then, hey presto, it is done! We'll have it later.'

'Really? I thought it took months.'

'Nonsense. Now, would you like to see my laboratory? I think the rain has stopped.' He didn't wait for an answer but headed out through a door that led into a small conservatory, which was filled with plants. Numerous strings held them up, though they were dying back rapidly. Olof plucked two small red fruits. He popped one into his mouth and handed her the other.

'Oh! Tomato!' she said.

'Yes. Not a poison apple, dear Snow White.'

'Snow White?'

'Yes. You've seen the film surely! First full-length animation. Made in 1937 by Disney. Based on a German folk tale that explores the Oedipal principle in the wish of the step-mother to get rid of the girl.'

He opened a door that led into the garden. They passed a tree heavy with pears, bamboo poles entwined with beans, and a carpet of orange and yellow nasturtiums that poured over the paved path, until they came to a shed.

'Of course, the apple has symbolism in the bible too. Everything has layers of meaning. Watch your step. And...' He threw his shoulder against the door and it juddered open. A terrible stench immediately poured forth, reaching Olof first, then Jude.

He waved his arms about as if that might clear the air. Jude stepped back several feet.

'Oh dear, that's somewhat pungent, eh? Perhaps we should retreat. Let it air.'

They returned to the house, Olof already thinking about something else, Jude bitterly disappointed.

'There you are!' Sigrid said.

'We were going to brew ink. No good. Nothing doing. Too stinky.'

'Ah, speaking of odd scents... Here, Jude, smell my hands. I rather like the smell though.'

Jude sniffed as Sigrid wafted her hands close to her face.

'It smells like the photo booth in the market.'

'Well, it would. Same process and chemicals. Ready for lunch?'

'Always!' Olof said. 'Always hungry. Always curious.'

'Yes, indeed. Who said curiosity killed the cat? What nonsense. It keeps you young. Keeps you alive! Ah ha, do I spy *Picklad rödlök*?'

They sat down to eat in the kitchen once more. Olof disappeared briefly and music flooded the room. A single violin, achingly lonely. For a moment, Jude imagined Olof must be performing, but soon he was back and the music continued.

'Sibelius. Gloomy as a rainy day,' Sigrid said.

'It's beautiful,' Jude said. 'Sad.'

'Too sad?' Olof asked, concern lining his face.

'No.'

'Jude told me a sad thing earlier. May I share it with Sigi?'

She was not used to this. No-one asked her permission, even when discussing her most private matters. She nodded.

'Jude used to keep a journal. Someone read it, then destroyed it,' Olof said, gravely imparting these pathetic facts with dignity. 'The criminal was her father.'

Jude closed her eyes, letting the music's swell and rise speak for her. She sensed Sigi and Oli exchanging glances. Then the sounds of cutlery, of plates and spoons, and the smell of yeast from the loaf baked that morning, and cheese, and apples. She opened her eyes.

'Help yourself,' Olof said.

Somehow, lunch drifted on. And on. Sigrid played a different record. Jazz this time.

'Miles Davis, *Kind of Blue*. More coffee?'

Olof remembered the book he'd mentioned, *The Bog People*, and put it into Jude's hands. She looked at the cover, which was predominantly red, with a monochrome photograph of a man's face. He was withered, sunken, the bristles on his chin as clear as if they'd sprouted yesterday. She opened the book, more to stop staring at the dead man than to read it.

'You can keep that,' Olof said.

'Only if she wants to,' Sigrid said.

Jude noticed for the first time that Sigrid seemed to be monitoring Olof's words.

'We have more than one copy,' Olof said cheerfully.

'Thank you,' Jude said, putting the book on the table in front of her.

'What did you, or he, do with the torn pages?'

Jude knew immediately what he was talking about. Her notebook. She remembered exactly what had happened. Her father lurching from the room, bumping heavily into the door as he went. How she had picked up every torn scrap of paper and hidden them in her pillowcase. Later she put them in an old toffee tin. She seemed to see herself doing this and now she had the strangest sensation that Olof had been there too, watching, guiding her.

'I hid them,' she said.

'Of course, you did. You kept them.'

'Yes. There were others he'd thrown on the fire, but it wasn't lit, so…'

'But these you kept. Just as they are?'

Jude nodded. How did he know that? Did he also know that she sometimes opened the tin and gazed at the jumbled shreds, sometimes focusing on a word or phrase but afraid to go further? She no longer knew who had written those pages. She could not be put back together.

'As therapy,' Sigrid said, 'you should let them go. Make a ritual offering. Burn them.'

'No!' Olof cried, 'You must put them back together. Discover what it was you wrote. Make it whole again. I will help you.'

They were both looking at her earnestly, patiently waiting for some response.

Then Olof abruptly got up and wandered out of the room.

With just Sigrid there, she felt she should clarify what she'd said, because it wasn't quite true.

'The thing is…' Jude began. 'It wasn't really a diary. It was just stories I'd made up.'

'But that's worse,' Sigrid said. 'Or as bad. He was destroying your spirit. Your soul!'

Jude thought about the night a year ago when she'd burnt what she'd written. Fear had made her do it. Or scorn for her pathetic self, her bruised and battered hopes.

Rain suddenly spattered heavily against the windows and strong winds rattled the glass.

'Listen,' Olof said, coming back into the room. He was holding a copy of the same book he'd just given to Jude, and without explanation he began to read aloud, 'We must exclude those who ended their days in the bog by accident, those who went astray in fog or rain and were drowned, one dark autumn day...' then he looked meaningfully at the windows as if he saw some dead soul outside trying to gain shelter.

Sigrid exploded with a scornful guffaw. 'You're not King Lear anymore, *älskling!*'

'I know,' Olof said. 'But I was.'

'You were. And you were magnificent!' Sigrid said, then turning to Jude, added, 'He played Lear with the Stockholm amateurs. I was Cordelia until they replaced me.'

'They should never have done that!'

'But, *älskling*, I was truly awful.'

He thought about this. 'Yes. You looked the part, but...'

'No need to elaborate.'

Another heavy gust whistled around the house and golden leaves danced across the sky, some plastering themselves on the window.

'They might have sacrificed those bog people in order to appease the gods, so that they would have good weather, a good harvest. Did you ever hear about the year without a summer?'

'No.'

'Ah. It was 1816. Caused by the catastrophic eruption of Tambora in Indonesia the year before...'

'Oli.'

'Yes?'

'Put another record on, something jolly this time.'

ERASURE

Jude spent more and more time with the Anderssons.

One day they took her with them to the Dogs' Home in Single-ton Park. She had not even known that such a place existed, that you could just march right up to the door, ask to see the dogs and take one away. It was clear that they knew the people there, had adopted dogs before.

'We always take the old dogs.'

'Or the ugly ones,' Olof said, gleefully. 'The ones no-one else wants.'

'Better than a puppy; the older dogs are house-trained.'

Jude looked at the many puppies in the cages, their big eyes pitiful. She knew she would have taken one of them if she'd been given a choice.

The kennelmaid took them to a cage at the far end, unlocked it, then after fastening a lead to its collar, brought out an old grey dog with a long solemn face and whiskery eyes. 'This is Nero. He's only been here for a few days. His owner passed away, so he's very sad.'

Their choice was quickly made, especially after Nero almost threw himself into Olof's arms when he stooped down to stroke the dog's bristly head. They filled in a form and less than ten minutes after entering the home, they were walking across the park with Nero.

Those days were like heaven. Sigrid would turn up in the Saab early in the morning to collect Jude. Sometimes she'd drop her at the house and disappear for a few hours. Olof would be in the kitchen drinking coffee and reading or making notes while Nero snoozed in a basket near the range. Or Olof might be preparing vegetables or fixing a clock with a black jeweller's loupe pressed into his eye. Every day it was something different. She would help herself to coffee and he would talk, explaining what he was doing or reading. Then they would take Nero out for a walk. Sigrid might be there when they returned and then if the weather was good, they'd all go out for the day.

Jude did not fully understand why they took an interest in her, why they were so kind and generous. She did not for a second believe she had any value – for them, for anyone. She was like Nero, a mongrel no-one wanted. Except that it made sense for people to adopt animals and Nero did what a dog will do; he greeted them when they entered, he padded faithfully beside Olof, his claws clicking on the red tiled floor, he rested his long head on Sigrid's lap when she sat in the armchair, gazed with loving interest at both of them. Jude's role, her way of expressing gratitude, was more difficult.

One day Sigrid surprised Jude with a gift.

'It's not my birthday.'

'It doesn't have to be,' Olof said.

Jude unwrapped the package. Inside was a beautiful leather-bound notebook.

'It comes with a proviso; you must write stories again.'

'No. I can't take it.'

'But it's yours. Look, Olof has even drawn a sort of book-plate for you.'

Jude opened the book to the first page. There was a drawing of some shaggy inkcap mushrooms inside a rectangle with a border of flowers and oak leaves. Beneath that her name was printed in capitals in a beautiful chiselled script.

She turned the page to find a pale-pink ribbon marker and faintly lined paper. She ran her fingers over it. Nothing like the cheap paper she'd used before, but smooth as silk.

'It's too nice,' she said.

'Nonsense. It's just a notebook.'

'I'll ruin it.'

'Well, you can keep it here if you like. Olof will be working on a translation. He likes to work at the kitchen table and he will enjoy your company.' Sigrid paused. 'And you may not believe this, but he will be silent for once. I have to be out quite a bit, so it would be nice to think of the two of you here, the only sounds the fire going in the range, the dog sighing and two pens busily scratching away… and the rain.'

'But…'

'There are all sorts of pens and pencils in this pot here.' Sigrid picked up a large jar full of writing implements and put it on the table in front of Jude. 'Tons of scrap paper here for rough notes,' she said, hefting an old Heinz soup box onto the table, 'and more there.' She pointed to a pile of cardboard cartons under the counter. 'Some of it's a bit old, some is already used on one side, but that doesn't matter, does it?'

Olof was indeed quiet, but Jude understood it, or thought she did. It was not a brooding silence that precipitated an explosion of rage, but the gentle silence of concentration. Having nothing else to do, Jude got a few sheets of the scrap paper and in pencil wrote the words 'A Vagrant Girl' at the top. She felt self-conscious at first. What was she doing? Pretending to be something, someone she was not. Yet in the act of pretending, words began to flow.

Days went by. They ate simple foods that required no preparation: bread, cheese, tinned soup, eggs. The dog took them out of themselves and out of the house, otherwise they might have turned to stone.

As the weather turned colder, Olof went outside to chop wood. Jude could hear the chunk, chunk, chunk of his axe echo in the frosty air. Then long silences. Once or twice, she saw Olof pass the kitchen window with a long tree branch over his shoulder. Then the noise of the axe continued.

Sometimes she felt suspended in time and space as if she were floating off across the universe in a space capsule. All that kept her tethered to here and now were the words that flowed onto the paper. The ink was a rope, a chain, a strand of embroidery silk.

One evening, while taking her home, Sigrid drove slower than usual.

'There's something I have to tell you,' she said, glancing briefly at Jude to be sure she had her attention, then staring intensely at the road ahead. 'I've been worried about Olof. I'm afraid his mind is beginning to fail. He forgets things. Oh yes, he could recite Shakespeare, he can translate from Latin to English to Swedish, he can give you the history of Carl Linnaeus's development of taxonomy, draw detailed floor plans of Kronborg Castle, but he jumps from thought to thought. Have you noticed that? You probably wouldn't; you'd imagine that is just how he is. I've looked at his translation work and it doesn't make sense. There are words in English, in Latin, in Swedish and French – even some Welsh words. He's struggling.'

'Oh,' Jude said. She couldn't think of what else to say.

'We don't know exactly what it is. Nor how much time we have before it engulfs him.'

Jude, hearing that word 'engulf', immediately pictured the school in Aberfan.

'Perhaps I should have told you before. You must think we've taken advantage of you. I could pay you, but I didn't want to insult you or spoil our friendship. I *will* pay you.'

Jude was silent. She didn't know what to think.

The car stopped outside the cottage. Sigrid switched off the engine, but kept her hands on the steering wheel, her eyes concentrated on the windscreen.

'Olof is a proud man. If he thought you were anything but a friend he would banish you from the house. He believes he is helping you. Promise me you'll think about it overnight. I'll come to get you at the usual time tomorrow.'

Jude lingered in the doorway watching her drive away. The car did indeed look like a whale, Olof was right. He was right about everything. He knew everything. How could that ever be erased?

ECLIPSED

They had settled into a routine. Every day Sigrid arrived to collect Jude and take her to the house where Olof and the dog waited for her.

Sigrid was absent for longer and longer, or if she was there, she locked herself away in her darkroom. There was talk of an exhibition sometime in the future.

Half of the kitchen table was filled with piles of books and papers. Olof barely spoke. He wielded a magnifying glass, red pens, black pens, various coloured pencils and a large dressmaker's pair of shears, which he used to cut long slips of paper. One Swedish-English dictionary bulged with hundreds of these markers. It looked as if the book was sprouting tendrils of new papery growth. The Latin dictionary was mummified with black gaffer's tape.

Olof's white hair had grown longer and wilder, too. He'd stopped shaving and his beard was, surprisingly, a mixture of white, grey and red hair. His eyebrows, still partially dark, were bushy and grew in all directions.

Aside from chopping wood, he was not keen on going out any more. Nero proved to be more successful at getting him to go for a walk than Jude, as the dog would bark and scratch and bother Olof until he got his way. Sigrid had insisted Jude not take the dog out on her own, even if Olof asked her to.

He no longer baked bread or prepared vegetables. Sigrid had usually made a cauldron of porridge before Jude arrived and it stayed warm on the top of the range throughout the morning. Olof spooned jam or honey onto it. Jude sprinkled hers with sugar. Lunch was tinned soup, Scotch Broth, Cock-a-leekie or Oxtail, which they ate with fat slices of Hovis. Then they'd have cheese and Ryvita crispbread, grapes and apples, but Olof ate less and less and was slowly losing weight. As he was already tall and thin, Jude thought he was turning into Nosferatu.

As there was nothing else to do, Jude got her leather-bound journal down from the shelf and sat toying with the pink ribbon attached to it. She looked at the first empty page but could not bring herself to mark it in any way. Invariably, she got a pile of the old paper and wrote her stories on that instead. She planned to transcribe the finished work into the virgin notebook when she was confident it was worthy.

She borrowed books from their house to read at home, always showing Sigrid in the car what she was taking and bringing back. Sigrid would nod disinterestedly, or say, 'That's okay.' Until one day, finally losing patience, she said, 'You don't have to tell me! We trust you! Don't you get it?'

'Sorry.'

'I should teach you to drive, really. Or pay for lessons. Get you a little car.'

Jude marvelled at that idea and hoped it would come to fruition, yet somehow couldn't quite believe it would.

A few days later, Sigrid asked Jude if she would stay overnight that weekend as she had to go to London. Jude was given the guest room above the kitchen.

'It's warm and you can hear Olof if he calls out. He's very restless at night, can't sleep like he used to. Lock the doors and bring the keys upstairs; I'm afraid he may begin to wander.'

They had no television set, but there were a couple of radios. Once it grew dark, Olof liked the radio to be on. He particularly liked 'Letter From America' and turned the sound up; mostly, though, it was all low murmuring. The background noise of other people.

Jude wrote and wrote. As a teenager she never liked the books 'for girls' but she discovered the readability of Dickens and tore through all his novels; next it was Hardy, then Trollope, the Brontë sisters and Jane Austen. George Eliot, Walter Scott, Wilkie Collins and Jules Verne.

Now, when she wrote, she found that what flowed out was (she feared) regurgitated eighteenth and nineteenth-century literature.

She fed the dog, she made porridge, she opened cans of soup and salmon. She boiled eggs and brewed coffee, she washed the dishes. When the bread ran out, they had rye crispbread or Jacob's crackers. Olof added more books to his pile, so that he sat nearly hidden on the end of the table. Hardly speaking, Jude thought he might just disappear one day. Or turn into a paper man. Nero, however, could be depended upon to rouse his master for a walk three or four times a day.

When Sigrid returned, Jude had expected her to notice how well she'd done, but she was distracted, gloomy and uncommunicative. Sometimes when Olof left the kitchen, Sigrid looked at the books and papers he'd been working on. Now she put her glasses on to read his notes. She took them off again and sighed.

'How have you been, Jude? Has he driven you round the bend?'

'No, not at all. He's been deep in his work as you can see.'

'And you? Did you entertain yourself?'

'I wrote a little bit.'

'Wonderful! May I see it?'

'It's not finished, but if you want…'

'Do you have to go back home tonight? I need to talk to you, but I'm dreadfully tired. I might be going down with flu or something. I'll ring my mother, but then I need to sleep. I could call you a cab, if you like, though.'

Olof came back into the kitchen with several more books. He barely acknowledged Sigrid, sat down and commenced working.

'I don't mind staying,' Jude said.

Sigrid went and kissed Olof's head, looked at him closely, then with a thumb, she smoothed his unruly eyebrows into place. She gently squeezed Jude's shoulder as she passed, then went up to bed.

The next morning brought terrible news.

Sigrid was stirring the giant pot of porridge. Olof had not yet appeared.

'I'm glad you're up,' Sigrid said. 'There's coffee in the pot.'

'Did you sleep well?'

'Not really. Jude, I have something to tell you.'

Jude added sugar to her coffee and stirred it, thinking happily about her next story and only half listening.

'We are leaving.'

'What?' Jude said.

'Leaving Wales. Going home to Sweden.'

'But…'

'My mother is failing. I should go back for her. And I think Olof will do better there. Among his own people. We'll take as much as we can, but the house will be boarded up, then eventually sold.'

'But the dog… you can't…'

'Nero will come too.'

'When?'

'Now I've decided, it will be as soon as possible. Within a month, I hope.'

'You can't just go!'

'We must. I'll get you cash from the bank to recompense you for all your trouble. You must gather everything that is yours before the house is closed up. Books and so forth. Indeed if there are any books from our library you would like you'll be most welcome. It can barely recompense you for all you've done.'

She should have expected it. Why had she ever imagined her life would go on in this easy manner?

As Sigrid had promised, they were gone before the month was out.

Jude got the contents of their food cupboard and fridge, around thirty books and a pine trunk full of Sigrid's unwanted clothes (she had promised to take them to the church hall for their next jumble sale but never did). Also, Olof's Harris tweed jacket as it was now too large for him. When she buried her nose in its rough fabric, she found it carried his scent still. She also took some of the ink he'd made from oak galls, labelled and dated like vintage wine. A few clean demijohns and assorted chemicals. An Anglepoise lamp, an Afghan rug and two cardboard boxes full of scrap paper, including the pages she'd written her stories on.

Sigrid and Jude loaded the car to take the stuff to Jude's.

'Ah, it reminds me of when my father drove me to college the first time. I felt so grown up, leaving home,' Sigrid mused.

But this is the opposite, Jude thought. You were moving forwards; I'm going backwards.

Just as she was leaving Sigrid gave Jude an envelope with two hundred pounds inside.

But Jude did not want money. All she wanted was to stop time. Fix everything in place.

Olof and Sigrid had shone on her like a life-giving sun and now a dark cloud had blotted them out and Jude, having tasted this, was lonelier and more bereft than ever before.

The last words Sigrid said to Jude were, 'Please write.'

PART THREE

1816

'The bright sun was extinguish'd, and the stars
Did wander darkling in the eternal space,
Rayless, and pathless, and the icy earth
Swung blind and blackening in the moonless air;
Morn came and went—and came, and brought no day,
And men forgot their passions in the dread
Of this their desolation.'

Lord Byron, excerpt from 'Darkness' 1816

THE WEB

October, 1816

In the morning, countless spider webs hung in the trees and shrubs; fine droplets of rain had gathered on their silky wheels, bright and sparkling in the diffuse light like a multitude of diamond necklaces. Daniel Matthew stared at the scene, momentarily filled with awe. He thought about a highwayman or a crew of shipwrecked Spanish buccaneers flinging away their plunder as they fled their pursuers.

He didn't think he had ever seen so many webs in one place before. Then again, it was only the endless drizzle that made the invisible visible. It hardly compensated for the dreary weather: the sunless gloom, the damp, the ruined crops.

The summer had not arrived; by August it had been given up entirely. Autumn was nearly over and there was still the winter to come. People talked of it fearfully. It was the end of the world, it was punishment for sin, it was a time for blood sacrifice and necromancers, for prayer and penance.

There lay the road to superstition and despair, so he turned his mind to the tale of Robert the Bruce in his cave. His schoolmaster had told him the story many times – how Bruce watched a spider try to spin a web six times, until on his seventh attempt he succeeded. The story was a moral one; it explained Bruce's determination, but little about the spider.

He had spoken to many rational people, among them Natural Philosophers, about the lost summer, but none could explain it, though theories abounded. The earth had shifted on its axis, an Arctic storm caused it, or sunspots, or a meteor, or a lunar eclipse. There was even a theory that Benjamin Franklin caused it with his lightning rods. He knew so little. He should know more. He would know more.

Tonight he was to meet with his new acquaintance, Thomas Baxter, an esteemed painter of fine porcelain from Worcester, who was recently settled in Swansea. Baxter was in the employ of Mr Dillwyn at the Cambrian pottery. He'd met him at a reception at Penllergare House, where the two were introduced by a third gentleman who explained that they had much in common. What this was, neither knew, aside from the fact that they appeared to be close in age and were awkward amongst that class of people, and clumsy at what was considered polite conversation. As Baxter had lodgings in the town and Matthew lived just two miles away in Sketty, they agreed to meet for dinner at the Mackworth Inn the following Wednesday.

Matthew might have walked there and back, had the weather been more clement, or indeed taken his favourite grey mare, but the fine rain would be good for neither the horse or him. He therefore settled on taking the donkey and cart with an oilcloth to drape across his lap and another to drape about his shoulders. It was as well that the Mackworth had a large stable, with plenty of water, blankets and hay.

Before setting out, he extracted a solemn promise from Mrs Curtis, his old nurse and housekeeper, that under no circumstances should she wait up.

Just as the fates are said to spin man's fortune and the spider her web, so the grim weather conspired to send Daniel Matthew out that night with the very means by which later events would be played out.

A VAGRANT GIRL

October, 1816

She went by Hannah. She arrived in Swansea on Tuesday, 8th October. She'd heard there was plenty of work, lots of rich folk in need of servants, but she had no letter of recommendation and there were plenty of local girls in need of work – the daughters and wives of men who worked in copper smelting, coal mining and shipping.

As Hannah rested by the roadside, an older woman, taking pity on her, asked for her help in exchange for a meal. The work involved climbing over a stone wall to gather coal in a sack. Hannah had no doubt it was theft, but hunger pangs were clawing at her belly and she did not think that Jesus would judge her as harshly as a local magistrate.

The old woman stood by the wall hissing instructions while Hannah staggered over the loose slag and coal, and dug with her bare hands for larger pieces. By the time the sack was full she was black from head to toe and exhausted. She lifted the sack onto the wall before climbing over. There were fewer toe-holds than on the perimeter side, so she slipped more than once, and did not notice that the old woman had grown very quiet, nor that the full sack of coal was gone. Only when she gained the top did she see that she had been taken for a fool.

The devil had tempted her just as Jesus himself had been tempted in the desert. She had failed the test and this was her punishment.

She walked on, with no idea where she was going, until she came to a horse trough. A dented metal cup stood on its lip. She hesitated before picking it up and dipping it into the cool, clear water. Was this the devil's work too? If so, this poor sinner would be punished. She forewent the cup and plunged her face into the trough, drinking deeply, then tried to wash away the worst of the coal dust. After that she mouthed the words she could still remember from a psalm: *we have sinned against you; we have done evil in your sight. We are sorry and repent. Have mercy on us according to your love. Wash away our wrongdoing and cleanse us from our sin.*

She was so lost in this pious recitation that she did not notice a flaxen-haired boy of seven or eight approach her. 'Miss,' he said. 'Miss!' He touched her elbow and at last she turned to see him. 'Mother says I'm to give you these.' He proffered a small heel of bread and a morsel of cheese as golden as his hair. 'She says if you would come to our cottage door there is milk from our goat, too; she's a-milking her now.'

Finding her quite beyond words, he tugged at her skirt and led her to the entrance of a humble cottage.

Hannah was in no doubt that he was the Christ-child himself come to save her.

Standing in the open doorway was the mother. Her brown eyes were large and seemed to swim with tears. Her hair was deep auburn, pulled from a centre parting in a neat line that disappeared beneath a blue kerchief. This must be Our Lady, the blessed Virgin Mary, Hannah thought with awe, hardly daring to look at her.

'*Mae hi'n ddu gyda baw!*' the woman said.

No language Hannah knew, but it must be what they spoke long ago in Galilee.

'She says you are very dirty,' the boy translated for Hannah's benefit.

'*Dyw hi ddim yn cael dod i mewn i'r tŷ!*' she said and put a pan of water on the step with a small rag beside it. '*Golchwch eich dwylo.*'

'You can't come in. You must wash yourself.'

Hannah did her best to clean herself, but the coal dust turned the water into grey soup.

The boy brought a three-legged stool outside for Hannah to sit on and a wooden bowl filled with warm, earthy-smelling milk. She ate and drank in a state of humble ecstasy. The boy stared at her in wonder until his mother beckoned him back inside and fastened the door against the poor wretch.

These being end times, it was expected that miracles and visions would occur. As the feeble light faded, a downpour of rain began, but Hannah was beside a domed, stone-built pigsty. Finding no pigs resident, she crawled inside and with some dry straw she made a nest and went to sleep thinking of heaven and the glory to come.

With dawn, she arose and set off before she could be discovered. Her plan was to find a church, to pray and to ask for parish relief. If the preacher was kind, she would also tell him of her meeting with the sainted Mary and her son, our lord and saviour. Yet she was so covered in coal-dust, mud, pig muck and straw, she dared not approach a holy place. She must make herself clean first.

As she journeyed on, the sound of rushing water caught her attention. It grew louder as she hurried towards it, her heart full of joy. Very soon the river came into view. 'Thine is the glory,' she whispered, stepping upon the old waterman's stair, hardly noticing the willow that bent low over it, keeping it in perpetual damp and sunless shade.

She took one step and her foot slid over the greasy stone. Her next step found no purchase either. She reached desperately for a branch but it was hopeless; she slipped over the edge and into the water without a sound.

The River Tawe was in spate; that year's endless rain had poured off the mountains in sheets and gullies, flooding banks and over-flowing streams, relentless in its urge to find the sea. It gathered Hannah up as if she were a mere twig.

Rolling and turning in the water, it was only her tattered red flannel petticoat that distinguished her from the fast-moving flotsam. Downstream a waterman caught her with his hook and hauled her onto the bank. She could not be saved.

As was the custom, he carried her to the office of the wherry-man, where she'd be laid out for identification. If her kin should claim her, they'd take her, but failing that it would be a pauper's grave for the nameless woman.

Word of the awful discovery passed quickly from mouth to mouth; they told of a working lass with callouses on her knees and hands, blue eyes, light-brown hair, ragged clothes, not even a penny-ha'penny in her pocket and a fraying ribbon around her neck. Anything else she'd possessed must have been lost in the water.

Now the river had washed her clean and she lay, nameless and alone, awaiting whatever fate would send her.

At gone midnight two gentlemen arrived in a cart, and after rousing the caretaker from his bed, they were shown the place where the dead woman lay.

'Ah, poor Eliza,' one of them said. He pressed some coins into the sleepy old man's hands and with his companion's help they wrapped Hannah's corpse in an oilcloth and carried her away.

Matthew was walking beside the cart to ease the donkey's burden. He was filled with an unsinkable feeling of dread. When they were a safe distance away, Matthew looked at his companion, who was holding the reins and gazing out at the darkened road. He almost swore he was smiling.

The day had begun, despite the gloomy weather, with hope, with the promise of friendship and perhaps shared interests; now, here he found himself, cold, wet and in the process of committing what could only be a most dreadful crime.

Baxter's confidence, his smooth dealings with the caretaker, even his quick invention of the girl's name, 'poor Eliza' – the words flowing so easily, so familiarly – were astonishing. Yet instead of simple awe, Matthew felt a ripple of fear and realised that in truth he knew nothing of this man. Indeed, he no longer recognised his own actions. What did he think he was about?

The clouds parted briefly and the gibbous moon lit their path with its cool light.

'Are you not well?' Baxter asked suddenly.

'I don't know. I feel as if I'm sleepwalking.'

'Then climb onto the cart; there's room beside Eliza, I'm sure.'

'Do not call her that.'

'Then what shall I call her? A thing? A corpse? Surely she deserves a pretty name and, who knows, it might have been her name when alive.'

Matthew fell into a surly silence.

The only sounds were the rolling clatter of the wooden wheels' iron rims on the stony path and the rhythmic shuffling clops of the donkey's unshod hooves.

'We must continue what we have begun, Daniel,' Baxter said.

'I would rather you did not use my Christian name. It is too familiar.'

'Very well, we shall continue like strangers, Mr *Matthew*.'

'Matthew will do.'

'And you won't call me Tom?'

'No. Nor Thomas either. Indeed, I would rather we walked in silence.'

But the silence could not be held for long, as their work that night was only half done.

PART FOUR

1967-1971

'A solitary being is by instinct a wanderer.'

Mary Shelley

WHAT THE RIVER TOLD HER

The river, innocent as a lamb, flowed from its source in the Black Mountain towards the sea, never expecting the deluge of filth it encountered on its way. Fish and fowl did not thrive in its lower reaches; mayflies and other insect hatchlings, small prawns, otters, salmon and sea trout all struggled amongst the outpourings of industry.

A curious figure was walking slowly across the concrete bridge that spanned the dense, churning river. Seen from a distance she might have been a wild nomad girl sprung from a Hollywood version of history, but closer to, the woman, despite her bright flowing clothes, was at heart, like the river, quite dead – a ghost. Or so she imagined herself.

She missed Sigrid and Olof terribly. For a short time she had felt whole, had felt needed, loved even, but as time went on, she began to feel that it had been an illusion, a vivid dream from which she'd abruptly woken.

'Please write,' Sigrid had said, but Jude hardly knew what that meant. Write to them in Sweden? Or simply write? She did not think they had given her an address but doubted herself, as a sort of fog had descended over her in those last days with them. Had the envelope with the money also contained their contact details? If so, they were lost. Sometimes she wrote them little notes, or pressed flowers for them, but these were letters with no destination. She continued with her stories, but these, too, had nowhere to go.

She stopped halfway across the river, took a folded piece of paper from its place near her heart, dropped it into the water and uttered a single word. She waited for a moment as if listening for an answer, then away she went, her velvet cloak dragging after her on the dusty ground.

An idea had been brewing in her mind for some weeks now. It felt sharp and clear, like the hopeful pinprick of light the gall wasp must see as he begins to break free.

The day was muggy and overcast, the air tinged with mingled coal-smoke and petrol fumes. When a slight breeze moved up the estuary from the sea, it blew loose strands of hair across her eyes. She brushed it away, pleasantly aware of the patchouli oil on her wrist and the scent of wood smoke that clung to her hair. She caught sight of her fingers, still smudged with brownish-black ink. Too late now to wash them. She should have done it before. Turning back would upset the order of *everything*. She was superstitious about such things. Fate couldn't be meddled with. Everything happened for a reason.

She quickened her pace. Felt herself flying forward into her future as if she were stepping through a magic passageway, while the past crumbled in her wake. No turning back now. She imagined the bridge cracking behind her, its concrete and iron girders falling into the water below; all the bad and shameful things ground to dust and swept out to sea.

The sun started to break through the low cloud and the sky began to colour; vapid grey-white thinning like a stretched cloth to reveal a pale blue. It was a sign that she was right. Today was the day.

She broke into a smile. She couldn't help herself.

If you want a thing done, do it yourself.

She reached the bookshop just as it opened and asked to see the owner. 'He isn't here,' the young assistant said curtly, and gave her a look of filthy suspicion. Jude left, biting back a flurry of swear words. She circled Castle Gardens three times, then sat on a concrete bench, brooding for a few minutes, before returning to ask again, this time, with a carefully cultivated smile. She was chit-chatting and extemporizing wildly, something about being friends with the owner's wife, about their mothers being old school-friends. No matter what she said, he just stared at her blankly, which only made her talk even more.

Then, for some reason, the young shop assistant asked her to wait in the office. He looked like some cheap Iago who anticipated an act of revenge. The door to the small room was marked *Private*. As his footsteps receded, she looked about her. A tall mahogany glass-fronted cabinet that dominated the tiny room held books; some were old and leather-bound, others had dust jackets. Jude felt, though she didn't know why, that these books were valuable. A leather-topped desk was against one wall, with a wooden captain's chair in front of it. Cautiously, Jude sat down and tried out the chair's swivel. Listening carefully for any approaching sound, she opened the top drawer to her right and saw a black metal cash box. She quickly shut the drawer again.

She knew she didn't look like the sort of person you put in a room like this. She could just as easily have waited on the shop floor. He was up to something. What that was, she'd figure out soon enough.

RINGS ON HER FINGERS, BELLS ON HER TOES

Helena was in the flat above the shop reading *The Driver's Seat*, the latest novel by Muriel Spark, when she heard Edward calling up the stairs. Her first thought was that it was the phone, but she hadn't heard it ring, just Edward calling in an unusually sweet singsong: 'Helena! Could you come down please?'

Yet when she saw him, he was his old, cold insolent self.

'Someone to see you,' he said in a flat voice.

'To see me?'

She looked around the shop. He nodded at the closed office door. She walked the ten steps there self-consciously, certain that he was following her with his mean little eyes. A part of her thrummed with the idea that it might be Christopher; Christopher home early from his trip, waiting to surprise her with flowers and plane tickets to Paris. Or just Christopher smiling to see her. That would be enough. Another part of her knew that this was impossible. Surprises were not Christopher's thing.

She couldn't imagine who wanted to see her. An old friend of hers? Unlikely. A business colleague of Christopher's? A disgruntled customer? Someone from the church begging a donation?

Nothing prepared her for what she saw when she opened the door. It was a woman, a very strange woman, and she was sitting in Christopher's chair, which was odd in itself. Or at least to Helena it was, as no-one ever sat there but him.

The woman was quite a sight in a long dress of printed fabric with a muddy and frayed hem and embroidered bodice of patchwork decorated with a multitude of small mirrors. Around her neck were several necklaces of tiny multicoloured beads, along with a crucifix, a hand of Fatima and an Egyptian Ankh. Twenty or more slender silver bracelets clanked and chimed on her wrists with her slightest movement. Her sandalled feet were blackened with grime. Instead of a coat she wore a moss-green velvet cloak that, judging by the distinctive pattern of fading, must have been curtains once upon a time. A strange scent accompanied her; it was musky and exotic, not exactly unpleasant, but its dark spicy notes were so all-pervading and unusual as to seem foreign and dangerous. Her hair was long and looked unwashed. One narrow strand was woven into a thin braid and tipped with a glossy red bead that looked to Helena like a tick swollen with blood.

She was shocked, but tried to hide it beneath a thin smile. 'Can I help you?' Her voice sounded flat and unfriendly, though she hadn't meant it to.

In reply the woman just stared. Her gaze was unsettling. Her eyes, which were as green and cold as a cat's, seemed to penetrate too deeply.

She echoed Helena's expression, yet her smile seemed a performance – a thing put on to give the impression of warmth and convention, but not quite succeeding at either.

Smile dispatched, without further ado or ceremony, the woman fished around in a large fabric shoulder bag and produced a manila folder. She opened it; inside were three pieces of old and yellowing paper. Each was a different size and type; all had writing on them, two in ink and one in pencil. At a glance, they seemed the work of different hands and showed crossings out and corrections.

'There,' the woman said, just as if Helena had expected her to bring them in. 'He said you'd look at them.'

Helena hesitated; the *he* must be Christopher. She looked helplessly at his chair as if it held the answer.

'Is this your chair?' the woman asked.

'Well…'

'You sit.'

Saying this, the woman stood up, her movement stirring the air so that the strange fragrance grew even more apparent and the excessive jewellery tinkled and rattled in earnest. The woman turned out to be surprisingly tall; she loomed above Helena in a way that was emphasised by their close proximity in the tiny space.

The woman hovered by her shoulder, leaning over to smooth and arrange the papers, her elbow coming a little too close to Helena's face for comfort, the cloth of her musty cloak grazing her bare arm.

She could hear voices coming from the shop; Edward ordering customers to leave their bags at the counter if they wanted to go into the back. She had always disliked that policy as it treated everyone as a potential shoplifter, yet now, for some perverse reason, Edward, who trusted no-one, had sent this strange creature into the office, unaccompanied, commodious bag and all.

Some days ago she'd come in to find Edward glowering at her from behind a copy of Robert Heinlein's *Stranger in a Strange Land*. The floor looked dusty and several leaves and sweet wrappers had blown in. Instead of asking him to clean up, she'd got the broom and then, in a brisk and what she thought of as a superior way, she'd done it herself. As she worked, Edward seemed to settle himself more comfortably in his chair.

'You really should take the time to ensure the place is spick and span,' she'd said, meaning to sound authoritative, but somehow the words came out in a whine.

He'd leaned over the counter and surveyed the shop floor languidly. 'Looks okay to me,' he said in a flat voice.

'Yes, *now* it does, but that wasn't my point.'

He stared blankly, blinking twice in innocent bafflement. Not knowing what to say and feeling entirely disarmed, she'd turned sharply on her heel and gone back to the flat. Was this another act of retribution? He'd started their war of attrition. She hated it, but still wanted to win.

Her best revenge would be to discover that the papers in her hands were rare historical documents. She made an effort to concentrate. All three were handwritten – the sloping angles of one had unusually long strokes crossing the t's and arching loops over the d's, another had ragged, ink-smeared words and the third had light, spidery left-leaning pencil marks.

She skimmed them briefly; none of what she read made much sense. The one in pencil mentioned a bookshop. What bookshop? This bookshop? Then again, there was the mention of 'a false sister'. This seemed an echo of the many fairy tales Helena had read. There was the false princess in the *The Goose Girl* and the little sister in *The Wild Swans* who was put in a bath with toads to make her skin ugly and blemished.

The papers didn't seem to have any clues as to authorship or any addresses or dates, nor did they read like diaries or letters.

'I don't know what to say,' Helena said.

'It's like a story,' the woman said.

'A story?'

'Yes.'

Helena saw no connection between the three. None had a beginning or end. There were no titles and none of the standard exposition found in stories.

'But they don't make sense,' Helena said.

'What do you mean? Can't you read the handwriting?'

'Yes. I can read it, but I don't understand what these are.'

'Papers.'

Helena sighed; did this strange woman take her for an idiot?

'I can see they are papers.'

'*Old* papers. Lost fragments from another age. A mysterious Gothic tale.' The woman's voice took on an almost comically rhythmic note when she said these words, as if she meant to haunt and spellbind her listener, as if Helena were a child and here came the big bad wolf.

'Yes. I see that, but I don't understand why you've brought them here. Or what I'm meant to do with them.'

'It's a lost manuscript. The story of a life. A real life. A tragic life. From the early nineteenth century.'

'Really? I think I missed that. I only skimmed them and there's a lack of context – you know, time and place.'

'There is a context. Definitely. Read them again.'

'Oh, I really don't think… I have things to do and I…'

'Please.'

Helena, immediately feeling uncomfortable about her lie – she had nothing to do – faintly murmured, 'Okay.' She picked up the last paper she'd read, which was written in pencil and was the shortest. 'Is there any order to these?'

The woman, smiling tautly, with closed lips, shrugged.

On a second reading they seemed to have a gained a sort of gravitas. *The lakes, the distant snowy Alps; leaving cares behind; shared blood; a false sister.* These stirred a remembrance of other books, works by Walter Scott or Dickens – or perhaps not Dickens as his writing was seldom stark. Thomas Hardy, then? Again no; many of Hardy's descriptions of landscape would carry on for several pages. It was predominantly the Brontës who came to mind, but it was so long since Helena had read any of them she couldn't be sure why parts of what she'd read today seemed to ring a bell. But perhaps it was just something to do with the language, which seemed to carry with it uncertain candlelight and rustling silk skirts and posies of drooping violets.

It brought back memories of herself sitting under a tree aged thirteen with a paperback copy of *Wuthering Heights* in her hand. No picture on the cover, just orange bands against white board, heavy black type and the Penguin logo. She'd felt angry she was forced to read a book that would be soul-destroyingly dull, but instead, as she read on, the book seemed to draw her in. It was magical, breathtaking.

An idea occurred to her: 'Do you think these are writing exercises?'

The woman's face changed; her expression seemed to darken.

'What do you mean?'

'Well, I just wondered if children were made to practise their handwriting by copying out prose or poems. People also saved passages from literature into what were called *commonplace books*.'

'Like what? What would they copy?'

'Gosh, I don't know – extracts from the classics? Homer or Sophocles? Shakespeare or perhaps the Brontës?'

'You think these are like bits from them – all those great writers of the past?'

'Well, yes, don't you think so? You obviously understood there was something special about them or you wouldn't have brought them here.'

'You think they're special? Like great literature? Like the classics?'

'I'm no expert, but that's the impression I get. Hang on, let me read these two again.'

Helena read the fragments once more and found that her concentration, her sense of intrigue as a reader, caused her impressions to coalesce. It now seemed possible that the papers formed part of a single story. She saw that the names from one paper paralleled those in others; Mary, Fanny, Mary-Jane, Claire.

'They seem to be about the same group of people, but written by different hands.'

'Yes! That's it. You've got it.' There was a strange tone of triumph in the woman's voice – more, it seemed, than the situation warranted.

Helena read the final paper more cautiously, saying nothing, making no comment, however bland or obvious. She still didn't know what she was expected to say or do. She finished reading, picked up the papers, slipped them back inside the folder and held it out to the woman.

But the woman didn't take it. Instead she stared at the proffered object dumbly as if she had never seen it before. They were locked in silence for an uncomfortable time, each uncertain how to proceed. Then, at last, the woman took the folder and Helena stood up with relief, certain that the whole business was over.

'Well, thanks for coming in. It was...' Helena searched for an appropriate word, 'interesting.'

'There's more.'

'More papers?'

'A lot more.'

'I see.'

'I think you should read them.'

'Right.'

'You really should. I'll come back.'

'I'm not certain what you expect from me.'

'I could bring lots more.'

'Well, I can't promise I'll have the time to look at them. There's the business to see to and I...'

'Three more, then?'

'Okay.'

'Four or five? Six or seven if they're short like the one in pencil.'

Helena did not know why she kept agreeing. She knew she should say no. Instead, she felt dazed and it seemed easier to agree for now, then later make excuses to avoid the woman. Her brief dream of discovering anything valuable had rapidly flown. She wouldn't know what to do with such documents or what their worth might be.

'See you next time.'

'I might not be here.'

'That's okay. If you're not here I'll try another day. I'll just come back until you are here.'

'But I still don't know what you think I can do because I'm really not an expert. You should see Christopher. My husband, that is. It's his business - I'm just…'

'When's the baby due?'

'Pardon?' Helena said, though she heard the words clearly enough.

But the woman was out of the office and halfway to the shop door, her moss-coloured cloak and unruly hair streaming behind her in a wake of patchouli-scented air.

PART FIVE

1814-1817

'The mind will ever be unstable that has only prejudices to rest on.'

Mary Wollstonecraft

WEDNESDAY'S CHILD

London, 1814

Mary-Jane Clairmont stormed down the passage, borne along by anger. Loud sobs and shouts had woken her and she immediately knew it was her step-daughter, Fanny, having another of her silly nightmares. Why must the useless girl live with them? She was no daughter of hers and no daughter of William's either. Her moping, miserable face was enough to frighten away customers in the book-shop so she couldn't be a help there. That William Godwin chose to keep the girl was an abiding pity and an endless source for her wrath. To be always stumbling across her weeping or fixed in some dreary mood was a thing to try even a saint, and Mary-Jane was very far from being a saint.

Why on earth, she asked herself, did those two bright creatures, Mary and her own daughter, Jane, or 'Claire' as the silly child insisted on styling herself, have to go and run off, leaving behind this melancholy wretch? She knew the answer very well, for it lay at the heart of the question and any fool could see it; Mary and Claire were attractive, lively and full of quick intelligence, while Fanny's face was marked by the smallpox she'd suffered as a child. Fanny was dour and weary-making, always fretting about house-work and money, of which there was too much of the former and not enough of the latter.

What man, even an ordinary man with little or no fortune, would be inspired to offer his hand to Fanny or seduce her?

Born on a Wednesday and filled with perpetual woe - that was Fanny. No wonder her scoundrel father, Gilbert Imlay, had abandoned her. And look at where and when she was conceived – the streets of Paris were still running with the blood of those thousands guillotined during the Reign of Terror! This must surely leave its mark, a depression like a thumb-print on the soul.

Mary-Jane had told William her own thoughts on the matter; at twenty-one, the girl was of age. She should be sent from the house and must make her own way in the world. But what would Fanny do then? Well, she would probably take three steps from their door, sit in the gutter and weep until she starved.

William stirred as she snuffed out the candle and got back into bed. 'What is it?' he asked.

'What do you think?' She kicked at the sheets angrily, for a wrinkle lay beneath her. She had perspired profusely while she slept and the damp bedclothes were now chilled.

'Poor child,' he said, his voice soft with pity.

'Poor child, indeed! Why can she not…' She sat up in bed, aggravated beyond reason. She smoothed the sheets, then punched the innocent pillow.

'Sleep, my love. You are working yourself into a fury for no reason. Calm yourself; here, let me comfort you.'

His comfort took the form of an embrace, then all too soon, the shuddering intimacy of his married love. After which he murmured, as was his habit, 'Forgive me.'

For some years, she'd wondered about his words. He surely did not ask forgiveness from God, for there was no God-forged manacle in his mind. It might be argued that he begged forgiveness from her – his poor violated wife who sacrificed her purity to his animal lust. But Mary-Jane was not immune to animal instincts herself; indeed she often wished he might 'use' her a little longer and not be so quick to start matters nor so abrupt to end them. No, she had long felt in a secret and bruised part of her soul that the subject of his apology was that no-less-of-a-god in their household, his long-dead and infamous first wife, the sainted Mary Wollstonecraft.

Could it be that every time he touched Mary-Jane, the woman he pictured in his mind was that other Mary? She was a rival impossible to fight off or frighten away; a rival who never aged, but seemed to grow in perfection and loveliness with each passing year. Her portrait hung over them in the study and all three girls, Fanny, Mary and Claire, had been in thrall to this immaculate and sainted woman for years now. *She* never had to worry about scolding them or cajoling them in their studies, or set them to sweeping the floor, or counting the pennies, or reckoning the household book, or quieting a silly girl like the eldest child, Fanny, who was as noisy at night as she was sly and sullen by day. No, the woman in the portrait was as serene as an idol, her eyes unblinking, her hair unruffled, her mouth shut in perpetual silence. It was enough to make Mary-Jane tear out her hair and scream.

GODFREY'S CORDIAL

1814

The moon was calling, waking her, dripping onto the floor in tiny pools. They were like sister moons created by the curtains' ripples. Each as white and nearly as bright as day. And beyond her window, a moon like the afterglow of a ghost tapping on the window glass was drawing a sharp line around the edges of the casing wherever it could find ingress.

Sitting up in bed. Creak of wood. Then softly, she stepped out, moved across the floor in whispers of movement to the curtain. Afraid. Then not afraid, standing so the moonlight fell on her toes. Looking down. How strange it was to see this cool illumination. Keeping still and letting the moon know her. No warmth from this lunar presence. Waiting. Watching. Then daring herself, she tugged the curtain open and found in the late August sky a great Harvest Moon.

Mary-Jane had left the bottle of Godfrey's Cordial out for her on the table by the window, along with a spoon. Fanny knew that it contained laudanum. She resisted its allure, as all too often she had resorted to it or been given it when too young to understand its danger. It had been a friend, a comfort. Yet when she saw it arriving in the hands of an enemy it was altered. Now it was poison.

She gazed out at the silent street. Here and there pale candlelight flickered through wooden blinds, but most of the windows, upstairs and down, were in darkness. Who else was awake at this hour? Who else in this great city of London ached for sleep? She knew of poor gentlewomen who, even by the poor light of a single taper, attempted to work. The mantua-makers, the spinners, the milliners all bent over their work, struggling to see in the dim light, their numb fingers pricked by the needle. She knew the story of poor Mary Lamb, who was driven quite mad by this work yet could not earn enough to live. Lamb was a young woman who, with piety, love and strength, cared for her paralysed mother and ailing father. She had deprived herself of both sustenance and sleep, but neither the body nor the mind can go on in this vein without let-up. Sadly, one fateful day, Mary Lamb, quite beside herself, having first terrorised her young apprentice, had plunged a carving knife deep into her mother's heart.

Fanny knew too well the mind that broke into pieces. Would she be capable of such lunacy? She felt it glimmering close by; an imp that might suddenly possess her. She uncorked the slim bottle and poured the brown liquid into the spoon, then quickly swallowed it, shuddering as she always did. Wearily, defeated in both mind and body, yet safely pacified, she returned to bed and was very soon asleep.

The morning brought a letter from her sister, Mary, addressed to Fanny. The joy she felt at being remembered lifted her heart so that it was like a lark soaring. She read it through three times where she stood by the door. The first time it was with a sort of happy greed, the second for the pleasure of her sister's turn of phrase, for Mary's descriptive passages about the rocks and valleys, the lakes, the distant snowy Alps. On a third reading, she found that the more vividly these sights were described, the more she felt the ache of not seeing them with her sister. To share such experiences, to go into the world leaving cares behind must be, would be, exquisite. Yet, unfairly, she had been denied this.

The letter was as damaging to her as the carving knife had been to Mary Lamb's mother. Hearing of the beauties of the world served only to emphasize the drab surroundings of Skinner Street, and no matter how many times she read the letter she never found the words she longed for: Come and join us, dear sister, we miss you and long for the pleasure of your company. We will send money and make all the arrangements. Make haste, dear Fanny, make haste!

Mary and she shared the same blood. The same mother bore them. Yet when Mary ran off with Shelley on that hot summer night, she had taken with her a false sister and left poor, dull, fretful Fanny quite alone.

PART SIX

1967-1971

'To keep your secret is wisdom, but to expect others to keep it is folly.'

Samuel Johnson

A RIDDLE

'That woman was here again.'

'Who?' Helena asked.

'Your friend, Jude. The hippie.'

Edward had the smile of an insincere game-show host. Or one of those chimpanzees in the adverts for tea.

'She is not my friend. I don't even know her name.'

'If you say so.'

This was the third time in a fortnight that Helena had missed a visit from 'Jude'. She had mixed feelings about this; she was intrigued about the documents and equally about the woman who'd brought them, but there was unease too, and this increased with each of Jude's visits to the bookshop. The first happened when Helena was out of the building for no more than ten minutes. The second time she had been at the market so she might have been gone for over an hour. Today she had been to the bank a few doors up and as it had been quiet there, it had only taken a few minutes. Sometimes she suspected that Edward was inventing all these visits purely to wind her up.

Edward resumed reading Robert Heinlein's *Orphans of the Sky* with its distinctive yellow dust jacket and red text. Helena watched him. He must have been aware she hadn't moved and was still facing him, but he ignored her, licked his finger and turned the page, reading on in that nonchalant way of his. Was he telling the truth? It seemed too coincidental that the woman would always show up during those rare moments in the day when Helena was absent.

What were the chances that this could happen three times? Slim, she decided, very slim.

Thinking this, her gaze had drifted from Edward to a spot just beyond his head in the lane. Something seemed to glint there, moving as if alive. She looked harder, trying to make sense of it.

'You look like you've seen a ghost.'

'I was just thinking,' she said, and saw that it was only a shaft of sunlight bouncing off the windows opposite, filtered by the moving branches of a tree.

'There is a ghost, you know,' he said and his voice, though flat, seemed to take pleasure in this fact.

'Really?'

'In this building, people say. Upstairs in the flat. In the lane, too – I thought maybe you'd seen it.'

'I don't believe in ghosts.'

'Maybe they don't believe in you.'

'What on earth are you talking about?'

'Just a joke. No need to get excited. It's a concept – you know, the idea that you are the ghost not vice versa.'

'Have you swept the floor?' she said abruptly.

'Have you?'

'No. It's not my job to sweep the floor.'

'Does it look like it's been swept?'

She looked down. It was clean, save for a single white feather that seemed to hang miraculously in midair between a bookshelf and the wooden floor. As she stared at it, the street door opened, making the feather spin rapidly in the breeze.

'Good morning,' a man's voice said. 'Is there a section on military history?'

'Certainly, sir. This way,' Edward said. Their voices faded as he led the customer towards the back.

Edward had two faces; one for those he respected, such as this well-spoken, middle-aged man, another for those he considered inferior. Christopher saw only one face; Helena was offered another, but saw both. When she'd broached the subject of Edward's insolence to Christopher, he had first laughed uproariously then, turning serious, said, 'My darling girl, you must learn to trust people and see the good in them, no matter what you've been through in the past.'

'The past is another country' was another thing Christopher said. But the past was in her head. She couldn't climb aboard a Boeing 727 jet to leave it, there was no temporary roll of barbed wire to leap over, no Berlin Wall to scale. She could not set off on foot with a knapsack on her back to escape the place in her head where the bad memories lived. She just had to live with it. But did it affect her judgment? Could she see things – people, situations, the truth – clearly? Trust was all very well, but could she trust herself? She no longer knew.

This train of thought fell into the category that was fiercely rebuked by Christopher: dwelling on things. She knew this, but her mind had a mind of its own. This last idea tickled her sense of the absurd and smiling to herself, Helena unlocked the door to the flat, escaping the dreary world of the bookshop for the domestic comforts of home.

When she'd first come to the flat, it had been dark and oppressive. Some of the rooms were done up with a sort of synthetic wallpaper that was meant to give the effect of wood panelling. Christopher's study still retained this dreadful stuff as he claimed he worked best in small, gloomy places. His study was further darkened by the very small window which looked out onto a narrow passage and the blind side of a neighbouring building. The largest space was the living room, which overlooked Wind Street. Christopher had given his blessing for her to oversee its redecoration and so decade after decade of wallpaper and paint had been stripped away to reveal a potted two-hundred-year history of wallcoverings. Helena had wanted bare floorboards, stripped and varnished, covered with a few brightly coloured kilim rugs, but Christopher had rightly pointed out that noise travelling in both directions between the shop and the flat would be intrusive. Instead there was a fitted, cherry-red Wilton carpet. The walls were painted white, the telephone was white, the Venetian blinds were white and the curtains were camel-coloured. A large glossy cheese plant stood in the corner near the right-hand window and the fountain-like spray of a spider plant spilled from a hanging clay planter.

The mantelpiece carried a procession of Egyptian faience figures: shabti and scarabs, and the amputated life-sized hand of a marble statue. All of these had been purchased by Christopher from one of his favourite shops in Drury Lane and given to her as gifts. She believed they were actually things he'd wanted. She wondered, in passing, what might happen if they were to divorce and find themselves in the position of dividing their possessions. An awful thought, but she had no doubt he would want them and she wouldn't really care.

She should have felt soothed to be back in the privacy of the flat, but she felt on edge. Exposed, perhaps; somehow permanently aware of the bookshop below. With Edward sitting behind the counter, his eyes, when they were not absorbing some absurd distant planet with its clunking space rockets and men from Mars, scanning the ceiling above his head, following the muffled tread of her footsteps as she moved from room to room. She did not like the sense of being listened to or watched, of being known. It made her feel as if she should justify her existence by being busy. The work she should do would be domestic, thereby demonstrating her worth as a good wife. But two of the tasks which were noisy enough to convey her industry through the floorboards were banned. Christopher had laid down the law on that score; absolutely no vacuuming and no running the washing machine during business hours. She thought she might go over the carpet with the Ewbank carpet sweeper, but it was an irritating, rattling thing, barely capable of picking up even a few crumbs and constantly clogging up with hair. Besides which, the carpet was fine and didn't need cleaning. And it was none of Edward's business. She should not let him, the shop assistant of all people; unsettle her with his sly remarks. That wild, strange woman, 'her friend' indeed! And a ghost in the flat! It was cruel and idiotic.

She glanced at her watch. A quarter to two. She switched the TV on for the news and turned the volume down until it was no more than a whisper. The lead story was the trial in Los Angeles of the Manson Family. Helena stared, fascinated, at the footage of four young women kneeling on a paved area in front of the court, their hands palm upward as if they were Buddhist supplicants. They looked so ordinary and innocent.

One spoke, leaning forward in order to direct her words into a microphone held by an unseen hand. Her voice was clear and intelligent, her expression both intense and sincere, yet what she said was chilling in its promise: 'There is a revolution coming very soon.'

Revolution, Helena thought, a revolution that began with the slaughter of pregnant women, with black-clad figures invading your home, putting a rope around your neck, stringing you up. The murders had been done with knives. Up close and intimate. Savage.

A different news story came on, a person tarred and feathered on the streets of Belfast, one fleeting image caught on camera like something from a horror film.

She drifted into the kitchen and pulled open a drawer. Carving knife, paring knife, fruit knife, bread knife. Edges muted or sword-sharp or serrated with teeth like a piranha. All here in the kitchen drawer ready for use, or misuse rather. Think too hard and it all became viscerally real, a razor edge cutting the fine skin of the throat, cutting muscle, tendons, veins, arteries, vocal cords.

A revolution is coming very soon.

She picked up the boning knife. This one, with its thinness, its flexible curving blade, always struck her as wholly alien. No-one ever used it, but there it was, waiting in the drawer, waiting for the hand of the murderer to snatch it up.

Her last moment of happiness would be this, standing in the kitchen frightened by news of events too far away to touch her. The Atlantic Ocean and the great mass of the North American continent stood between her and the deceptively pious-looking girls on that street corner in California. Yet they looked like the students and teenage girls in her town. Long hair, freshly washed and gleaming in the sun. One was wearing a blouse with a sort of bubble effect made by rows of elastic thread. Helena had looked at a blouse exactly like that in Chelsea Girl just the other day. Although she'd thought it pretty, she decided it was too young for her. Not that she was exactly old.

She was twenty-two, and more to the point married to a man almost twice her age. She was the respectable wife of a respectable man with his own business. And possibly pregnant, too. Not that it showed.

Yet that woman – Jude – had asked, 'When's your baby due?'

She hadn't had a chance to question her and now she wondered if she'd imagined what was said. Or misheard. A Freudian slip working on incoming information instead of outgoing.

She went into the bedroom and opened the wardrobe door to see herself in the full-length mirror. Her breasts seemed slightly fuller, but her stomach, while not flat, did not look like that of a pregnant woman. Her face was the same – no telling glow. Indeed, she thought she looked paler than usual, with blue-black shadows showing beneath the paper-thin skin around her eyes.

This pregnancy was, to her mind, not presence but absence. She had missed two periods; that was all. Her periods had always been erratic. Stress seemed to freeze her body, to shut down her internal system.

She stepped onto the bathroom scales and the needle lurched violently then, quivering, settled on six stone, twelve pounds. Last time she weighed herself she had been just over seven stone, so, in a reversal of the expected pattern, she was losing weight instead of gaining it.

It occurred to her that she had somehow, impossible as it was, imagined herself pregnant. But that strange woman, Jude, had known. But there was no way she could have known. Helena had gone to the surgery, but she'd only spoken to the receptionist. Only asked to make an appointment. She didn't think she'd said what the appointment was for. In answer to the question of whether it was urgent or not, she'd said quietly, no, it's not urgent.

Did her condition show in ways unimaginable? In her eyes – the child appearing like a dark spot on the iris? She leaned closer to the mirror so that her breath misted it. Around the black pupil of her eye, a starburst of rust faded into pale yellow-green. The iris had patches of grey sea-green and an outer ring appeared like a smudged crayon of darker grey-green. One spot showed up like a stain in the area near the pupil, but it was tiny. No-one would notice that in the ordinary way.

She stepped back again and studied her body. Turned to the left, then the right. Looked at her ankles, which she knew could become swollen with pregnancy, but they looked as they always did. Slim and pale, bone showing beneath the skin, quite ugly if you thought about it too much.

So, she must have misheard what the woman said. Or the woman said those things all the time to every woman she encountered regardless of their condition or age. Threw those words out randomly, experimentally, insulting those who were overweight, shocking those who were young and innocent, and mocking those were long past the possibility of such a condition. Sometimes though, as in her case, the words met a receptive target and her question was answered with an expression that said, yes. That was how women like her gained secret knowledge.

A sharp sound, a double knock, RAT-TAT, broke the silence and was followed by an abrupt shout.

'Helena!'

Edward was halfway up the stairs when she looked down.

'I've been calling for ages.' His face showed anger.

'I didn't hear you. Sorry. I was...'

'She's back. Your little chum. Your bosom buddy.'

'Jude?' she asked uncertainly.

'Yeah, Jude. She's just dying to see you.' His voice, rich with sarcasm, matched the sneering expression on his face.

She wanted to say something withering to him. To reprimand him. But his tone of voice and his particular arrangement of words were not tangible enough to prove to a third party his ongoing aggression towards her, his war of attrition. It was his word against hers. If she told Christopher he would laugh as he'd laughed away her other complaints. 'Oh, it's just Edward's way. He's being playful. He thinks the world of you!'

As she began to descend the stairs, he retreated, ducking quickly out of sight. No doubt returning to his throne by the till, back to his book and a secret journey to yet another fantastic planet. Well, he could just stay there as far as she was concerned.

Jude was standing between two of the tall bookshelves, head tilted up, as she scanned the Ancient History section. She reached up and took one book down, opened it and began reading as if that was all she had come there to do. Helena turned to see Edward behind the counter, his elbows on it, his head bent over the book he was reading.

On the top of his head she noticed that a small circle of his strawberry-blonde hair was thinning. This gave her such a moment of joy that she almost forgot everything else. Then came the pangs of guilt. To be heartened by another's physical deterioration was very low indeed. Unworthy. She looked at Jude again; today her hair was in two schoolgirl plaits held in place with narrow elastic bands. Over her shoulders was a Spanish shawl, silky black with a pattern of red and orange flowers and a fringe of long black filaments. Yet, incongruous as ever, beneath the shawl she was wearing a pair of faded jeans which were torn on one knee and frayed at the hem.

Helena felt for a moment as if she was suspended between these two humans, Jude and Edward, who while they were evidently physically present, were also not there at all. One was transported forward in time to the shiny or dystopian future while the other had gone backwards, travelling through the dust of centuries, past the marching feet of soldiers and shifting borders and toppled empires and babies born and graves opened and bodies toppled in, taking with them all hope, all pain, all triumph and tragedy. Only Helena existed in the here and now, marking her days in endless waiting. Reading the newspapers, watching the television news, watching the serious programmes on TV and the rubbish too, hearing the tinned laughter, seeing the strained smiles, tuning into Coronation Street and Top of the Pops, Play for Today and The Sky at Night, then, as if it were something nourishing to sustain her through the night, the National Anthem.

'Hey, you!' Edward's voice seemed to roll past her to his target, Jude. No matter how much he seemed to be lost in his reading, Edward was always aware of what was going on around him. So he knew that Helena had been standing there like a fool, waiting for someone or something to jog her into action.

Jude turned to face her, a half-smile tilted on her face, but Helena's eyes were drawn irresistibly to her chest. The top she wore was tight and low-cut and her breasts swelled up like two magnificent mountains, tanned and gleaming and without doubt enviable to any woman who saw them and desirable to every man. Unexpected too, though exactly why, Helena couldn't really think. Except that it didn't chime with her first impression. Not one bit.

'This is the fourth time I've been,' Jude said. 'I keep missing you.'

'You were here earlier?' Helena said, feeling underneath her uncertainty about the strange woman the warmth of being sought out and wanted.

'Yes. He said you might be gone for hours, but here you are.'

'Yes. Here I am.'

Edward knew she had only popped out to the bank earlier. That she would be absent for minutes, not hours – so was he trying to help her in some way by putting this woman off? Or, if he truly believed Jude was her friend, being obstructive?

'I've brought more of the manuscript.'

'Manuscript?'

'The papers. Or letters. Or whatever they are.'

'Ah. Of course. When you said "manuscript" I immediately thought you meant the manuscript of something you'd written.'

Jude scowled.

'Sorry – of course, I'll be happy to look at more of the papers, but honestly, as I said, I'm no expert.'

Edward, eavesdropping, made a sort of guffaw at this, but as she turned to confront him, he turned it into a pretend cough and thumped his chest as if something, a bit of food, an evil thought, a tiny alien spacecraft, had gone down the wrong way.

Helena led the woman to the office again and unfolded the wooden step-stool so that her visitor could sit. Helena arranged herself in Christopher's chair, resting her elbows on the arms and lacing her hands together over her stomach. She smiled.

Jude perched on the stool and lifted her patchwork bag onto her lap. There was no dark perfume evident today, rather an apple-crispness as from shampoo, and the woman wore no clanking bracelets, nor even a single necklace.

'Now,' she said, patting the velvet bag importantly. 'Here's the thing... do you remember the first papers I showed you?'

'Yes, of course.'

'The names of the people mentioned?'

'Well, only vaguely. There was a Mary, a Fanny... Claire? Was it Claire or Cathy? An Anne?'

'But the man's name. The surname, do you remember it?'

'Ah, was it Thomas? Thomas Good? Michael – no. Remind me.'

'It was William.'

'Yes. Of course, I should have remembered – that was my grandfather's name, but he was always Bill…'

'William Godwin.'

'Yes. I see.'

'*William Godwin.*'

Helena tried to absorb this information. The woman's emphasis seemed to suggest that there was more substance and importance to the name than Helena could at first perceive. She grabbed a pen from the pot in front of her and some scrap paper, wrote down the name. Jude repeated it.

Helena wondered if the name was some sort of riddle, a cryptic crossword clue to be unpicked. She wrote it with the letters spaced, thought about scrabble tiles and what words she could make. She divided the two words into smaller parts and almost immediately she came up with an anagram; a three word phrase, philosophical in its premise:

Will God win?

Or more pleasing in its surety there was:

God will win

However there were three leftover letters; I, A, M. So:

I am God. Will win.

Jude was talking still, '…and he had two daughters, Mary and Fanny. Married again and had a step-daughter, Claire.'

'Yes, I think I got that. I just couldn't remember all the names.'

'But the names are the thing – William Godwin. Mary Godwin. Fanny.'

Jude was staring straight into Helena's eyes. It was an unwavering gaze – intense, unsettling.

Helena laughed nervously, 'Oh, I'm hopeless. Sorry. Do the names mean something? Are they distant relatives of yours?'

'WILLIAM GODWIN.' She spoke the name louder, giving each part careful emphasis in a way that suggested the name should be instantly recognizable.

Helena frowned and shook her head.

'You've never heard of William Godwin?'

'No.'

Suddenly Jude had a look of gloating triumph. 'William Godwin. Author of *Political Justice*? Author of *Caleb Williams*? *Lives of the Necromancers* … and *Memoirs of the Author of a Vindication of the Rights of Woman*?'

Helena shook her head.

'Husband to Mary Wollstonecraft? Father of Mary Shelley – author of *Frankenstein*?'

'Oh. Oh yes, Mary Shelley! And the other name rings a bell too, Wollstonecroft?'

'*Craft*. Not Croft.'

'Yes, Wollstonecraft, I think I'd heard of her, but not Godwin. It may not have been studied at my school; we did a lot of Chaucer and Shakespeare and in history it was the Tudors, religious persecution, that sort of thing. So, I…'

Helena let her voice trail away. She shrugged, then gave a sort of helpless smile.

Jude was still staring at her, her eyes glittering with what might have been anger or triumph.

'You own a bookshop and you've never heard of William Godwin?'

'It's my husband's business so I…'

Again, Helena's voice trailed off. It dawned on her that this strange woman was enjoying herself, that Helena's ignorance about this particular author seemed to prove a point of some sort.

Helena, confused and defensive, was uncertain what to say. Then the woman seemed to catch herself, and like one of those impressionists on the TV, she instantly changed. She rolled her eyes heavenward and chuckled, 'Oh, listen to me! I get so involved in these things. I forget that the rest of the world isn't interested. I'm sorry.' Her voice was pleading, full of self-mockery. 'What a complete idiot I am. You must think me awful. He's pretty obscure these days. You know, not like Dickens or George Orwell. So, it's hardly surprising you haven't heard of him. And you're so young, too. I can see that now. I just assumed you'd know. How old are you?'

'Twenty-two.'

'Twenty-two? Oh, you're just a baby, aren't you?'

'Twenty-three in two weeks.' Helena realised how pathetic that sounded even as she said it.

'Well, the thing is …'

The phone began to ring. There were two extensions, one by the front desk, one in the office. Helena looked at the phone, then decided Edward could pick up in the shop. The phone rang on – two, three, four times.

'Aren't you going to answer that?' Jude asked.

'No. I…' Contradicting herself, she snatched at the handset awkwardly, managing only to lift it from the cradle and juggle it for a second before she dropped it, cutting off whoever was calling.

'Damn.'

Edward opened the door, peered in, looked at the two women, then the phone.

'She hung up,' Jude said with a tight smile.

'You hung up?'

'No… yes. Accidentally.'

'I was waiting for a call. An important call. From a rare book collector. You hung up?'

'Accidentally.'

'I don't understand. Isn't it my job to answer the phone? Aren't I the one running the shop while Christopher's away?'

'Yes, but I thought…'

'It only rang twice.'

'No, there were four, five rings, so I…'

'You should have been quicker,' Jude said to Edward.

'Excuse me. Who are you? What does it have to do with you? You wander in off the street and tell me how to do my job?' His voice grew louder with each sentence.

'Well, if you don't know how to do your job.'

'Please stop.' Helena said.

'Don't you dare tell me I don't know how to do my job. What are you? Tell me, just what are you? Nothing, that's what you are. Rubbish. Have you looked at yourself in the mirror lately?'

Jude began to rise from the stool and Edward took a step

forward into the tiny office. Helena was trapped between the two.

'Please,' she said. 'Please stop.'

Then, as if in some perfectly-timed farce, the phone began to ring again.

'I'll get it! Don't touch it!' Edward shouted. He bounded away leaving the office door swinging open. The two women listened to the receding sound of his feet pounding on the bare floorboards, and the tring-tring, tring-tring of the two phones, a rattle as he picked up the receiver.

'Hello, 25258, Quarto Books.'

'As I was saying,' Jude began.

Helena was reeling. Hanging up had been an accident, but Jude had made it sound deliberate, an act of war against a lazy employee. But it was Jude who had more or less told her she should pick the phone up. She had fumbled because she had felt nervous. And she was nervous because she was always nervous these days. She should tell Jude to go. Tell her she had no right speaking to Edward like that. Then she should apologise to him, try to explain. But he'd invited Jude into their office in the first place. Why had he done that? It was so out of character.

Jude piled a new stack of papers on the desk. Helena looked at them but did not make any move to touch them.

'Read them, then,' Jude said, and Helena meekly did as she was told. It was easier to do that, easier to obey whoever ordered her about.

SCAPEGOAT

Jude left Helena alone for less than ten minutes while she read the documents, saying she would look at the books in the history section, as she wanted to discover clues as to the documents' dates. Then she was back, talking non-stop, her words implacable despite the fact that Helena was still trying to read.

She was lecturing Helena – names and dates came out of her mouth: 1806, London, The French Revolution, Burke, Godwin, Paris, the American War of Independence. Helena watched Jude's mouth; it formed the words she heard, it linked them in sentences, in paragraphs too, probably, yet made no sense.

'Do we speak in paragraphs?' Helena thought. 'In sentences obviously, but…' Then her mind drifted off, away; it left the office and floated through the bookshop and up the stairs then snuggled up on the couch under a soft white blanket. A little cloud.

'So, what do you think?' Jude said.

'Oh. Fascinating.'

'It is, isn't it?'

'I used to like history, but it's one of those things you leave behind once school's over,' Helena mused.

'Those who don't remember their history are doomed to repeat it.'

'Ha, yes. I had to re-sit my O-level history.'

'That's not what I meant.' Jude stared at her. It was hard to see beyond the stare, to understand it. It did not invite engagement. It seemed to have neither negative nor positive emotions; it just swallowed you up. Coldly. Dispassionately. Eternally.

It was easier for Helena to think beyond Jude, beyond the encroaching walls of the office, past the legions of books and the plate-glass windows at the front of the shop, beyond Wind Street, beyond the places it led to and from: Castle Gardens with its fountain and floral displays, and Boots the Chemist with its three floors of bath cubes and soap and medicine and toys, beyond the market with its tubs of black slimy laverbread and pale orange cockles, and further away – past the dark railway bridges and docks and huddled terraces, past the bald, dead hill of Kilvey and the filthy river Tawe, on towards that wider world, east to London where Christopher was, then west to Los Angeles where those hippy girls were sitting on the street proselytizing, preaching death in the name of peace. Beyond all that imagining, Helena was nowhere.

She was a tethered goat and Jude was the wolf.

Helena stood up suddenly, not even aware that she had sent a message to her limbs to flex, to unfold and straighten, to lift herself from the gravity of sitting. The chair glided back on its castors a few inches and seemed to pull her in its wake. She swayed precariously; the blood drained from her head and a high-pitched noise sounded in her ears.

'Are you alright?' she heard and Jude's face seemed to loom and swell, a pale balloon on a fragile string in a collapsing world. Then Helena's knees buckled and down she went, surprisingly light and slow, a half-risen cake sinking.

She woke in a daze as they were carrying her out of the office, Edward hooking his arms around her upper body while Jude took her legs. Her body sagged between them, chin fallen onto her chest, hair covering her face. They laid her in the empty space in front of the counter and opened the shop door so that the cool air might revive her. They quarrelled half-heartedly about who should phone for an ambulance, whether she should be on her back or on her side, if one of them should slap her and how hard? Then in a rare moment of accord they agreed that water should be administered and Helena woke up wet and spluttering, her head lifted in the crook of Edward's arm while he poured water into her mouth and down her chin, soaking her clothes.

They helped her up and sat her in one of the spindly old bentwood chairs that Christopher had bought from the Mission House.

'You fainted,' Edward said. 'I'll get you upstairs. Shall I ring Christopher?'

'I don't know.'

'I'll stay with her,' Jude said. 'Make some tea. Put her to bed.'

'No. You've done enough, thank you. I need to close the shop.'

'She didn't say you should.'

'I don't need her to tell me that. Are you alright there, Helena? Can you sit? I'm locking up the shop.'

'I should stay,' Jude said. 'We were in the middle of…'

'No. Leave it. Go on. Go.' He half-guided, half-pushed Jude through the open door.

'I'll come back tomorrow at around…' she called.

The door was closed and beneath the rattle of its locks and the jangle of the spring-loaded bell, the end of Jude's sentence was lost.

Edward followed Helena up the stairs. The world was coming back into focus with all its stark clarity, but she held the handrail uncertainly and stepped slowly.

'Will you lie on the couch or on the bed?'

She didn't want him in the bedroom, that was an intimacy too far. 'The couch. The couch will do.'

She lay down and realised that her clothes – her blouse and jumper – were quite wet. She'd change once he was gone.

But Edward had little intention of going.

'I'll make tea,' he said and disappeared into the kitchen. She lay very still, closed her eyes to see if sleep might come, but she knew it was a sham. She wasn't tired. Not in the least. If anything, it was the opposite; she was alert but anxious. Why had she fainted? Why had she allowed herself to be lectured by that strange woman? Or bullied by Edward? Had her body shut down in a final act of power-lessness? It didn't seem a positive result if one looked at it from the standpoint of evolution and survival. Such a response would quickly cause people like her to die out very rapidly in a harsher world.

She heard footsteps coming from the kitchen and feigned sleep. She listened as cups and saucers were placed on the coffee table, then the TV was clicked on and the leather armchair creaked as Edward sat in it. The news began; there was a story about a train crash in India, then the Manson trial in Los Angeles again. She heard the news presenter explain that Manson's girls, the so-called Family, had shaved their heads in sympathy with their messianic leader. She opened her eyes.

The girls on screen must be the same girls as before, though now that they had shorn themselves of common femininity they'd lost the prettiness, the innocence, the ordinariness they had previously possessed. How could they do that? she thought. Now they looked ugly, as capable of evil as the crimes suggested. She sat up.

'Oh, you're awake. There's tea there. I put three sugars in it, for shock.'

She sipped from the cup, though it seemed more like a solution of hot milk and sugar than tea. She stared at the TV screen, the news: a parade of the monstrous, the unlucky, natural and unnatural disasters, wraiths of history, which, like newspapers, would eventually be forgotten, mere paper for wrapping fish and chips in.

'I'll ring Christopher at six; he should be back at the hotel by then. Or leave a message with reception if you think it's urgent?'

Her mind went back to the accidental hang-up. 'Was that him on the phone earlier?'

'When?'

'When I dropped the receiver.'

'I don't know, do I? You hung up.'

'But was it important, something to do with the business?'

'What?'

'The phone call to Christopher. Can I help?'

'I'm ringing him about you. About that funny turn you had. He'll want to know.'

'But I'm fine.'

'You weren't fine half an hour ago.'

'It was nothing.'

'I have to tell him.'

'I'd rather you didn't.'

'Why's that?'

'I don't want to worry him.'

'He has to know. I have to tell him. What if next time you dropped dead?'

'I'm not going to drop dead.'

'You drop dead and he finds out you fainted before and no-one told him? It would be like I'd murdered you, wouldn't it?'

'Hardly.'

'Negligence on my part.'

'I'm not a child. I'll tell him when he gets back.'

'No.'

'No?'

'He always says, when he goes, make sure Helena is okay.'

'What?'

'He says, "Keep your eye on her, keep her busy, interested, she's..."'

Helena leaned forward, appalled at this. 'She's what? What does my husband say I am?'

'He's concerned.'

'About what?'

'About you, about his wife. Like any man would be.'

'What did he say?' Her tone was becoming shrill.

Edward sighed. 'He said you suffered from nerves. That it was a female thing. A bit irrational at times, you know, like all women are. Like...'

'Like?'

'Like those women on the news.'

'What women?'

'Those ones that were just on. The ones with the shaved heads. Do they know how mad they look?' He smirked, unable to resist, then adjusted his expression into a sympathetic smile. 'He's just worried, that's all.'

'This tea's bloody awful. I'm going to make myself a coffee.'

After saying that, she almost apologised. Almost. She held back the 'I'm sorry', held back her fury, held back the tears, too. 'You can go back downstairs. Open the shop. We can't afford to lose customers.'

He considered this.

He's probably thinking about how soon he can get back to the stupid book he's reading, she thought.

'No. I think I should stay here. Christopher would want it.'

She set off for the kitchen, put water and coffee in the moka pot, lit the gas beneath it and went into the bedroom to change out of her wet things. When she got back to the kitchen he was in there, peering into a cupboard. He'd found a pack of Kipling's Viennese Whirls and put all six on a small plate, then nodding to the pot on the stove said, 'I wouldn't mind a coffee.'

As she waited for it to percolate, he went back into the living room. The volume of the TV went up; he was watching one of those programmes for schools, something about Shakespeare. She took the coffee through. All but one of the Viennese Whirls were gone. He had his feet up on the footstool and did not look away from the TV screen as she entered and, as she saw it later, 'served him' his coffee.

ARTHUR'S STONE

Christopher came home the next day wearing a look of fierce agitation that might have been concern, but, Helena thought, was more likely anger at being dragged away before his work in London was completed.

His initial enquiries into her health were met with Helena's reassuring answers of, 'It's fine. I feel fine. Everything's fine.'

He stared hard at her and said, 'Is it your brain?'

She didn't know what he meant by that. Christopher liked to talk about brains. It was his thing. He talked about good brains and bad brains, about men's brains and women's brains. Dogs' and cats' brains. About brain size. Quoted statistics about how much of the brain is used. He was no expert but perhaps because he had been told once that he had a very good brain, he clung to this.

'Why would it be my brain?' Helena asked. She was perplexed, uncertain whether he was referring to her mind as the organ of consciousness or as a physically faulty organ. To her this idea created two distinct possibilities; either she was disturbed and thus the fainting was an emotional reaction, or her brain had malfunctioned, cut off her supply of blood or oxygen and this had caused her to black out.

'I was upset,' she said.

'Upset? What on earth do you have to be upset about? You know I have to go on these business trips. Have to keep the ship afloat, can't be pandering to invalids.'

'I am not an invalid. I told Edward not to bother you, that…'

'He did the right thing. Don't you start all that nonsense about

Edward again; I won't have it. Do you hear me? I won't have it.'

'But darling, all I meant was…'

His look cut her off. He sniffed loudly, his way of marking an end to the discussion.

Her silence, her downcast eyes must have seemed to him a sign of her acquiescence, but her thoughts roiled on. It seemed that Edward had said little to her husband about the circumstances leading up to her collapse. She knew if he had mentioned Jude at all he would have distorted the story, would have referred to the woman as Helena's friend, not as a stranger who had wandered in off the street with some curious old papers to discuss. Surely Christopher would have asked about this woman if he knew. Or would he? Not if he felt he had all the information he needed from Edward, who, being a man, had a good brain and could be trusted to give a rational account of her actions.

Perhaps the two of them had not spoken of it in such bald terms, but she suspected that Edward acted as Christopher's spy, paternalistically watching over her in his absence.

Watching her heart too, perhaps.

Christopher picked up the newspaper, shook it out and disappeared behind it. Today it was *The Times*. He also, on different days and in different moods, bought copies of *The Guardian* and *The Telegraph*. Always a broadsheet. He regarded the tabloids as comics, only slightly more complex than *The Beano* or *Dandy*. Maybe there was a perceived manliness in manipulating the huge pieces of newsprint, of holding it in two outstretched arms like a personal shield. He was like a bather undressing behind a white towel, his naked emotions hidden behind a scrim of newsprint.

'Can I borrow the car today?'

The paper was slowly lowered to reveal a questioning face.

'Or perhaps we could go out together? Blow the cobwebs away? I'd love to see that prehistoric tomb again, the one on the hill? You took me there when I first came to Wales.'

'Arthur's Stone?'

'Yes. That's it. Let's do that. Oh, please!'

His expression seemed to soften, but still he hesitated a moment, then shook his head to dismiss the idea out of hand.

'Oh, darling, you've been in London, in smoky old streets and dusty auction rooms and shops, and I've hardly been out at all! It will be good for both of us.'

At last he smiled. 'Go on then, but put something sensible on this time. No heels!'

'I will. I'll change now.'

She hurried into the bedroom to change into slacks and walking shoes. She was feeling a burst of happiness – a sense of hope and renewal, but then, as she tied her shoes, she felt the unfairness of his remark about not wearing heels.

She remembered that awful day, nearly three years ago now, when he had told her he was taking her out for lunch. Somewhere special, he'd said, so she'd dressed accordingly, in a smart black cocktail dress, stockings and stilettos. She was thinking he might propose or introduce her to his family and friends. He had been such a gentleman, insisting on the propriety of her staying at a hotel for her first visit to Swansea. She desperately wanted to please him.

He was sitting in the reception area of her hotel when she came down from her room. He had looked her up and down, raised an eyebrow, but said nothing. She thought his expression was one of approval, of desire. He took her elbow and led her to his car.

'Where are we going?' she'd asked.

'It's a surprise.'

In the car, she checked her make-up in her compact. Her lipstick was cherry red, a bit strong for day but she was so certain they would be going to an expensive restaurant she had made a big effort. Pencilled brows, eyeliner, mascara, powder, a touch of rouge. A pearl necklace. It was the sort of costume designed to make her look older and more sophisticated than her twenty years. She didn't want to let Christopher down, to embarrass him.

When he drove out of town she didn't question him. They sped along the Gower Road through villages whose names meant little to her – Sketty, Killay, Dunvant – past terraces of cottages, and suburban semi-detached homes, and here and there large houses set further back from the road with tree-lined drives and beautiful gardens. Past a red brick school that teetered high above the road, until finally the last houses fell behind them and they were on a vast, almost featureless plain where the sky grew big and milky with low clouds.

Wild horses stood in groups grazing just feet from the road; sheep wandered here and there, seemingly ownerless and completely free. She wished he would slow down so she could enjoy the view more, but he must have made a reservation somewhere very select, very much in high demand even at lunchtime.

The road straightened out revealing a long strip of black tarmac narrowing like a triangle in the distance.

'Hang on to your hats!' he said and, changing gear, accelerated. The car crested a hillock then dropped sharply down. Helena's stomach flipped. 'Yee ha!' Christopher yelled and the car climbed another slope and again dropped suddenly. The sensation was like that of riding the Big Dipper, creating a physical reaction that should have been unpleasant but wasn't. It was thrilling.

'Last one!'

She screamed as the car seemed to fly up then fell into space and her body escaped gravity for a second and hung above her seat before collapsing into the ordinary world once more.

They drove on in silence, climbing a steady incline until they reached a nondescript place where a few cars and an ice cream van were parked. Christopher turned off the road and the car bucked and lurched over the uneven ground. He pulled on the handbrake, smiled and winked at her, then got out of the car and stretched. She sat waiting, her black patent handbag on her knees, her hands on top of it, neat as a cat's. He shut his door, then looked at her curiously through the windscreen. She smiled back but did not move. She had an idea he was going to find a gents' toilet, or as that was unlikely, a nearby tree to relieve himself. Not that there were any trees, just low gorse bushes and bracken and crab grass. Going to the toilet, even when it was al fresco, was not the sort of thing people with good manners ever stated aloud; instead, euphemisms were used, for example she might say she was going to powder her nose, he might say he was going to wash his hands. So she sat in the car patiently smiling, and looking, as she now saw, like an idiot.

He walked around the back of the car, got something out of the boot and opened the passenger door.

'Table for two, Madame?' he said and gestured to the picnic basket and tartan rug he carried. He looked so happy, so pleased with his surprise that she could not protest, only step out of the car and stumble after him.

As he led the way they passed other walkers – couples and families dressed in shorts or slacks, all of the women in sensible shoes, flat pumps or brogues or sturdy crepe-soled sandals. They seemed to look at her with surprise, taking in her narrow sheath dress, her over-done make-up, the foolish shoes. Their surprise quickly turned to scorn. Stupid girl, she read in their faces, vain creature, ignorant woman. There were darker judgments, too, that seemed to see in her unsuitable dress the remnants of the night before, of unhealthy pursuits, of whoring, drink and drugs – because why else would a young woman be done up like that in the middle of the day? Even the modest pearl necklace, which had seemed such an elegant and understated touch, now felt like some flashy cheap adornment, a plastic trinket from Woolworths, or something won at the fairground.

It doesn't matter, she'd counselled herself, these people are strangers, you'll never see them again as long as you live. Her consoling thought was short-lived, cut down by the approach of people who evidently knew him.

'Christopher! Chris, my dear, I thought it was you!'

'Elizabeth! What a surprise.'

Two women hurried toward them, a pair of black spaniels dancing at their feet. They looked the same age as Christopher; one was tall and wore a navy slash-neck sweater, ski pants and canvas shoes. She was strawberry blonde with a long skull-like face, large pale-blue eyes in deep hollows, prominent cheek bones and a slightly masculine chin. No make-up. She gazed warmly at Christopher, but took only sly sideways glances at Helena. The other woman was not quite so tall and a little overweight. She wore a houndstooth jacket, a tweed skirt, ankle socks and brown lace-up shoes. On her head was a Tyrolean hat with a pheasant feather in the band. This woman also barely looked at Helena, concentrating her gaze on Christopher with a fixed smile, though behind the smile, her eyes seemed dead.

Only the dogs paid Helena any attention, running at her then scampering away again.

'Of course, you haven't been to the club for weeks, have you?' Elizabeth, the taller woman, was saying to Christopher. 'Such a scandal about Harry Butcher. His poor wife, was all I could think, but you know I'd always thought he was a bit odd. He was arrested in a gents' lavatory near the swimming baths. It's where they go, you know, to…'

The dogs ran off, oblivious to the scandalous news. One had picked up a long stick and the other had somehow also got its teeth into it, and they raced away, side by side like a team of horses, splashing into a puddle then disappearing into a thicket of gorse. One popped out seconds later without the stick and raced straight for Helena. Grateful in a childish way to have some sort of attention, she bent and offered him her hand. A mistake, as the dog pawed and scrambled at her legs, tearing a hole in the knee of one stocking, making a ladder in the other and getting wet black mud on both, as well as on her hands and dress.

'Down, Prince!' scolded the shorter woman. 'Bad boy!' And she struck him on the rump with the leather leash she carried. He whimpered and his body seemed to shrink. The woman looked hard at Helena. 'You shouldn't tease him. He's a working dog, mustn't be fussed over.' Her voice was crisp and impatient.

'But, I only…' Helena began to protest weakly.

The woman glared and shook her head, reducing Helena to silence. When she spoke again it was to her friend. 'Right ho, Betty. Time for these chaps to go back to the car,' she called, starting off at a run, the one dog following, the other bursting out from the undergrowth at a whistle.

'Oh, well,' Elizabeth said. 'Must be off.' She put her hands on Christopher's shoulders, pulled him to her and pecked his cheek. 'Don't be a stranger,' she said warmly, then with another puzzled glance at Helena, took off with long determined strides.

Christopher watched her go. 'Wonderful woman,' he mused. 'A damned good head on her shoulders.'

He marched along, pleased with himself, barely noticing the bedraggled Helena in his wake. Only when they had reached the place he'd chosen for their picnic and laid the blanket on a patch of dry grass did he seem to notice Helena.

'Oh dear, what's happened to you?'

'The dog. It jumped up and...'

'Oh well, no harm done, eh? Come on, sit down. We've a proper feast.'

'What's that?' she asked, nodding at the great triangular stone ahead of them.

'Arthur's Stone,' he said in a tone of surprise at her ignorance.

'Is it a burial mound?'

'Something like that.'

Helena sat down awkwardly. The dress she wore was tight and rode up her thighs. Her stilettos caught in the fibres of the tartan rug. For ten minutes, they ate in silence.

Helena felt every bit as out of place as the naked woman in the painting by Manet. What appetite she'd had was gone. She ate a grape. A tiny portion of cheese. If only he had told her it was to be a picnic. If only he had taken the trouble to look at the clothes she'd put on and then suggested something more practical and rustic. It would have taken her seconds to run back up to her room, to scrub her face and throw on some slacks and a sweater. Do men never notice women's clothes, she wondered, or are we all just invisible to them?

'You didn't introduce me to those two women,' Helena said.

'What's that?'

'You didn't introduce me to your friends just now.'

'Didn't I?' Christopher said this in a vague off-hand way. He was searching through the picnic basket, a deep frown creasing his brow.

'No, you didn't. They kept looking at me. I felt very awkward.'

'Ah, that's probably why they were looking at you.'

'What?'

'Well, people who look awkward draw attention to themselves, don't they? You know, it's that awful self-consciousness some people have; it screams "Look at me", doesn't it?'

'But it was the fact that you didn't introduce me that made it awkward. Made me awkward. They didn't know who I was, what the situation was and...'

'Darling, don't go on and on. You're spoiling our day.'

'But I'm just trying to explain.'

'Really. This is becoming silly and childish now. I've said I'm sorry.'

'No, you didn't.'

'Didn't what?'

'You didn't say you were sorry.'

'But I just did.'

'No. You said, "I've said I'm sorry" not "I'm sorry."'

He did not answer but threw the contents of his cup into the grass and began violently screwing the lids back on the jars of milk and sugar, tossing Tupperware boxes and tin foil packages back into the picnic basket.

She watched him as she nibbled morosely on a ham sandwich. It was good ham and there was mustard on it but it seemed to have lost all its taste. She might have been chewing cardboard.

Christopher stood up.

'Are you done?' he said angrily. 'Quite finished?'

She shook her head. He tugged at one end of the rug viciously, but as all her weight was on it all he managed to do was to distort the loose weave of the fabric, pulling it out of shape. With as much dignity as she could muster she stood up and threw the rest of her sandwich into a puddle. He tossed the blanket over one shoulder, picked up the basket and set off towards the car. She tottered after him, stumbling and fighting back tears. His pace was even faster than before, his long legs taking giant strides. The distance between them grew. There was no danger of her getting lost as the path was one long, straight one. It crossed her mind that, in an absolute fury, he might just drive off without her and then what would she do?

The parked cars again came into view; she could see the ice cream van and also a VW camper with its roof pushed up like a piano accordion. There were five or six cars, one of them red, the others blue, grey or black.

More walkers passed her; she tried to avoid their eyes, but felt their attention drawn to her irresistibly, and who could blame them – she looked ridiculous. At last she was close enough to make out Christopher's car and him in it, sitting behind the wheel, as motionless as a tin chauffeur in a toy car.

That first impression of her as an idiotic girl during the disastrous picnic had been hung around her neck against her will, an albatross. She had not been the one responsible. If Christopher had simply told her he'd planned a picnic, the chain of circumstances would have been altered. No, it was not she who had shot the albatross, though she carried it all the same.

The phone rang and Christopher picked it up in his study. He'd left the door ajar and she listened as he said, 'Yes. Yes, that's right. I see. Today? Yes, of course. One o'clock. The Pines on Gower Road? Yes, I know it. Yes. See you then.'

He hung up and turned to where she stood in the hall. 'Sorry darling. I have to…'

'I heard,' she said sharply.

'It was Professor Hayden's widow, she wants rid of his books ASAP. I can't…'

But Helena didn't wait to hear the rest of it; she returned to the bedroom and shut the door. She pulled off her shoes and wriggled out of the slacks and put on the clothes she'd been wearing earlier. She grabbed her bag and, hesitating by the open study door, saw he was counting out a stack of pound notes. She waited until he was done, knowing how furious he got if interrupted. She watched as he worked, noticed the liver spots that had begun to appear on his hands. Finally, he wrapped an elastic band around a stack and made a note in the account book. Quickly, before he could begin any other work that couldn't be interrupted, she said, 'I'm going out.'

He waved his hand, not even turning to look at her.

She walked the short distance to Castle Gardens and sat on a bench in front of the fountain. Its slate-coloured sides were metal, each panel impressed with a vague classical decoration while the centrepiece was a two-tiered structure with a spluttering pipe at the top. It should have been in some Italian garden, shaded by tall cypress trees, sparkling under a deep blue Mediterranean sky, instead of here in the middle of the municipal flower gardens, alongside the concrete benches, under the gaze of the broken castle and its parasitic ugly sister, the newspaper office.

She'd no sooner thought this than she felt bad – even a small pocket of green lawn and shrubs and flowers was an oasis of sorts and the town, or so Christopher had told her, had been nothing but a giant bombsite after the war. Well, so had London, so had Coventry; there were endless places still pockmarked by the doodle-bugs and incendiary bombs.

She remembered that someone had told her there was an aerial photograph of the devastated town centre on display in Boots the Chemist. As Boots was just across the road from the gardens and as Helena was at a loss for anything else to do, she made a beeline for it without a second thought.

The shop had expanded its provenance far beyond a simple apothecary's remit and its range of goods expanded over three floors. In the basement there were toys, while the ground floor boasted medicines and numerous make-up counters, and stacks of different items to soothe or support or enhance the human body. Various manufacturers blazoned their names across a variety of signs; there was make-up by Mary Quant and Biba and Miners. This last, being cheap, was always surrounded by a swarm of very silly teenage girls on Saturdays. The girls shrieked and pointed and touched everything and had to be watched carefully as their grasp-ing fingers went easily from fondling a palette of lurid eye shadow to dropping it into a pocket. Helena had witnessed this the very first time she had innocently entered the shop to buy an antifungal cream for Christopher's athlete's foot. It had struck her then that all the lipstick and scent and beautifying of young girls might end in such banal errands as hers.

On a weekday, at least until four o'clock, the store was filled with more civilized shoppers and had a dawdling quality which made one want to linger and inspect the goods on sale at one's leisure. After she had sniffed delicately at a number of products – Aqua Manda with its fresh orange scent and Night in Paris which was too pungent for her liking – Helena took the stairs to the basement and ruminated over the many board games. Christopher would never approve of these – only chess or backgammon could be tolerated – but if they had children? That would change everything.

She retraced her steps to the ground floor and then on up to the top floor, where she'd never been before. At one time, there had been a lending library there; she'd seen old books with a shield on the spine with the words 'Boots Library' picked out in red. At one end of the sales floor there was a record department with numerous wooden boxes of long-playing records, and on the far wall, plywood listening booths in which one could hear a record before purchase.

While taking all this in, Helena was also perusing the walls of the shop for the aerial photograph she'd been told about, but it was nowhere to be found. She might have given up but on being approached by a salesgirl who asked if Madam required assistance, she made her query and was directed to a second set of concrete stairs. On the wall above these stairs were numerous album covers and posters for records, then at the turn in the stairs she found the incongruous picture: a town blasted to rubble, flattened and empty, as grey and bleak a black-and-white photo as one could imagine. It was almost impossible to think that this was the town just twenty-five years before.

She'd seen photographs of Hiroshima after the atomic bomb was dropped. The same vista of grey rubble broken only by a few wrecked skeletons of buildings told its miserable tale. She had been born just a few years after the end of the war and at times it seemed as if the conflict belonged to the distant past, at others like only the opening fanfare of far worse to come. To live you had to forget about it, otherwise what was the point of anything? Plans for the future, the getting of an education, learning to read, to appreciate the classics or be knowledgeable about architecture or music, and buying houses, having babies, working towards some worthy goal or even a self-interested one – all seemed pointless. Yet little towns like Swansea had picked themselves up, buried their dead, rebuilt their shops and houses and worried about their children's 11+ exams and how to make a shirt as white as a neighbour's with Daz or Tide or Persil. Bob Dylan sang his protest songs and in Vietnam the destruction and death raged on.

Her own petty worries seemed like nothing in the face of this destruction, but that did not lift her mood one iota; instead, it was darkened to a ghastly blackness, a sense of futility. Perhaps it was also the effect of a cold concrete staircase with no windows. Feeling angry with herself for lingering, she resolved to get back into the air and sunlight.

SMALL WORLD

She turned sharply, ready to hurry down the stairs, and there was Jude. It seemed as if Jude had just been coming up; she was two steps down from the half-landing, but she might also have been standing there for a long time. Perhaps she'd followed Helena all the way from the bookshop, through the gardens and on her wandering journey around the store.

'Oh,' Helena said.

'Fancy seeing you here,' said Jude, with a pleasant smile. 'Doing a bit of shopping?'

Their voices echoed unpleasantly in the stairway.

'No, not really. I came to see this picture.'

Jude, as if by invitation, moved to stand next to Helena in front of the photograph.

'I used to look at it when I was a kid, then I stopped seeing it after a while,' Jude said. 'It's just there, do you know what I mean?'

'I think so. It's depressing anyway; probably better not to look.' Helena made to leave.

'Where are you going now, back to the bookshop?'

'No, I'm just…'

Jude waited, her head tipped slightly on one side, a half smile on her face.

Helena had been about to say she was 'killing time' but the phrase, with its murderous intent, its blank vacancy, had withered on her tongue. Besides which, she didn't want to reveal herself to this strange woman. She looked more carefully at Jude. Today she seemed normal. Her hair was tied back neatly and her dress was a simple brown woollen shift. She looked like a young housewife. None of the extravagant jewellery was in evidence and she carried no pungent scent, no whiff of joss sticks or patchouli.

'I just came out for a breath of fresh air,' Helena said at last. 'And to see this picture. Someone mentioned it was here.'

'I was going to come and see you.'

'Oh, really?'

'Yes, though of course he doesn't like me, does he?'

Helena wondered at this. Her first thought was that 'he' was Christopher, but Christopher didn't know anything about Jude so how could he dislike her?

'Anyone would think he owns the place. He's just a snotty kid.'

'Oh. You mean Edward?'

'That's his name, is it? Miserable little toe rag.'

'He's alright,' Helena said, feeling it correct that she should defend Edward, defend Christopher and the shop, despite her own feelings about them.

'If you say so. Do you want a coffee?'

'A coffee?'

'Yes, we can go to The Milkmaid. Or The Kardomah, that's not far. Then I can show you the new stuff I've found.'

Going for a coffee with a female friend. That was a distant memory and one that had somehow been snatched away from her when she moved to Swansea. No-one tells you how when you get married, when you don't work in an office or go to college, you can easily become isolated. Especially if you live above the shop in a small Welsh town, if your husband is much older than you, if he is away a lot of the time, and busy when he is home.

'Alright. Let's go to The Kardomah.'

If Jude had looked as she had on those other occasions with her jangling bracelets and necklaces, her hippy skirts, her Spanish shawl and heaving bosom, then Helena would have been ashamed to be seen with her.

As they walked, Jude said, 'It's not the same one, you know.'

'Sorry?'

'It's not the same one Dylan Thomas and his friends used to go to.'

'Oh.' This meant nothing to Helena. She knew Dylan Thomas was from Swansea, but otherwise he was just a dead poet as far as she was concerned.

'But it's funny in a way, isn't it?'

'How so?'

'How so! You talk posh, don't you?'

'Not really.'

'Don't blush.'

'I'm not.'

'You are.'

Helena felt the burn rising in her face. It was true, she was blushing. But she didn't like having that pointed out. She hated being told she talked posh.

'It's rude to draw attention to someone's way of speaking and other things about their person,' Helena said stiffly, thinking about Jude asking when the baby was due – it was either guileless and childish or manipulative and insulting. '*Very rude*,' she added.

'Is it?'

'Yes. But what did you mean anyway, what were you going to say?'

'Oh, it's funny that we're going to The Kardomah to discuss literature and stuff, just like he used to.'

'Dylan Thomas?'

'Yes.'

'Well, I suppose there are lots of places where different writers met and spoke and wrote. The Lake District, Dove Cottage, Stratford upon Avon, the Parsonage at Haworth. And London, of course.'

'See?' Jude said, 'You do talk posh.'

Helena shook her head. Jude was right, but completely wrong, too. How can anyone engage in a conversation when every word is scrutinized and thrown back in one's face?

They'd entered the café, which was thronged with a predominance of female customers. It smelled richly of coffee, tinged with cigarette smoke and frying fat. They found a table by a window overlooking an alley and a blank wall. Helena looked about her, the babble of conversation a constant rumble. A rattling cart bearing cakes was being wheeled ceremoniously up and down the aisles between the tables. On the inner wall, there were copper decorations that showed workers gathering and roasting coffee. Near the front was a large stone carving of a boy carrying two tea chests on a yoke. The tables' Formica surfaces had a geometric pattern grid of black coffee beans on white backgrounds.

A waitress appeared, order book in hand, pencil poised.

'Two coffees, please,' said Helena, looking at Jude for confirmation.

The waitress wrote this down and continued to look expectantly at Helena.

'Thank you,' Helena said.

'You have to order food. It's lunchtime.'

Helena looked at her watch. 'It's almost two o'clock.'

'I'll have a cheese and tomato sandwich,' said Jude.

Helena sighed. 'I'll have the same.'

The waitress spun on her heel and was gone.

'I suppose they have to make their living,' Helena mused.

Jude was unruffled and poked about in her bag until she pulled out a sheaf of papers. She looked through them and passed one across the table to Helena.

Helena recognised the same off-white paper as before, the same slanting handwriting. She did not read it but cast her eyes over the lines of words as if to confirm their existence.

She looked up at Jude, who was watching her with excitement.

'And…' Jude said, presenting another page with a flourish.

Here was the same paper, the same hand. Helena held the two papers awkwardly. She didn't want to place them on the table in case of spills and didn't feel able to concentrate enough to read them properly. Aside from the noise and the comings and goings around them in the café, she needed a context, an explanation. She could see that Jude had at least twenty similar sheets of paper and she would have preferred to look at them all at once to see if they were consecutive.

But Jude seemed too excited, too much the magician controlling what was seen and in what order.

'And…' Another paper was presented. Helena skimmed it, caught the odd word, 'Elsinore' and 'swarming' and 'silhouette.' A paper on Hamlet no doubt. Or a letter reporting a visit to the theatre.

The coffee and sandwiches arrived. Jude held out her hand for the return of the papers and it was a sort of relief for Helena to return them to her.

Jude put three spoons of the dark brown sugar into her milky coffee before attacking her sandwich as if she were starving. Helena pushed her plate towards her.

'Have this. I wasn't really hungry.'

'Are you sure?' Jude said and moments later both sandwiches were gone. She didn't say 'thank you'. Helena noticed this fact with a sort of prim distaste that she also noticed and didn't like about herself. It was like one of those endlessly repeating pictures where the subject holds a picture of themselves holding the picture. Endless regression, endless awkward self-awareness.

'So,' said Jude, picking up her coffee cup and dipping her head towards it, her eyes, bright and bird-like, fastened on Helena. 'What do you think?'

'I don't know,' Helena said wearily.

'What do you want to know?'

What Helena wanted to know was what the hell Jude wanted from her, but, of course, she could hardly say this. She thought about a simpler question instead. 'How many are there?'

'What, here?'

'Well, yes.'

'About twenty-five I think. And more in the house. I keep finding them.'

'They aren't all together?'

Jude looked unsettled by this question, though it had seemed a perfectly reasonable one to Helena.

'No. Why would they be all together?'

'I don't know. Because people tend to organise such things, put correspondence in a desk drawer or box or...'

'Maybe they were hiding them?'

'Why would they do that?'

'I dunno. Because they held secrets, because someone didn't want anyone to know they were being written.'

'I suppose that's possible, but how are you managing to unearth them now?'

'I look in the attic. The cellar. The wall cupboard. I was tidying, you know. Sorting stuff. There was this one nook, it had been papered over. Only saw it when I pulled the paper off, little hidden space in the wall like a safe or something. That's where I found those first ones I showed you.'

Beneath the gushing excitement Jude seemed nervous, as if she was hiding something. Helena wondered if the papers were not Jude's to take. She realised that she knew very little about this curious woman. Jude might be lodging or working in someone else's house and going through their belongings to take, bit by bit, a legacy that was not hers. Surely if these had belonged to some member of her family there would be some strand of distant lore about them. Even Tess Durbeyfield's impoverished stock had managed to keep an old spoon that bore the D'Urberville crest. But then some families had secrets – the criminals, the suicides, the insane and illegitimate they would do anything to hide lest the taint, even a hundred years later, should ruin their reputation.

'So you have no idea how many there are altogether? Nor who wrote them or anything?'

'No, not yet, but a picture is emerging. Like I said, a story.'

'I suppose it would be bound to. Inevitably. But it doesn't mean that it will make sense.'

Jude flashed with an anger that seemed to bear no relationship to Helena's mild and faintly cautious words.

'What do you mean? Can't you read the writing?'

'No. I didn't mean that. I just meant that the bigger picture might still elude one.'

'Because it's crap, is that it?' Jude said in a loud voice.

A few heads turned.

'No,' Helena said in an urgent pleading whisper. 'You misunderstand me. I just meant that without knowing who the authors of these papers are, we can't place them in terms of time and relevance.'

Jude seemed placated.

'You think they are authors then?'

'Well yes – of course. That's obvious, isn't it?'

'Really?'

'Yes.'

Helena saw how pleased this seemed to make Jude, but she once more felt that the woman was unbalanced; that there was something dangerous and primitive beneath the surface. Even the clothes she wore seemed to represent an instability of the self. It seemed as if each day Jude woke and dressed herself as if she were a different person. Helena had heard about cases of multiple personality disorder where one person was inhabited by several distinct person-alities and, as she understood it, each one knew very little of the others' existence. They seemed to experience blackouts where whole days, perhaps weeks, went by and they found themselves in strange towns never knowing how or why they had got there. Yet despite the different clothes, Jude was always Jude and her goal of getting Helena to read the papers she'd found was consistent. Unremitting, even.

Helena saw that she must be cautious; a pleasant chat and a cup of coffee was never, in this case, going to represent anything resem-bling a normal exchange. Jude might be a thief. She might be on drugs or insane or part of some weird cult or hippy terrorist group. Yet what on earth did Helena represent for Jude? She was not rich or powerful. She was just a young married woman expecting her first child. Unless ... Helena thought, her imagination swerving into the most sinister and horrifying conjectures ... unless it is my unborn child the cult want ... She shuddered, remembering the horror of the film *Rosemary's Baby*.

No. It was absurd to be thinking that, as she sat here in a Swan-sea café, among chattering women in pink chiffon hats and navy suits, with their shiny court shoes, their carrier bags from David Evans and Lewis Lewis, their hair permed and blue-rinsed, fancy brooches on their lapels, plastic rain-hats in their handbags – just in case – and always a folded cotton handkerchief in a pocket and smelling salts in a tiny glass bottle. But those were exactly the sort of people behind the satanic cult in *Rosemary's Baby*.

'Cake?'

The dessert trolley had rattled up to their table and the waitress stood over them, pastry tongs in hand.

'Not for me,' Helena said, trying to remember the special dessert Rosemary had been drugged with in the film.

'I'll have the lemon meringue pie,' Jude said, and it was plopped onto her side plate and the item added to the small chit that lay between them on the table.

'Cake?' the girl said to Helena.

'Do I have to?' Helena said, remembering the stern 'you have to order food' directive from earlier.

'Go on,' Jude said.

'Oh, okay. I'll have the apple tart.'

It came with a whirl of very sweet confectioner's cream.

Once more Jude demolished her lemon pie in a matter of minutes. Helena ate a little of the apple filling, a little of the cream and none of the pastry, then put her fork down.

'Don't you want it?' Jude asked.

'I'm really not hungry.'

Jude snatched up the plate, opened her paper napkin, dropped the tart onto it, wrapped it up and put it in her bag.

Helena watched, appalled, and noticed that a middle-aged man and his wife at a nearby table had also seen. Their sour faces blatantly showed their opinion of such behaviour. 'It's easy to judge,' thought Helena, and indeed the man's clothes – a hand-tailored pinstripe suit, very fine black socks and a striped tie with a repeated heraldic motif that surely represented an elite school – suggested that he might be a magistrate or judge. Yet the pie would be paid for whether it was eaten here or elsewhere, and if Jude was hungry, then why should good food go to waste? It was disgusting really to discard food with so many starving people in the world. Helena frowned at the couple, but they had already turned their disdainful noses away. She stared, almost willing them to say something so she could tell them what she thought of their prejudice and assumptions. He was quite red in the face, from too much port wine and whisky, probably. His wife's face was thick with powder and her fuchsia-coloured lipstick had bled into the wrinkles that radiated from her sour-looking mouth. If they noticed Helena staring at them, they chose to ignore it.

Jude was again rearranging her precious hoard of mysterious papers.

'Here. Read this one.'

Helena took it. 'I'm not sure if I can concentrate here,' she said. 'It's so noisy.'

'Really? I can concentrate anywhere,' Jude said. 'I had to, growing up where I did.'

Later Helena realised that this might have been an opportunity to find out more about Jude. But she missed her chance, saying instead, 'Let's go somewhere quieter, shall we?' and handing the paper back.

'What about your flat?' Jude asked, as they stood pondering where they could go. Castle Gardens might have been nice, but a slight breeze had begun, sending clouds skittering across the blue sky. That the wind would do the same to bundles of loose paper was certain.

'Oh no. Not the flat,' Helena said.

'Why not?'

'I'm a bit sick of the sight of it to be honest.' This was true but Helena also hesitated to have Jude there, especially as Christopher might turn up at any moment. Jude looked presentable enough today to be asked to dinner. Christopher had a habit of doing that, taking some people at face value and going too far, too fast. It was idiotic really. There had been that old Colonel with the handlebar moustache that Christopher had cashed a cheque for. A cheque for fifty pounds from no less than Coutt's Bank. It was forward-dated two weeks, but by the time Christopher could pay it into the bank, the Colonel had mysteriously disappeared and the cheque, naturally, bounced.

Even then Christopher had said, 'Poor old chap. Might have been his heart, you know. They'd freeze his account if something happened, wouldn't they? Sudden death, something like that.' Later there was a story in the paper about the man and his various disguises, frauds and embezzlements.

'What about the reference library?' Helena suggested.

'No!' Jude said this so definitely that Helena didn't even attempt to question the decision.

'Then, the Glynn Vivian? I'm sure we could find a quiet corner there in one of the upstairs galleries.'

They crossed town and on entering the gallery went straight to a small room upstairs. Finding a wooden bench, they sat side by side beneath the gaze of portraits by Evan Walters and Alfred Janes.

Jude took out her sheaf of papers but before she had a chance to select one, Helena said, 'Can't I see all of them? Why don't you look around the rest of the gallery while I read?'

Jude twisted her mouth and looked doubtful, then seemed to come to a resolution.

'Alright. But I know how many there are, you know.'

'What? Do you imagine I'm going to steal them? Or lose them? What sort of a person do you think I am?'

'Oh. I'm sorry. I'm sorry. I didn't mean that. I didn't. I just… well, they're so important. And in the past…' Her voice fell away. She gave Helena the papers and, taking the apple pie out of her bag, drifted off, carefully unwrapping the sodden napkin. Helena wanted to say that eating in the gallery was probably forbidden, but Jude wasn't a child, even if she had all the attributes of one with her quick mood swings, her enthusiasm and eagerness, her flashes of stubborn anger.

Helena searched through the papers trying to see if any contained headings or addresses or even page numbers, but there were none. All she could do was begin reading – then, if possible, find a logical thread through the labyrinth of words.

There was writing on both sides of the paper and it was easy to see that one side read on from the next. Sentences flowed, one following another, but the pages often began and ended in mid-sentence, a thought or action arrested just as if it had fallen over a cliff edge. The difficulty lay in finding an order that flowed between each sheet of writing. Helena tried for some time to read those cliff-hanging sentences then locate the rest of the sentence where it resumed on the next sheet. Two seemed to match. Just two.

She had laid papers on either side of her on the wooden bench and would have liked to spread out more, but the art gallery was obviously not the place for this.

An attendant came and stood near the open door, and gazed at her unashamedly. She looked up and gave him what she hoped was a confident smile. He tipped his head but continued to stand there overseeing her.

Was it permissible to use the gallery in this way? She really didn't know, so she gathered up the papers and, holding them against her chest, moved to stand in front of the portrait of the poet, Vernon Watkins. He looked like an Elfin King, she thought, a long face, pointed chin, huge ears with peaks at the top like Mr Spock's on Star Trek. Thoughtful eyes, however, as one would expect.

'Dissertation?'

The voice seemed to come out of a fog. Or it was the sound of the prompt standing in the wings as Helena, the actor who has forgotten the next line and is frozen and wordless, must be moved into action again. She turned. The attendant had moved cat-like until he was nearly at her elbow.

'Sorry?'

He nodded at her sheaf of papers, 'Dissertation? You're doing research?'

'Oh, yes.'

'Art College or University?'

'Neither.'

'Ah. Not school, surely?'

'Gosh, no. It's just private research. For myself.'

This seemed to please him. 'Very admirable,' he said, smiling warmly. 'What subject?'

Helena saw that Jude had returned and was watching them.

'History?' Helena said and then, as if by explanation, she wafted the papers in the air. The guard, thinking she meant to show him, reached out to take them.

Seeing this, Jude nearly flew the short distance across the gallery and shouted, 'You can't have them!' The guard, in surrender, put both of his palms in the air and stepped backward, shaking his head. He looked hurt, turning his eyes on the two women in turn, until his position of authority reasserted itself. 'Perhaps it's time you both left,' he said, grimly.

'Why?' Jude demanded. But Helena moved towards the door saying, 'Yes, we must go.'

As they walked along the balustraded upper gallery, Jude said, 'Why were you going to give them to him? Who is he?'

'I wasn't. I don't know who he is. He's just a guard.'

'I saw you!'

'I was just talking to him. For goodness' sake, calm down! What on earth would it matter anyway?' Helena stopped walking and stared at Jude. 'Really,' she said, 'what do you think he's going to do? Steal them? Do you imagine I'm in league with him? Here. Take your blasted, precious papers!' Then, none too carefully, she pushed the papers at Jude, while Jude, who was unprepared, struggled to hold them. Some fell; one sheet, as Jude flailed for it, wafted over the balcony and floated, lilting, down into the main gallery below. Jude picked up the rest of the papers then rushed down the stairs, her footsteps echoing loudly. Helena, feeling quite literally above it all, watched her from the balcony. Jude collected the lost paper, put it with the rest and without looking up, tucked them safely away in her bag. Then just as another gallery attendant moved towards her, drawn by the unseemly noise, Jude disappeared through the exit.

'That's the last I'll see of her,' Helena thought, but it seemed a bitter triumph. Or not a triumph at all, but a lost opportunity. She could have helped her. Might have taught her that not everyone was her enemy, that trust was possible. Helena went down the stairs slowly, casually as if to prove her difference from the other woman. She knew how to behave in a gallery, she knew you didn't run or raise your voice above a whisper. She went into the room on the ground floor where there was an exhibition of watercolour paintings. She moved around the walls, stopping to look at each picture in its turn, but not seeing, not really. In one corner, she noticed a few shreds of white paper and scattered crumbs. Jude had stood there eating the apple pie. You didn't have to be much of a detective to know that. Or to know that there was something off-kilter about Jude, something damaged and perhaps irredeemable. Helena looked at her watch. It was nearly four o'clock. Time to go; there was supper to be made and she hadn't even thought of it until now. Oh well, it could be corned beef hash. Again.

She walked into the main gallery and paused to look at a sculpture. The female guard who she'd seen earlier walked deliberately across the open space in her direction.

'Excuse me, but were you with that other woman?'

'Yes.'

'Do you know who she is?'

This was hard to answer; to say Jude was a friend was a falsehood as much as saying she wasn't. What was she, though?

'She's a customer… at my husband's shop, Quarto Books on Wind Street.'

'What were you doing here with her?'

'Well, I don't think that's any of your business… did she do something she shouldn't?'

'You know nothing about her?'

'Not really, no.'

'Be careful with that one,' the woman said ominously and made to go.

'Hang on, what do you mean?'

'Just that. Watch your step. Oh, and don't bring her back here again.'

With that, the guard turned on her heel and walked at a brisk pace back to wherever she'd come from. Helena looked around. The male guard was standing on the balcony watching, but as soon as he saw her looking, he stepped back out of view.

Days passed and it seemed that Jude would soon become a distant memory. This was a relief but seemed an unsolved mystery, one of those riddles like The Bermuda Triangle. If it were ever solved it would be… almost disappointing.

THE GOOSE GIRL

Helena was alone in the shop, idly turning the pages of an oversized book on the counter. She found herself looking at Victorian fashion plates of women in enormous puffs and ruffles of fabric, wondering how they managed to move or get anything done.

'Like painted dolls,' Jude said.

'Oh, goodness! You startled me!'

'Sorry,' Jude said, but she was grinning and her eyes rolled up briefly into her head, making the apology mocking and clownish.

'What did you say?'

'They're like painted dolls.'

'I don't understand.'

Jude was leaning with both elbows on the counter. She was far closer than any normal person would be, and Helena shifted away from her, but subtly, for all the world as if she were the one who was breaking a social taboo.

Jude jabbed her chin in the direction of the open book. Helena looked again. The women in the fashion plates did indeed look like painted dolls with tiny rosebud mouths, big doleful eyes and plump cheeks. Their severely centre-parted hair and the tight ringlets, which hung by the sides of their faces, made them seem rigidly unnatural.

Helena hadn't really thought about it. Or rather she hadn't thought of them as real women; she'd been wondering more generally about the shapes of the dresses, how they narrowed in the Regency period, then got bigger and bigger until they had those absurd crinolines, followed by bustles which in turn became sack-like Edwardian dresses. Hundreds of years of women's legs being covered by inconvenient skirts, then POW! along came a World War and following in its wake, the roaring twenties, and out came the legs.

'Why do you think they make them look like that?' Jude demanded.

It seemed a rhetorical question, but Jude continued to glare at Helena, waiting for an answer.

'Well...' Helena said.

'I'll tell you why – it's to keep women in their place. To pretend they aren't even real!'

'Ahm,' was all Helena managed to say, as she had begun in a rather sluggish and stupefied way to wonder how and why she was engaged in this odd conversation.

'But they were real, weren't they? I mean they had desires, they had brains!'

'Yes, of course, I agree. But Jude, why are you here?'

The mildness of Helena's tone seemed to calm Jude.

'It's the documents. I've found even more. I knew I would. I said I would, didn't I?'

'You also said that you didn't trust me.'

'No, I didn't!'

'Not in so many words, but that day in the gallery you...'

'Oh, that.'

'Yes, that.'

'Doesn't matter. Forget it.'

'But...'

Helena wanted to say that it wasn't forgotten. Not one bit of it was forgotten. Oh, and by the way, when had she ever signed up for this nonsense? Why did Jude keep showing up and pestering her? They weren't friends. Never would be. Helena was a married woman with a business to run, a family to think about. While Jude was ... Who knew what Jude was? A changeling in some ways. A mad woman. A dangerous person, possibly. Certainly no-one to be trusted.

'Will you read them? You must read them.'

'Must I?' Helena had meant this reply to carry an edge of irony or sarcasm, but somehow it emerged plaintively, the words of a small child questioning the need for bad-tasting medicine.

Seizing the upper hand, Jude said, 'Yes,' and stepped back to dig into her shoulder bag, this one a green army-surplus knapsack with a variety of straps and pouches.

More papers were pulled out and set on top of the open book. Then more fishing around produced a second set. Helena, watching Jude's hands, a safer target than the woman's face, noticed that her fingers, particularly the forefinger of her right hand, was ink-stained. The colour of the ink was a brownish black, as was the ink on the documents. Or on most of the documents; some were in pencil. Her first thought was that Jude, in her ignorance and clumsiness, had somehow got ink on her fingers while she was reading the papers. That was the thing about this woman, she kept on and on about how precious these were, then threw them into a tatty old bag and trudged about in the rain, going here and there, shoving bits of cake in the same bag. Who knew what else she threw in – greasy chip paper, bags of meat, cockles and bruised fruit she'd collected from the market rubbish bins, probably. Then she had the nerve to accuse Helena of trying to steal the documents. 'And,' Helena thought, 'I'm probably not the only one she's bothering with these. I've told her I'm no expert; she's probably showed them, or tried to show them, to anyone she can draw into her madness. The only difference is that I'm the only fool to actually read them, or listen to her.'

'So, he's away again, is he?' Jude said. She had finished the business with the papers and they sat in a loose pile, thirty or so sheets of old-looking letters. Once the papers were before Helena, Jude stood back a few feet. Today she wore a cheesecloth blouse with embroidered flowers, purple loons and plastic flip-flops. Her hair was pulled back and tied with a colourful pink and purple scarf. Eyes black-rimmed with kohl. A scent like English roses hung about her in a heady cloud, old lady-ish and cloying.

'Sorry,' Helena said. 'Who do you mean?'

'Him. Misery guts, that sits there like he owns the place.'

'He's off. He's gone to a festival thing …' Helena stopped herself from saying more.

'And the other one?'

'I don't know who you mean.'

'The other one. The man, what's-his-name, Mr Quarto himself.'

Helena laughed softly at Jude's mistake. She wasn't the only person to think that Quarto must be a surname.

'No, that's not his name. Quarto is an old term for a particular type of paper.'

'I know that,' came the angry reply.

Nothing was ever soft with this woman; everything, even the blandest statements, must be seized upon and taken as an accusation or insult. It was exhausting to talk to her; to say a single word was to tempt damnation.

Helena looked glumly at the top sheet in the higgledy-piggledy heap. A few words seemed to rise up and catch the air of the moment she was in. Or so it seemed.

'Why, we should find shelves for them or at least make a more tidy pile. Perhaps we might also read them.'

The words gave her that feeling of déjà vu. Or not déjà vu, but something like a telescoping of time, of a hand reaching from the past to touch hers. She felt slightly giddy; perhaps it was from bending her neck to read, or from not having eaten yet. She blinked and looked up. She was going to tell Jude to go. She would lock the door and pin a sign on it, 'Back in 15 mins', go upstairs, eat a yoghurt and some toast. But Jude had already gone. She saw the summery flash of white embroidered blouse and purple flares pass the window and disappear. The shop door stood wide open. The documents were still there on the counter and the sight of them caused a sort of sickness to come over her. Hurrying, she scribbled out a sign on a piece of old cardboard, locked the door, rushed upstairs and before she had a chance to eat anything, knelt over the toilet bowl, dry retching and heaving and feeling as sick as a dog. She was hot, then cold, then hot again and lay down gratefully on the floor with her cheek against the cool pedestal of the sink as the spasm slowly passed. The doorbell rang once but the thought of merely lifting her knees to begin the process of standing up was enough to convince her to ignore it. It rang again sometime after. There were days when no customers at all came into the shop, yet Christopher insisted they stay open from nine in the morning to five o'clock for six days of the week. Closing on any day for any reason sent a very bad message, Christopher said. A customer only had to come once and find the shop shut to go away and never come back. But Christopher was never here, not day after day, hour after hour, because the real trade, the real money wasn't in tatty paperback copies of Chaucer for undergraduates, or novels or maps of Wales, or Roget's Thesaurus, or the Michelin Guide to the South of France, or the history of the occult and the odd copy of a dark-blue clothbound 'First Aid in English' which someone had written all over, either filling in the answers or with crudely pornographic doodles.

It could all go to hell, she thought, sitting on the bathroom floor, legs stuck out straight like a wooden doll's, chin lolling on her chest, arms just flopped and useless by her sides. She had never wanted to work in a bookshop, never wanted to serve customers, or to stand behind a till and take their money, put their purchases in a pink and white striped paper bag. Listen to some doddery old man grumble about how spoiled young people were and how National Service was the thing! And bring back the birch and hanging and what a fine gentleman Enoch Powell was, and what about all those foreigners?

That had happened yesterday and she had to just stand there, weakly smiling and nodding and loathing the racist pig, and hating herself too, for the hypocrisy of her smile. Yet the students and hippies terrified her too. As did the greasers who hung around by the Double Ace café. And the skinheads in the pedestrianized part of College Street with their ox-blood Doc Martens and braces and shaved heads.

There was no tribe for her to belong to. She wasn't even really Welsh. None of it was as she had envisioned it. When Christopher had been wooing her in London it had been dinners and dances, theatre and classical performances, cocktails with his friends. Visits to the cinema and galleries and jazz concerts. A weekend in

Boulogne. Flowers. When had he last bought her flowers?

Flower power, she thought, letting her mind drift from one association to another. 'If you're going to San Francisco be sure to wear some flowers in your hair.' Peace. Love. On the Kings Road and near Carnaby Street she'd seen them, the drifting girls with daisies painted on their cheeks, the beatific men with bottle-green lenses in their round metal sunglasses. But in Swansea in the rain, in the winter dark, the same sort of bedraggled kids, in dog-wet Afghan coats, trailing crochet waistcoats with dangling damp fringes, seemed foolish. Schoolboys in enormous army overcoats with sweet faces under a blur of facial fuzz, with hair growing like a curtain down past their shoulders, could seem like angels. At other times like devils.

The feeling of nausea had passed. She stood up carefully and cupping her hand under the tap she splashed water over her face. Then, worried about the shop being closed for too long, or worried rather about Christopher somehow finding out, she grabbed a banana from the kitchen and made her way downstairs again.

For a time she sat doing nothing but scanning the people meandering along outside, certain that at any minute Jude would be back. A woman in a creased raincoat wanted a book whose title she couldn't remember, whose author she didn't know, but it had something to do with children and birds. 'A Kestrel for a Knave?' Helena suggested.

'Is that set in China?' the woman asked.

'I don't think so. Is the book you're looking for set there?'

'Of course, it is!' came the brisk reply. The woman rolled her eyes when Helena said she had no idea what the book might be and bustled out of the shop as if she'd been insulted.

Would Edward have known the book? she wondered. Or Christopher? Perhaps the book did not even exist, but was a figment of the woman's imagination.

An hour later, a young man came in looking for a book by Herman Hesse. They had two books by Hesse, but not the one he wanted. He bought a copy of Siddhartha anyway. As it happened that was the only book they sold that day, so the entire takings were fifteen pence.

She lifted the large book and, using it like a tray, moved the pile of papers to one side, being certain not to touch or disturb them. Jude had said she must read them, but the chances were she'd be back raging and rampaging no matter what Helena did. If she read them it would have been done in the wrong way. She'd be accused of mixing them up, of damaging them, of losing one or two or a thousand pages. Of sharing them with MI5 or even Russian agents. The CIA. The East German Stasi. Cuban spies. Or with spirits from the other side, or perhaps the ghost of Wind Street that Edward had mentioned.

No, she would not read the papers. She was done with all Jude's nonsense. The situation was quite absurd.

Five o'clock came limping along; she watched the hands of the dial move until, on the hour, she rose from her chair, went to the door, locked it and turned the sign to closed. That done, she sighed and seemed at once to relax. No more Jude today, no more crazy conversations and mind games. Instead she would have a light supper, a warm bath, watch TV or read, then have an early night. She was halfway across the shop when something – curiosity or the idea that Edward would see them – made her return to the counter, gather up the documents and carry them off to her secret lair upstairs. Yes, that was exactly how she felt, she thought, like an animal dragging its dead prey to the den where it could eat in seclusion. But it was also, she rationalised, a way of being certain to keep the papers in order and not lose any. The first thing she did was count them. There were 36 sheets, all with dense writing on both sides. Some might have been the papers she'd begun to look at that day in the gallery, but now there were even more, and again, it was hard to tell at first glance if one piece of text flowed to another. Sentences on the top and bottom of the pages began and ended mid-stream.

Helena sorted the sheets into piles, those with sentence ends and starts, those which began or ended mid-thought. There were twenty-nine of the latter. Making sense of them was fairly easy once the correct next page was found, but not infallible, especially where one page ended with a final paragraph and full stop and another began with a capital letter.

There was no numbering on any of the pages, but she got a pencil and with the lightest of strokes began to add numbers to the top right-hand corner of each sheet. She stopped her work after a few hours and opened a tin of chicken soup and ate it with toast at the table, looking up every now and then to survey, at a safe distance, the papers where she had spread them over the floor, the sofa and coffee table.

She had resisted the impulse to read much more than the threads at the tops and bottoms of pages, but these, besides being keys to the puzzle, also gave tempting hints to a truly fascinating story. Which was just what Jude had kept promising.

Then, somehow, she found something else; why had she missed it before? A torn envelope, pencil writing on one side, but on the other, typewritten words – unmistakably modern.

Miss J. M. Hopkins
Ferryman's Cottage,
Hafod,
Swansea,
West Glamorgan

Helena turned the envelope over. On the back in pencil was the phrase, 'She makes a luxury of her melancholy.' It was repeated six times, but each one varied, sloping back, then forward, with round characters then narrow, some with extravagant loops and long curving tails on the y's and others without. It looked as if someone had been trying out different styles of handwriting, as a teenager might, and one of the versions was very like the script used in one of the manuscripts she'd seen. Why would anyone copy out that sentence so compulsively?

Boredom, Helena supposed; it was no more complicated than that. Like doodling the same shape over and over. She herself drew spirals and chevrons. In the margins of her old school exercise books they were still there, evidence of distant days, the hand and pen busy, while the mind flew away on daydreams.

Later, much later, she would remember finding the envelope and wonder at her stupidity. Why had she not seen what was plain to see? Was it because her own prejudice stood in the way? She knew Jude was odd and probably mentally ill. She suspected, too, that Jude was probably dishonest. And possibly dangerous. But Helena had greatly underestimated her intelligence, her skill and cunning, judging her instead on all those superficialities of her dress and way of speaking, her attitudes and nonadherence to social niceties. Jude was without doubt, uncommonly common in one way – rude, obnoxious, uncivilised, in short. The easy conclusion therefore, was that she was not very bright. And perhaps that, too, was part of her plan.

After hours of putting the papers in what seemed to be the right order, Helena made them into a neat stack with what she judged to be the first on top, then had a shower and got into her nightgown. At ten o'clock the phone rang. She picked it up within two rings, but the caller hung up. Christopher, she surmised, using the payphone in some smoky little pub in London, The French House in Soho or Dirty Dick's on Bishopsgate or The Coal Hole on The Strand. He'd taken her to these when she'd first started seeing him; there and to restaurants in Chinatown, steamy, cramped places with shiny golden-brown ducks hanging in the windows, or Italian cafes with hissing Gaggia coffee machines, or Greek Tavernas or The Lorelei near Soho Square.

Sometimes when he rang and told her where he was, she liked that she could picture the place, wherever it was. His city, with its curiously named pubs, its funny little lanes and alleys. And its private members' clubs and bars that, when she was in London with him, he could only point at. 'Sorry, darling, can't take you in. It's pretty stiff in there anyway, a bit of bore. Old codgers dozing off behind the *Financial Times*.' It had seemed as if it had all belonged to him somehow; he told her how he'd seen Bob Dylan trying out guitars in Denmark Street in the early sixties, that he'd happened to be there when Jimi Hendrix was turned away from Kew Gardens because of how he was dressed. The bombsites that still riddled London, the tramps waiting to enter the crypt at St-Martins-in-the-Fields, some of them women, or as Christopher cruelly put it, 'creatures who were once women.'

Sometimes when Christopher rang, he didn't have loose change for the phone. Twice he'd reversed the charges and she, panic-stricken, had accepted the call, practically shouting at the telephone, only to hear his casual words: 'Sorry darling, couldn't change a pound note anywhere!'

He would ring again, she thought, and curled up on the sofa with the blanket around her shoulders and a mug of warm milk, and the documents, the precious letters that Jude had mysteriously abandoned to whatever fate Helena chose for them. She might throw them away, burn them, sell them, deny she'd ever had them.

'I'd never do such a thing,' she said aloud as if someone besides her and God could hear. That was the first sign of madness, wasn't it, talking to oneself? Though singing was allowed, oddly enough. The rules and strictures of society really were all nonsense, she thought, then pictured again those American girls on the news, as they sat on a city pavement, kneeling or cross-legged, grinning like a set of Cheshire cats at nothing except some mysterious ill-founded joy. Even more frightening than the hippy girls was their leader, a bug-eyed man with a great mop of filthy-looking hair who stared defiantly at the camera. His picture was always shown at the same time as that of the beautiful Sharon Tate with her gleaming blonde hair. If he was evil personified then she was without doubt an angel.

Helena hadn't watched the television news for a couple of days. It seemed a deliberate act of avoidance, a plunge into the sort of wilful ignorance that Christopher despised, but it unsettled her too much. Soldiers would continue to die in Vietnam and Northern Ireland, as would ordinary people. There would still be bombs and earthquakes, volcanoes and murders. Hearing about it on the day it happened did not help anyone, nor could it stop the next terrible event from rolling forward to destroy whatever was in its path.

She turned the envelope over in her hands. The J. M. Hopkins named on it must be Jude. She was the sort of person Helena expected to be living in some cramped bedsit in Mount Pleasant or Brynmill. Helena imagined her moving from one shabby furnished room to another, with a shared bathroom, a slot meter for the gas fire, another for the electrics, a store of candles for when there was no money and cold baked beans eaten from the tin underneath the black patch of mould on the ceiling, beside the broken window covered by a cereal box, with upside down Tony the Tiger facing into the room. But Jude had said she lived in an old house and 'Ferryman's Cottage' certainly sounded old. If there was any trouble ahead, at least now she knew where Jude lived and her full name.

She put the envelope in a carved Indian box in her bedroom. This was the place where, amongst cheap jewellery, she kept her most precious mementos: a lock of her hair from when she was five, letters from her mother sent the year before she died, her grandmother's wedding ring, a love letter from her first boyfriend, an empty bottle of scent. Pressed flowers. A lucky stone. Some shells. An acorn. It crossed her mind that putting anything to do with Jude amongst such relics was like introducing poison to something pure and unsullied, but she countered this notion rapidly with the equally obscure and ridiculous idea that her mother would protect her from whatever evil flowed from Jude. Her mother's letters were the three drops of blood on a handkerchief carried by the princess who would become the goose girl in the fairy story – as long as she possessed them she would be protected.

With that comforting idea, she went to bed and lay for a little time with disconnected thoughts roiling through her mind: Jude, the papers, her mother, Christopher and the goose girl. She remembered how in the story the blood-stained handkerchief had fallen into the river to be swept downstream; after that the girl became powerless. Helena would be more careful. She would survive.

PART SEVEN

1814

'The chief sea port is Swanzey, a very considerable town for trade, and has a very good harbour. Here is also a very great trade for coals, which they export to all the ports of Sommerset, Devon, and Cornwal, and also to Ireland itself; so that one sometimes sees a hundred sail of ships at a time loading coals here.'

Daniel Defoe 'A Tour Through the
Whole Island of Great Britain'

MELANCHOLY

From the edge of the bed Fanny could see herself in the looking glass. The mirror was speckled and distorted, making her face a ghostly mirage. The slightest movement altered it, making it plump, then long, then unevenly bloated. There was one reflection, however, that she fixed upon. Her eyes were slightly enlarged, her nose shortened and her rough, pockmarked skin looked smooth. Chance and science made her appear thus, she knew, but if she could have kept this face she would. If by some magic a paper could be adhered to the glass making an impression of this reflection, whether by chemistry or of as-yet-unheard alchemy, she would treasure it forever.

This is how I truly am, she would say, proffering the mirror's fixed image to all she met; this is my truth, my goodness. See? My soul is not scarred and rough. I am not ugly, not worthless. I am every bit as deserving of love and attention as other women.

A pair of faces sprang to mind with that thought, one slim and fair, the other dark, with plump rosy cheeks and an ample bosom; the two were both laughing and whispering together, their eyes dancing merrily. Her sisters, Mary and Claire.

'She makes a luxury of her melancholy!' she overheard her father saying once, and she'd been so ashamed. Had she created this melancholy, stirred it up inside herself and fed it day by day? So that now she suffered beneath its weight and the sting of its whip, just as a packhorse suffers under the command of a cruel master. But why? Why would she choose this path? This road of bleak and weary suffering?

When she heard the first hue and cry go up about the doves, she hardly stirred. Only when her own name was called did she go down through the house, out of the door and into the lane. She took two steps, her head bent low in misery as it always was. Her gaze was upon the beaten earth so that she saw the bird immediately: its plump white body, its scaly pink legs sticking up side by side almost comically. Its head had been severed neatly, and lay a few inches away staring back at itself without pity.

Once upon a time, this sight would have driven her to wild sobbing or trembling fear. Now she felt only indignation that life destroys life in order to live. She looked more carefully. There was very little blood, only a sort of red collar at the bird's breast and a matching scarlet ruff around the neck.

In the distance, far away it seemed, she was half aware of her name still being called.

'Fanny!' she heard. 'Fa-nee!' Her name broken in two, so that it sounded alien and unconnected to her. She stooped and picked up the dead bird, its body in one hand like a crown of elderflowers, its head in the other, a ball of white wool.

'Where are you? Faa-nee!'

All the commotion was at the back of the house and here she was on the lane at the front. Her senses, muted as they were by melancholic lethargy, seemed to distort space and time.

'I'm here,' she whispered, her voice croaking with little use. 'Here I am.' She seemed to say this to the bird's senseless head, its lifeless eyes. Some blood, still sticky, smeared her palm.

She did not go back through the house but slowly walked up the lane, then turned in at the gate, following the curved wall of the dovecot until she was in the yard.

'There she is.'

'Where have you been?'

As ever, she had no response to the words that flew at her. She heard them well enough, but they seemed to penetrate so deeply into her being and to suggest so many replies, that she lost track and could not speak. Where had she been? Since when? She had been on the path seconds ago, before that in her room, before that in a wood, before that, long, long ago, on a ship, the ship on the sea, and once, she'd been rocked jig-a-jig, gallop-a-trot on Man's knee as he sang to her and whoosh, down she went. But he always caught her for it was only the lovely game he liked to play. Another time she had lain in a fever, burning up, then icy cold, her teeth chattering, then another time she was hiding behind the sofa and listening to the man's words. Not Man, but another man. Man was her father, others were just men. Not that Man had married her mother. No. Man just was. Then he wasn't.

So where had she been? Poor knotty head, its insides were as tangled as a naughty child's curls.

Where had she been?

She came at last to the perfect answer and began to speak. 'Oh, nowhere.'

But her quiet answer came too late. They advanced towards her, the two men and the kind old woman, all of their faces twisted and strange at the sight of her. Their eyes burned her.

'What have you done?'

'Oh, Fanny, what is this? What cruelty have you wrought?'

'Poor creature.'

'Poor creature!'

'She has wrenched its head from its living body with her bare hands.'

'She's a monster.'

'A monster!'

The youngest of the two men took the torn bird from her hands and threw it into a pile in a straw basket.

At first, she had taken this for laundry, white sheets and red ribbons all tumbled about and ready to be put on the washing line, but now she saw that the basket was filled with nothing but dead birds.

She breathed in deeply and closed her eyes. Listened. Yesterday, or perhaps it was this morning or a thousand years ago, when she'd stood on this spot she could hear the roosting birds within the dovecote, hear the rustling, the curious creaking noise of their wings beating the air as they flew off. Now there was only the drone of bees, the chirrup of crickets. And the voices.

'Oh wicked, wicked!'

'Why, Fanny, why?'

She was falling through a dark tunnel and the voices grew distorted. Then nothing. She fainted.

THE MOONCALF

Only one memory of her mother stuck in Fanny's mind and it was bitter-sweet. Mary had just been born so it must have been 1797 and she, little more than a child of three, had crept upstairs to the room where her mother had been shut away. She remembered vaguely how she was drawn there by unfamiliar sounds and the sight of a strange man who carried a closed basket into the house and up the stairs.

She had spoken of this with Mary and Claire during the time when they were so enamoured with Mary Wollstonecraft that every chance they had they lolled about by her tomb in St Pancras grave-yard like pagans around an idol. Mary had at first believed her. Her eyes had grown large with awe and perhaps a little envy as she listened. Then Claire said, 'Oh Fanny, such fibs! You are such a ninny! Don't listen to the silly mooncalf, Mary!' and with that the spell was broken. Yet could it be true? Had she embroidered the memory from scant facts, from words read or heard? To consider this notion was to strip away her last connection to her mother. She would not do it. Could not.

As she recalled it, she had heard the cries of her new baby sister and Papa had shown her the elfin creature in its crib, but these new sounds were higher, sharper, and sounded at times like a chorus. She'd happily followed the noise as she clambered up the creaking wooden stairs. As she neared the top, two women and a man came out of the room with her father. Not noticing the child, they went a little way down the passage and lingered there, speaking to one another in mysterious and urgent whispers. The door to her mother's chamber had been left ajar. She slipped through and tottered over to the high bed where her mother was. There on the floor was the empty wicker basket.

She heard a sharp yelp, then answering it, her mother's voice, low and soothing: 'There, there, my little one.' Fanny, certain that it must be she who was thus addressed, ran closer and climbed onto a footstool placed near the side of the bed. Such a sight did she behold! Her mother was propped up on a number of pillows, her bosom exposed and her hair loose and wild, and at each breast a tiny puppy suckled. More puppies nestled nearby, one fast asleep, its black nose still shiny with watery milk. Her mother's cheeks were flushed and her eyes were closed but she was not asleep. The fingers of her right hand played gently with the smooth fur on one of the puppy's heads as if to encourage and guide its suckling.

Fanny was at that age when reason is still only in its early formation so she took it as a matter of ordinary course to find her mother thus engaged giving suck to a litter of puppies. If someone had told her these black and brown and white mongrel pups were her own brothers and sisters she would not have blinked an eye. No, to her all was wonder, all was adventure, all beauty. She could not recall how long she watched this happy scene, only that one puppy, being sated, let the nipple fall from its mouth and very quickly its sister, an all-white pup with a single black patch over one eye, took its place, lapping, then eagerly sucking.

But then there came the nurse's voice full of alarm. 'Oh, the child is here. Oh, sir. She must not see!'

Strong arms gathered her up and bore her away, then her father appeared and she was passed to him without seeing who had first removed her.

'Fanny, you naughty child! Your mother wants her rest. You must not pester her.'

In the corridor, she was set on her feet and the maid roughly took her hand and led her downstairs complaining of her wickedness all the way, until at last Fanny began to weep and the maid, taking pity on her, gave her a small piece of honey cake. This halted her sobs, though tears still fell from her eyes even as she ate, salting the sweet morsel and making it, or so it seemed, even more delicious.

Was that the cause of her melancholy? Might a child that devours her own tears always be fated to eternal sadness? Her sister Mary had a sunny disposition and their father looked on her with favour. She had never swallowed her own tears. She is the sun and I the moon, Fanny thought. She is day and I am night. She is summer and I, winter.

FOX

The boy had killed the fox, catching it first in a trap of his own construction, then stabbing it with a sharpened stave.

'Tha varmint, thou! I'll teach thee to get amongst our squabs!'

That her aunt could believe that Fanny had, in a fit of madness, gone wild among the birds, ripping the head off one and goring many others in diverse ways, was an astonishment to her. She knew very well that Eliza and Everina had wished to adopt her after her mother died, yet could not understand why they did not want Mary. When she was with one or the other of the aunts, she felt both better and also less herself, as if suspended between two lives neither of which was really hers – both borrowed and ill-fitting.

Her wits, she knew very well, were unsteady, not fixed and solid as they should be. But perhaps this was because of her being, as some tended to put it, 'a poor motherless girl.'

No-one begged her pardon when the destruction in the dovecot was discovered to be the work of the fox. Even when she ventured to speak to her aunt on finding her alone in the schoolroom, and said plainly, 'Aunt Eliza, how could you think that I could hurt those poor creatures?' the answer was sharp: 'Well, there you stood in the yard, blood on your muslin gown and slippers, and the broken bird in your hands and that wild moonish look on your face. What else should I think? Thanks be, that the mistress did not either send you back to London or dismiss me. She knows my good reputation and honest work, but you! Why, if she knew!' Here she hesitated and, flustered, drew in breath.

'But I did naught!'

'No child, doing naught was not your work. Oh no, you must interfere, you must pick up the pieces of that bird in your bare hands and then parade about the lane and yard with them as if they are some papist relics. You know not when to stop. Which might have been also said of your poor mother, excepting that...'

'Mrs Bishop.' A voice came from the doorway, commanding but not unkind.

Fanny and her aunt turned to look at the mistress of the house, Mrs Ellis.

'The girls are in want of distraction. Pray be so good as to take them for a ramble. Perhaps as far as the village?'

'Of course. My niece shall come too and make herself useful.'

Mrs Ellis, without so much as glancing at Fanny, nodded in assent and turned from them.

Of the five Ellis children, the four eldest were girls. Each of them had dark hair and brown eyes like their mother and all were in the thrall of the oldest girl who seemed seeped in the local superstition, a result of the influence of their previous nursemaid, one Bess Meredith who still dwelt on the edge of the settlement, near the woods.

All was well for some time, the sisters walking arm-in-arm ahead of Fanny and her aunt. Then they came to a fork in the lane and at a shrill cry from one, all four set off running along the bank toward a rude dwelling.

'Girls! Girls, stop at once. Stop!' cried Eliza.

'Shall I follow them?' Fanny asked.

'Yes, yes. Be quick. Tis Bess Meredith's place and they are drawn there as moths are to candlelight.'

Fanny clambered up the bank and ran after them. She saw them enter the hovel and minutes later she followed, plunging on into the gloom and stench beyond the rough door.

She heard the babble of the girls' excited voices but could not at first see anyone. She found herself in a long, low passageway with an earth floor. On one side were a number of crudely-made cages; inside one was a pair of rabbits, in another a young fox. More held magpies, crows, ravens and a solitary snowy owl that seemed to wink at her. The rabbits scuttled around frantically as she passed; one crow cawed and attempted to fly, succeeding only in battering itself against the cage. The fox, its broom mangy and grey-looking, pressed its sharp muzzle towards her, eying her, though whether its intent was to lick or bite she could not tell. A cat appeared at one end of the corridor and stalked boldly towards her; it had a pretty face and rich tawny fur. It stopped in front of her and made a singularly un-catlike noise that sounded like human words posing a question.

Fanny stepped closer and the cat fell on its side in an attitude of abandon, its four legs stretched out east and west, its body an attenuated curve of soft downy fur. Fanny knew better than to touch it. She had met cats before who seemed to offer their delicate bellies for a caress, only to pounce upon the benevolent hand with claws and teeth. The creature was in her path, however, so she had to either step over it or give it a gentle kick. The caged animals had quickly settled down again; the fox lay down in a tight ball, its broom half covering its face, its eyes sad and resigned. As she regarded the cat, considering her course of action, she heard the first discordant scrape of a bow upon a violin, then before the ugly sound had died away it transformed itself into a wild fiddle song. A few girlish shrieks accompanied it at intervals, then rhythmic claps.

Alarmed, Fanny nudged the cat with the toe of her shoe. It was less a kick and more of a determined push. The cat got up like an affronted duchess, quivering with fury, then it crouched low and sprang up onto the owl's cage where it draped itself lazily, letting its long tail dangle like a threat into the owl's domain. The owl, whose enormous eyes had been wide open as if astonished, slowly closed them.

Fanny moved towards the music. It grew faster and louder and the accompanying shrieks were bolder. This is how demons are raised, how the dead are stirred into dreadful half-life, how the innocent are seduced into evil, she thought.

Bess Meredith had her back to the doorway. Her loose black hair rippled like a stormy midnight sea and reached down her back to the base of her spine. The hand that supported the fiddle's neck was brown and thin, the fingers that moved over the fingerboard agile and quivering. The bow, played by the other unseen hand, jabbed and thrust at the air.

The three younger girls stood before their enchantress, their heads bobbing, their faces flushed, each wearing expressions of wild ecstasy as they clapped and whooped. Matilda, the eldest girl, was at the centre of them all, spinning around in a dizzy dance, her hair flying out behind her, her face a blur of movement, now visible, now not.

'Matty!' Fanny cried as loudly as she could, but her voice was drowned out by the tumult and noise. 'MATTY!' she tried again, but even her own ears could hardly register the sound.

Frantic now and caught between this frenzy of noise and movement and her nagging awareness of her aunt waiting outside, she gathered all her energy and strength to scream the name of the girl again. Her intake of breath, long and deep, coincided with the final dark vibrating note of the music and the first part of the girl's name flew out of her mouth into clotted silence.

It was as if she had suddenly screamed aloud in church. Fanny, so shy, so withdrawn, who, if she could, would forever go unnoticed, passing like a wraith through the world, had sent out a noise that was harsh and piercing, the shriek of a Medusa when she glimpsed her terrible reflection in the polished bronze of Perseus' shield seconds before he severed her head.

Bess Meredith did not turn at first, but stood very still. The Ellis girls all stared at Fanny with expressions of unrepressed astonishment.

There was a moment of uncertainty as if the girls were fearful as to what she, the niece of their governess, might do. But all they saw in Fanny's face was fear and discomfort, and very quickly their faces were transformed by smirks of cruel triumph.

Before Fanny could recover or find any words to admonish the children, Bess, twisting her head strangely in order to inspect the interloper, turned her gaze on her. Her eyes were the colour of violets, the eyelashes and brows dark as crows' feathers. Her unruly black hair covered her lower face like a veil. Fanny was reminded of a painting she had once seen, of the penitent Mary Magdalene washing Christ's feet with her hair – except the saint's eyes had been upraised and glimmered with a searching and pure light, while these eyes expressed its opposite, evil.

'She curses me,' Fanny thought. 'Now upon this spot I will surely die.'

Then the youngest girl, Elizabeth, giggled and another suppressed a laugh, and Matty, always the naughtiest, pointed at Fanny and said, 'What a silly face!' Then all of the girls were laughing at her, and Bess Meredith turned fully to face her, drawing the hair from her face and tossing her head so that the great mass of her black tresses was thrown behind her like a widow's cape.

Bess raised her right hand and the four sisters were immediately silenced. Such obedience, Fanny thought; never before had she seen it in the unruly girls, not at their mother's command, nor at the strict words of their governess, and certainly never in response to Fanny's plaintive appeals.

'You have crossed my threshold without invitation,' Bess said, her voice proud and intimidating.

'I beg your pardon, Madame, I...'

'Madame?' Bess repeated, then laughed with such genuine amusement that her face was quite transformed and she looked beautiful.

'I have misjudged her,' Fanny thought and she upbraided herself for her quick prejudice, but this was spoiled as suddenly as milk when lemon is added.

'The milksop calls me Madame! How dainty she must find me! How elegant in my jewels and silks! It must be the rich surroundings of my drawing room with its expensive furnishings, its hand-painted wallpaper, its silk drapes, its gold and silver ornaments.' Bess kicked at the rushes strewn underfoot to draw the girls' eyes and intelligence to her meaning. 'Not forgetting the fine Turkey carpet...Or perhaps it was my array of servants whom she met in the hall, my lady's maid and footmen, the housekeeper and stable boy, the droll butler with his winking eye and sharp beak?'

Everything hung on this moment. Or so it seemed to Fanny. She stood gasping for air, taking in breath after breath of the woman's cruel wit even after her last words were spoken. Some could swallow such words then spit them back in the face of the one who spoke them, but not she, for she was meek. Lacking courage, she stood unspeaking as the words sank deep inside. Their meaning seeped through her being slowly and once absorbed, they quickly soured her stomach and poisoned her blood, flowing into her heart where they festered into self-loathing.

'Take her away,' Bess said. 'She offends my eyes. Go quickly, my little loves, take her before she faints.'

So it was that Fanny found herself once more on the road by her aunt's side, watching their young charges skip away ahead of them like a band of sprites.

'Say nothing of this to their mother,' Eliza said in a low whisper. 'She will blame us instead of that woman. The girls will say nothing of their naughtiness for they know very well they are not allowed to see that wicked woman or even mention her name.'

'I will forget it,' Fanny said and the next day her aunt sent her back to London as if to ensure her niece's silence and her own position.

But Fanny never forgot. It was another bead of salt water in her cup of sorrow.

PART EIGHT

1816-1817

'Thither write, my queen,
And with mine eyes I'll drink the words you send
Though ink be made of gall.'

William Shakespeare, *Cymbeline*

REBORN

Swansea, Winter 1816

'Once upon a time,' Fanny wrote, for she had been inspired to work at a story for children. The pen scratched the paper and in her hurry to write the first sentence she left the 'c' out of the first word and had to insert it floating over the line, so that the entire page looked ugly and childish.

Her father wrote, her stepfather wrote, her mother wrote, her stepmother wrote, her half-sister wrote, her half-sister had run off with a poet, her step-sister threw herself at a poet, and wrote. This is why she felt compelled to write. Yet it also repelled her. It was a burden.

She had seen her father's manuscripts; sometimes he rewrote and crossed through parts when work was in the composition stage, but then the last version was always done in a fair hand and was flawless. Her impulse was to tear up the paper and throw it in the fire. To watch it burn and let herself weep. To hold her hand as close to the fire as she could bear. And weep. And pluck the pages from her most beloved book and weep. And wish herself a saint or martyr or an innocent woman accused of witchcraft, tied to the stake with flames licking at her toes, and weep.

And weep. And weep. And weep.

Or.

Begin again, and again, writing slowly, carefully, breathlessly.

Once upon a time there was an enchanted princess and she lived in a place called Summerland. All of the people of Summerland were happy and the weather was always…

She hesitated there, glancing up hopefully at the window. She wished for sunlight, the warm rusty glow of a spring evening that she might describe accurately from observation; the whitewashed wall that blushes pink when the sun's low red gaze is upon it. But it was dark, the sun even at midday shrouded in gloom. This terrible weather had begun in the late spring of that year, drawing a grey veil over the world just as it must have before the Flood. Perhaps it was not an angel who told Noah to build his ark, but the weather. What a sense of purpose he must have had, Fanny thought, to continue with his project while all around people laughed at him. And how loving and faithful his three sons, Shem, Ham and Japheth were to join him in his work! What if Noah's wife had said, 'Oh, no, tend to the sheep, fix the latch on the door, sweep the yard, grind the corn. Worthless man. Useless dreamer.'

How would Noah have fared if he had been a mere woman such as she had been just months ago? A struggling woman in this year of failed harvests. The price of food had gone up again and again. It seemed as if the spring would never come and summer would be held forever in winter's thrall. Then Mary and Claire had run off again, leaving her behind. With little money and many debts, she, unable to do work of any sort, tried instead to be a careful house-keeper. She was condemned to the chopping of vegetables, to sweeping floors, to begging for more credit at the butchers or for a sorry bone scraped clean of almost every ounce of meat and then to creep homeward and make a sorry soup. A soup too salty, fed as it was by tears. Her father had come upon her time and again, catching her weeping. It must have wearied him, to discover her thus.

'Crying again, Fanny?' Papa said

'No, I swear it is only the onions. They sting my eyes.'

But he had gone from the room already.

These thoughts, these memories must be banished, yet they were the source of her story.

All of the people of Summerland were happy and the weather was always fine. Even the rain was polite and arrived only when the crops needed it. When it was time for the corn and barley to ripen, the hay to dry, the sun shone. All were fed and happy in Summerland. The children grew up strong and healthy; mothers and fathers rejoiced. Only one person in the whole kingdom was not happy and that was the king's eldest daughter, for she was under the spell of a wicked witch and wept from morning until night, day after day, month after month, year after year.

'Why do you weep, my child? There is nothing to give rise to sorrow here in Summerland, only good things.'

'Oh, Father, I do not know,' the poor girl said, as tears spilled down her cheeks and made a salty puddle at the King's feet. 'I know I should be happy, but I cannot. I think I must have been born sad.'

Fanny looked up. A bare tree hung in the mist beyond the window; the soft curve of its uppermost branches seemed to belie the true nature of its material. From a distance, she could imagine running a hand over it as one would a dog's head; it might be as smooth as fur or bristly like a hog-hair brush. She knew it wasn't, but somehow her mind went tumbling through thought after thought, finding metaphors, likening one object to another so this could fix what she saw and felt, as if preserved in aspic.

Then her thoughts ran to Greek myth, to the nymph Daphne who was transformed into a laurel tree to escape her pursuer. Did Daphne know she was a tree? Did her mind go on, did her soul pulse? Was it better to be a tree? Or was her transformation into a tree like death?

The only escape from her troubles that Fanny had finally seen possible was into the arms of oblivion and death. Before Matthew and Baxter had found her, she had been as dead as a tree. Or not dead, but without consciousness – which is like the condition of a plant. Alive but with no senses, no soul, no intellect.

With his friend's help, Matthew had, God-like, brought her back to the world. Given her a new life in a place that was like Eden. She was free here. Free of cares, free of Papa's money worries, free of Mrs Clairmont's sharp words, of her carping and scolding. She was reborn. Made anew.

She remembered what he had said in those early days: 'This shall be your room. It was my sister's. Look, here is the table she placed under the window. Here are her books. Here is paper and here ink. Here is her old doll. Very tattered and torn, but she is still smiling and pretty. My sister called her Lottie. Ah, but you frown, you are too old for dolls, of course. I only thought... well, never mind.'

He was so good and kind. As was the other man, his friend. They had done it together, their good deed, lifting her from the maw of death and somehow – she could not think how they had arranged it – persuading everyone that she was indeed dead. He'd shown her the Cambrian, the newspaper that told of her death. It was a 'melancholy discovery' and she was a 'most respectable-looking female'. Her suicide note was recounted too – all of it – every pitiful word except for her name.

Matthew had told her that Baxter had torn off the strip of paper from the bottom of her note and placed it in his breast pocket.

'Why did he not burn it?' she asked, the second time he'd told her the story.

'Why? For security, to be certain your name was kept secret, for sometimes a guilty scrap may not be entirely consumed by fire. But perhaps his reasons were superstitious, too. Baxter is a man of genius and well-read; he is a man of rational thought who yet appreciates the mysteries of the unseen and the unknown.'

'And he still has the strip of paper bearing my name?'

'I believe so.'

'But why? Does he mean to expose me? To harm me?'

'Harm you? No! My dear child, I believe he is a good man. He was the very architect of our scheme; it was he who set all in place, he who knew the best means to bring you back to life and he who arranged all matters after.'

'But you...'

'I was merely his aider and abetter. Chance meant that I was the one who had a home to offer you and thus the means to give you asylum and make you well. His position is very different. He dwells in rented accommodation and has a wife and several children. Each of us provides what we are able; the one genius and wit, the other bricks and mortar, a warming hearth and good whole-some food. One without the other is lost, is it not?'

'Yes.'

'Are you not grateful? Did we do wrong? Do you regret our actions?'

'You mean, I suppose, do I regret not succeeding in my aim?'

'Do you?'

'It would seem I have succeeded and also failed. The world believes I am no more and yet here I sit, blood still pulsing in my veins and, I confess, sad thoughts still flying in my head. But sir, I am aware that I am indebted to you. How shall I ever repay either of you?'

'That is easy! Your good health and restored spirit shall be our only due and recompense. That is enough.'

'But I must make shift for myself. Though I am little skilled for useful employment, I had a scheme to write a tale for children. It was something my mother did. She wrote books.'

'Did she indeed! And that would make you happy?'

'It would be something – if only as a banishment of idleness. I began an attempt this morning, but it is a very poor thing.'

'Then set to and try again, dear child. You have all you need?' She nodded.

'Very good, then. When it is finished and ready, I will read it and offer such advice as I am able.'

Fanny had 'set to' many times, but each idea, each fresh attempt, each moral tale, each guiding story for an innocent child, had fallen away two or three sentences in. The story about Summerland and the weeping princess was the longest she had done so far and yet she faltered; where was the story going? Many paths occurred to her; a prince from a faraway land might see the princess, fall in love with her and discover the source of her enchantment – an old witch who lived in a cave below the escarpment of the castle. He would run the witch through with his sword thus releasing the princess from the spell. Or he might overturn the witch's black caldron which held all the tears the princess would cry for the rest of her life. But tears, Fanny knew, are not merely an excess of salt water that the body must purge. Tears are the result of sorrow and pain.

Perhaps the princess needed to learn how to be happy. Yet, except by some magic, how can happiness be learned? And she was the last, indeed the very last, person on earth who should attempt to write such a story. So far from discovering her own happiness, her attempt threw up a white sheet on which only the outline of her own limp hands could be seen and never the phantasmagorical creatures of the shadow puppeteer.

It is not enough to say the princess is enchanted. Or that she was born under a bad star. But I am, Fanny thought. How can I learn to be happy if all I see is sorrow? Conceived near Paris while the blood-letting of revolution went on, the illegitimate child of an American man, who some called an adventurer, and a woman described as a hyena in petticoats, a bluestocking and worse. With a stepfather who claimed I made a luxury of my melancholy. That is me and I cannot be undone. A 'sorry occurrence' to be born, a 'sorry occurrence' to die.

A gentle knock at her door stopped all these thoughts at once. She put down her pen, turned to greet her saviour.

'Fanny?' Matthew said. 'Are you busy? Baxter has come to pay his addresses.'

A WINTER'S TALE

'Miss…' Baxter said, his courteous greeting cut off by a remembrance, a riddle. He knew her surname as it was written on her final letter to the world. He knew too, that it must not be spoken aloud, but as she was yet to be baptized with another name he had faltered into silence. They must consider a new name for her. Baxter and his friend Matthew were in some degree like fathers to this new-born being and as such were charged with the solemn duty of bestowing the subject of their patrimony with a name. But Baxter, in his vast, his quicksilver intelligence was also acutely aware of the importance of rank and the rules of polite society, and therefore knew that 'Miss' would not do.

'Miss Frances,' he said at last.

He caught her eye momentarily. Immediately she looked down and colour rushed to her cheeks, betraying something – shyness, embarrassment – or perhaps the heat of affection. He found his own face burning, but then he had just walked through the icy December air through the lanes that rose steadily upward to the village of Sketty and into his friend's warm parlour.

He was also, how could he not be, acutely aware of this young woman's body. She might not remember, but he had held her in his arms, the light cotton shift she wore falling away from her shoulders to expose her breasts. He had seen her on the brink of death, an intimacy of another sort. And he had seen her quite naked. Touched her bare flesh which, he remembered with a shudder, was cooling rapidly. It reminded him of clay, cold to the touch but malleable. Her skin was imperfect; no smooth complexion for this bone china shepherdess; grog or sand had been added to the clay used to make her. The scars of some childhood disease had roughened her skin, but perhaps, like sand in clay, it added strength too.

'My dear,' Baxter said, 'forgive me. The circumstances of our first meeting were unusual. Yet I have thought of nothing since, so distracted have I been with hopes for your recovery and, ultimately, your enduring happiness.'

Happiness, thought Fanny, there it is again. I would pursue it like a rare butterfly on a summer's day if I glimpsed it just once.

'Do sit with us, dear Fanny,' Matthew said, pointing to the chair by the fire. Fanny sat. She was obedient in this, but kept her back straight, her hands clasped together on her knees, her gaze lowered. This was how a well-bred lady should sit, shyly and with humility and deference, withdrawn from society, a grey moth with its wings folded, silent and still.

The servant brought tea.

'Baxter, will you join us tonight? Rebecca, tell Mrs Curtis there will be one extra for dinner.'

'No, no, my dear friend; I cannot impose.'

'Nonsense, Baxter, I insist. Rebecca? We still have that excellent ham, do we not?'

'Yes, sir, and the boy brought a brace of sea trout this morning.'

'There, you see, Baxter, we are in great need of another at our table or we shall be forced to send good food to the pigs!'

'Mrs Curtis said that the leftover trout would do for a fish paste tomorrow and the ham scraps have been promised to me for to take when I goes to my mother on Sunday,' Rebecca said in a rush, undermining her master's words.

'That will do, Rebecca.' Matthew attempted to sound stern but he could not rinse the boyish sweetness from his voice, so his words seemed like gratitude rather than censure.

Fanny did not look up, but watched the servant's feet as she fussed with the tea things. Her skirt was grey and its hem was turned under perhaps twice or three times, producing a thickness and clumsy weight. Her stockings were coarse and wrinkled. Her shoes were of a soft brown leather that showed the outline of the girl's toes straining against the material. The dress, being a little too short, showed the girl's bony ankles and an inch or so of her slender legs. She is young, Fanny thought, and still growing. Wanting confirmation of her assessment, Fanny glanced up, her eye roving quickly past the two young gentlemen to the girl. She was indeed very young and small in stature; her head seemed to be on the same level as the seated men's. Tiny she was, and yet evidently not quite a child as her bosom was already well developed.

Perhaps feeling herself observed, Rebecca met Fanny's gaze and her expression seemed to instantly change into something very fierce and fiery. Fanny dropped her eyes and felt the old burning shame that came from a sense of being watched. And judged.

'Now, Rebecca, that is all. On your way.'

The girl's feet did a little hesitating dance.

'If there's nothing more then, sir.'

'No, we have everything. Thank you, Rebecca.'

Finally, the feet, curled and crimped in their too-tight shoes, retreated and the door closed.

'Hah!' Baxter said. 'So I am to be excluded from dinner so your cook can make fish paste and that girl can take the ham for her family to feast upon!'

'Don't mock the poor child. She lives in terror of Mrs Curtis. As do I.'

'That is why you need a wife. A wife would soon put Mrs Curtis in her rightful place.'

'She needs new shoes,' Fanny said. She had not meant to speak these words aloud and they produced in the two men a sort of spluttering astonishment.

'I beg your pardon? What was that?'

'New shoes for the proposed new wife? Is that it?' Baxter asked.

'Who needs new shoes?'

'She does. That serving girl, Rebecca.'

'But when did she tell you that?'

'Just now.'

'Did she? I heard no words pass between you.'

'Not in words. But in how she looked and moved.'

'Is that so?'

Having said her piece, Fanny shook her head and turned her body so that she was nearly facing the wall. The wall was good, she thought, pretty to look at with its rose-sprigged wallpaper, and it did not look back at her, nor speak. I will alight on one flower, Fanny thought, settle all my concentration there.

'Call the girl back,' Baxter said.

'No.'

'Yes, you must. I wish to observe her for myself. This shall be a matter of science.'

A bell sounded distantly and after a matter of minutes the door opened and the same hesitant feet drew towards them.

'Yes, sir? Did I forget something?'

'No, no. But could you adjust the window shutters? I fancy if they were folded back more closely, greater light might be admitted.'

'They are well back already. As far as they will go. I did them myself this morning.'

'Oh, please do not stand there arguing. Indulge me. Go and check them.'

The windows were on the far side of the room and thus permitted an extended study of the girl for the purpose of Baxter's scientific observation. Fanny did not watch the girl cross the room, but heard the clatter of the wooden shutters, the crisp turning and returning of metal clasps.

'They are all tucked back, sir, as I said they were.' There was an unmistakable petulance in her tone.

'Very well. Come back here then, Rebecca.'

'Yes, sir.'

'Now stand there, if you will.'

There followed a long silence and Fanny imagined the two men looking at the girl's poor feet and their glances at one another, the silent confirmation of a proven theory.

'Have I done something wrong, sir? The gloom is due to the weather, which cook says comes from it being the end of the world. There's hardly a crack of light through the clouds, no bit of sun to be had,' the girl, loquacious as ever, said in a rapid stream of lilting words.

'No, no. You've done nothing wrong. It is only that one of our company has drawn attention to your shoes.'

'My shoes, sir? Are they dirty? I did wipe them over this morning with a rag.'

'No. They are not dirty, but they are too small. Do they not injure you?'

'Oh, yes, sir. They do hurt like b…'

The girl stopped herself from using whatever crude term had been on the tip of her tongue.

Pretending innocence, Baxter said, 'Hurt like b…?'

'Hurt like bee stings, sir.'

'Ah, like bee stings, very good. I thought you were going to say something else.'

'No. Not I. Bee stings – yes – like a thousand bees is trapped inside my shoes and they's a-stinging and a-biting all the day long.'

'Then you should get new shoes.'

'I've got new shoes!' This was said sharply, the girl's pride and sense of injustice seeming to rise to the surface in her words. 'I got new shoes from my sister, who got them from the Dillwyn family who she's indentured to, as their youngest girl quite outgrew them before she'd even had them a month.'

'And they fit you?'

'Like a glove, sir. My sister did say it was as if they'd been made for me and only worn once, she said.'

'Then why on earth aren't you wearing them?'

'Yes, why?' added Baxter. 'Are you saving them for your trousseau?'

'No, sir. I am not.'

'Oh, don't tease the poor girl, Baxter. It is very cruel, is it not?'

'It is, sir. Very cruel. Especially when a poor girl's toes are in such torment and grief, too.'

'So then, why not wear the new shoes?'

'They are red, sir. Red as fresh blood. And Cook says…'

'Ah, I understand.'

'Cook says I must put blacking on them if I wants to wear them. But sir, I can't. I can't! They are so pretty and what if the Dillwyns, who must have paid a great deal for them, for they are from a master shoemaker in Bath, my sister says… what if the Dillwyns should ask for them back? What then?'

'I do not think the family will ask for them back.'

'But sir…'

'Do you have the shoes here?'

'Yes, in my room, hidden under my bed, lest Cook should get ahold of them.'

'Then pray go upstairs and fetch them. We will decide if they will do or no.'

Fanny followed the pattern of rosebuds on the wall as she listened to this drama unfold. The flowers formed a sort of grid, each one exactly like every other and therefore unlike anything in nature. These painted buds did not move, they did not breathe as living flowers seemed to when a breeze stirred them. Their petals would never fall, no insect would ever drink their nectar. They were stark and sterile, mere pigment on paper. Fanny remembered a painting she once saw. It was a still life of flowers in a terracotta pot painted in astonishing lifelike detail. Roses, poppies, convolvulus and foxgloves with their speckled hoods. And there amongst the twining, tumbling stems and flower heads were butterflies and moths, spiders, beetles; a universe entire. Someone said, in that special tone of voice that meant, remember, remember, 'This is the work of a Dutch lady.' But who said it was lost to her. She had liked to think it had been her mother, but that couldn't be possible.

'Ah. Here she is!' Matthew's voice announced the arrival of the maid. Fanny's eye set off on a subtle trail from the wall, across the hearth and Turkey carpet. Skimming past chair and table and Baxter's legs. Her gaze arrived at Rebecca's feet, which were now clad very prettily in red shoes. She wore the same stockings as before, but they were less wrinkled now. The girl bounced on her heels as if suppressing a peasant dance of raucous energy.

'Well, now. Are they quite comfortable?' Matthew asked.

'Yes, sir.'

'Step back a little. Now forward as if you were bringing us tea.' The girl did as she was bid.

'So, Baxter, what do you think?'

'They are indeed very red. As red as a ladybird's shell. In China, the colour is thought to be very auspicious. Though in the science of pottery, making true red is elusive.'

'Hmm, but it is acceptable for a servant of all work to be so shod?'

'I should say that the choice between a girl half-crippled by her shoes and one able to move freely suggests that the work shall be better done by one unhobbled.'

'Indeed.'

'And they are very pretty. Very eye-catching. They set off her slender ankles exceedingly well.'

'I think those are Mrs Curtis's objections.'

Both men laughed.

'There, then. Tell Mrs Curtis it is my express wish that you wear the gift from the Dillwyn family and that they shall be invited to dinner shortly and will wish to see the shoes as scarlet-hued as on the day they were bought.'

The girl bobbed a curtsy and turned to go.

'It was Miss Françoise here whom you should thank, for it was she who noticed how ill-fitting your old shoes were.'

'Oh,' the girl said on an intake of air. There was a pause and Fanny felt compelled to look up. 'Thankee kindly, Miss.' The words were spoken with deliberation but the young girl's eyes remained cold.

'Tis nothing,' Fanny murmured, quickly dropping her gaze again to study her hands where they lay laced in her lap. Pale hands, not roughened or reddened by work. Hers, Fanny's, was the worst position – educated and intelligent yet without any money, nor hope of money. Too full of airs to live as a poor girl and be accepted among the common folk. Too ruined by scandal to live amongst her equals. Her face disfigured by smallpox scars, yet not so much that the lepers should welcome her. Motherless, fatherless, sister-less too. Now the object of pity and kindness and perhaps the subject of the latest scientific scheme undertaken by these two gentlemen. An experiment in humanity and natural philosophy. Brought back from the dead, as Lazarus was, to walk amongst mankind again. But the world remained the same. Nothing had changed. Death still waited. Death's work was postponed, but not, for all the rejoicing at the raising of Lazarus, cancelled completely.

Thinking of the red shoes, of precious worldly possessions,

she remembered the gold watch from Switzerland and more importantly, her mother's corset with its embroidered initials of MW. Left behind in that wretched room at the inn. Left behind with a note, and the empty laudanum bottle: all she possessed – even her corpse.

Yes, here lies Françoise Imlay, Frances Wollstonecraft, Fanny Godwin. Dead she is, poor creature. Her skin leached of colour, it is white, then a sort of vapid blue, then powdery green, and where she lies on her back there are livid pools of deep blue, black, burgundy – like bruises made by a giant's fist. Nothing beautiful there. Though as she was never a beauty in life, death can hardly bring any improvement.

It was unsettling to consider one's own death, though Fanny had considered hers for many an unhappy hour, but how much more unsettling it was to discover that one had succeeded, and yet lived to see that success!

Sometimes, she thought, this must be an illusion. An ongoing dream from which she would never awaken.

There were voices beyond her consciousness, drifting around her ears – the rumbling baritone patterns of the men's conversation. At times, it was pleasant to be almost like a child, seen but not heard. Or, for that matter, a woman who was not meant to grasp the complications, the breadth and depth, weight and wisdom of male knowledge.

With only half her attention in the room, and half-floating and sinking by turns, she heard what they said only in snatches.

'But with economies, for example if the firing time could be reduced and if wastage could be cut... yes, coal is cheap and plentiful, but my role is that of an artist...'

'The cost of improvements would run into hundreds, but the house is entailed. You know what that means!'

'Now, here is a nautilus shell. Here a common snail and a razor clam – such variety must be nature's design!'

'No – my Grand Tour ended in Amsterdam with news of my father's death. I had disembarked only hours before...'

'And this experiment proves the principle of...'

'Aeschylus was the father of tragedy and died tragically too.'

'But all death is surely tragic.'

She had grown up hearing such conversations and better. She had taken in, along with her mother's milk, the claims for women's equality with men. She'd listened to William Godwin debate political justice and numerous great men on the issues of the age: suffrage, equality, revolution, slavery, American independence. She'd heard Coleridge read 'The Rime of the Ancient Mariner' while the ink was hardly dry upon the page. Yet what good did any of it do her?

A thought occurred to her from this swamp of present sensation and past memory; it came to her as a bright-eyed child, or with the astonished eyes of Eve as, fresh-born of his rib, she gazed at Adam. How did I get here? What was I before? What will become of me?

MEN OF SCIENCE

With that thought, Fanny rose from her chair. She had a sensation of floating upon an unseen river. She was certain there was some ceremony she should perform before departing, even if it was only to offer a good night, but she was speechless with weariness. The current carried her downstream, past the two men, deaf to their words, their questions. She navigated upholstery and carved chair backs, no longer noticing the prim lattice of the wallpaper, seeing instead an out-of-focus screen of bushes and trees and dappled light. Her name was called, distantly, as when a sound was heard in the night mimicking a voice, but was merely an eloquent creak.

'Fanny?' the younger man said. His name, she dimly recalled, was Matthew.

'Françoise,' the other said.

'My dear, we have tired you.'

Both men rose from their chairs when she stood. They followed her to the open door and into the dark hall. Then followed with their eyes as she, a stately galleon, sailed up the stairs towards the harbour of her room, and out of sight.

'Well,' Baxter said. 'Well, well.'

'She is under the spell of melancholy. We cannot expect her to behave within the confines of what are merely manners and trifles.'

'Quite so, but even primitive friendship inspires common courtesy.'

'But she is uncommon. Quite the most uncommon creature I have ever encountered, and Baxter, it is you and I who made her so.'

'We have saved her! Liberated her. Given back the thread of life and, and...'

'...and cut it also.'

'How so?'

'The person that she was, that desperate young woman who condemned herself to an early grave, is still there beneath the appearance of life.'

'Nonsense. We have swept away her old life. We are giving her a second chance. A clean slate.'

'I cannot begin to imagine what it is to be a spotless slate – all past identity wiped away.'

'I can. My God! To begin again, all mistakes swept aside, all prejudice, all assumption, all family association.'

'So, you would sweep away your marriage, your children, your mother and father? Cast yourself on a desert island? Become a Crusoe with no friends, nothing but the clothes you stand in and your wit?'

'Try me!' Baxter cried. 'I would triumph and thrive; though if Man Friday could be made Woman Friday I might also seed a fresh population for my new-found land too.'

'I see that you would, but my dear friend, you are cut from a very different cloth than most men.'

'As are you.'

'Perhaps. But as men we can only glimpse or guess at the mind of womankind. More especially one such as she.'

With that, both men looked at the spot where the mysterious creature had sat. Matthew sighed. Clapping him on the back, Baxter said, 'You promised something stronger than tea last time I was here.'

'I did. Indeed, I did.'

Fanny, in the room she had been given, wearing a borrowed dress and borrowed shoes and borrowed petticoat, stood and looked at her reflection in the glass. If she had imagined herself in a new situation, it was in Ireland. In a school for girls and young ladies, herself as their teacher. A spinster lady, serious and sometimes stern with her charges, but never cruel. They would never admire her, she knew, but a modest portion of something like love might be her due.

Leaning closer to the mirror, she searched her face for her mother's features. No-one had ever remarked that she resembled her mother. Never. But perhaps they did not see beyond the pock-marked skin, did not chose to linger over her features as they might another's. If she remembered how her mother had looked it was more from the painting that hung in her father's study than from any true recollection. It was the same with her father – her real father – who, it was said, she used to call 'Man.' Not Father. Not Papa. But that starker word in which there was no apparent relationship, no ties, no particularities, only plainly, anonymously, that generic term for all his gender: 'Man.'

That being so, Fanny considered, she must, as a child, have known that his importance in her life was limited, that this 'Man' was merely one among many.

He lived still for all she knew. Her mother had last seen him in London and their parting had been dull, almost that of the most distant acquaintances. There was nothing left between them, no spark of affection or love, no duty or passion, no shared sympathy.

Unnatural child to be the result of such a union. To be the only remaining trace and then for each to be occluded, one by death, the other by removal to whatever remote sphere he dwelt in now. He had been born in the New World in a place called New Jersey. At times she had a fleeting fancy to gain passage on a ship bound for the Americas, to seek out the man who had abandoned her and her mother. Yet that must be impossible.

His likeness then, was it there in her eyes, her mouth, her colouring? We cannot make something from nothing, lest it be lightning from the firmament, sparks from an anvil. He had made her. Fastened her in her mother's womb then, rogue that he must have been, he'd fled.

'I am half-rogue, half-hyena in petticoats; no wonder I have difficulties in finding my place in the world. I am badly made, stitched from parts that do not belong together.'

She sat once more at the table under the window. Turned the pages to where she'd begun to write her children's story and now scratched out the words in haste.

'Half-rogue, half-hyena. Very good. Go on. Who are you,

Fanny? Write it lest you forget.'

'I am a watch mechanism thrown together from the cogs and wheels and springs of other timepieces. Nothing quite works, the teeth of the cogs do not lock together, time cannot be measured. It is unhinged.'

'Delve deep. Somewhere in your beginning is the key. Find the key and the door to your current self will fly open. All will then be seen, be understood.'

HER LIKENESS

Mist painted over the scene at her window, muting its colour to a limited palette. All the talk was, or so Mrs Curtis said, of spring never coming again, nor summer. 'Preacher Ingram says tis end times and the final judgment is nigh. I says to him, "Wait and see. One bad year don't make another." Now up, my girl, and I will brush your hair! Mr Baxter is coming this morning for to make a picture of my master and you are to give them your company, lest they grow restless.'

Fanny got out of bed and Mrs Curtis helped her into a warm wrap and sat her at the dressing table and began to brush her long hair very tenderly.

'I suppose my mother once did this.'

'Bless you, yes, she must have done, and washed and fed you and told you stories such as all mothers do.'

Fanny closed her eyes and tried to imagine herself a very small child once more and the hands which lifted and brushed and smoothed her hair, the fingers now and again grazing the bare skin of her neck, her cheek, to be those of her own mother. She tried to animate the painting by John Opie but her mother's gaze in that picture looked askance and it seemed that her mother could never be made to turn and look her in the eye, nor indeed could she move in any degree – not walk, nor speak, nor laugh, nor touch, nor kiss. Always she was looking at something just outside of the frame of the picture. An unseen object, an abstract object perhaps, a dream or an idea that was there almost tangibly to her left. When the picture had hung in the study at Somers Town, she had often tried to discover which object held her mother's gaze; was it the bookcase? And if so, which volume did she gaze at so steadily, so meaningfully? When Fanny crossed the room to discover which book it was, and looked back at the painting, she found that her mother's gaze had then shifted, so that she now looked beyond the bookcase and her secret message to Fanny was withheld.

'Father,' Fanny asked one day. 'What is it that my mother is looking at in her picture? I had thought she looked long and hard at the bookcase over there, but when I go there and look again I can no longer tell.'

Godwin sometimes warmed to conversations about his absent and most beloved wife, at other times he grew morose and closed the subject as resolutely as he sometimes shut a book he found displeasure with, but that day he was his best self and laughed a little at the question.

'Well, now, let us see. Come stand next to me.' Fanny obeyed and the two looked up at the painting. Godwin raised his hand and pointed with two fingers to represent Mary Wollstonecraft's eyes and drew a steady line at a gently inclined angle across the room where they came to rest at the line of books in the middle of the shelf. 'Now then,' said he. 'Go you, Fanny, and stand where I point.'

She did as she was bid, feeling a wondrous pride in the experiment and anticipating an answer to her long sought-after enquiry.

'Now, Fanny. Turn if you will. There, step one inch to your right and keep still.' He swept his arm back and forward, pointing from where Fanny stood to the portrait of her mother. Three times he did it, with the child's eyes following the tips of his fingers each time. 'Another half inch to your right. There! That is it! I have it! Now I see what she is gazing at so lovingly, so seriously.'

'What? What is it father? What?'

He smiled condescendingly. 'Why, can't you guess?'

'No. Tell me!'

'Why, I swear it is none other than you, her dear daughter. You, Fanny.'

Fanny's reaction was to run again to the spot where he had stood and to see what he had seen, but of course, as she had removed herself there was only the bookcase to soak up her mother's interested gaze.

'You have spoiled the illusion, Fanny. Look, let me try. You stand here and do as I did.' He crossed the room and taking a chair sat so that his head was in the approximate position that the child's had been.

'Now follow the line of her gaze as I did. Yes. That's it! Does she seem to look at me now?'

Fanny nodded, but understood the flaw in the experiment, for anything, any object, any passing person might become the subject of the portrait's gaze. Herself or her father, her sister Mary, any of the visitors to the house, a book, a servant or even a scampering mouse. He was indulging her, she saw, treating her childish query with pretend seriousness.

'Well now,' he said, drawing their tête-à-tête to an end. 'Papa has work to do.'

Once he had gone, she lingered in the room gazing at her mother's picture, then despite the disappointment of the experiment, stood in the spot by the bookcase with her eyes closed, letting her mother gaze at her for many minutes at a time. In silent communion she said, 'See how I've grown. How I love you, dear mother. I think of you every day. I will never forget you. Never!' For a flickering moment she felt a nearness of spirit, a consanguinity of their two selves: mother and daughter reunited. Yet it was quickly extinguished. The sudden dark remembrance of where her mother's body really lay, decomposing in the cold earth of St Pancras churchyard, came like a sudden draught blowing out the flame of imagined life. These extremes of thought inevitably made Fanny cry. She knew she would be chided for such, and yet she clung to the idea that her sorrow was legitimate and her mother should know of it, should see it and feel it, lest she think herself forgotten.

'There now, Miss. Your hair shall shine very prettily. Hold still and I shall dress it.'

'Do you have a daughter, Mrs Curtis?' Fanny said, looking at the kind old woman's face in the glass behind her.

'Bless you, what a question!'

'Is it impolite to ask such a thing? Have I offended you?'

'No, no. Tis only that a question asked in a handful of words may provoke just one word, a simple no, or a stream which may prove unstoppable.'

Fanny frowned, uncertain if she had been answered, or rather led away to a remote stone-built pen as sheep are, so that their liberty is corralled.

'Oh, Miss, you look puzzled. All I meant was that your question provoked the telling of a very long story.'

'So you do have a daughter?'

'No more, I don't.'

'But you did once?'

'Yes, I did. I had six daughters and three sons, too. But therein is the tale, or many tales, rather.'

'Did they...?' The word, even unsaid, seemed to fill the room. How else does one lose one's children except to death? The old woman answered without hesitation.

'All are gone over to the other side. All nine of them are at peace and feel no pain.'

'I am very sorry for your loss, Mrs Curtis.'

'Oh,' the good old woman said, then paused and cast her eyes downward, sighing deeply. Fanny watched her and waited. Mrs Curtis seemed to rouse herself, 'I shall tell thee about them one day, Miss. If you should like to hear.'

'Yes, I should.'

'And I shall elaborate, too, on the shades of them that linger.'

'Oh?'

'Not to alarm you, Miss, but they are all of them with me still.' Here, as if to illuminate her point, the housekeeper looked around. Her gaze alighted in turn on particular spots in the room, some close by, others at its furthest reaches, and her face wore a warm smiling countenance as if she were greeting old friends. 'But if you would, Miss, I beg you do not mention this to the master.'

'If that is your wish, but...' A knock at the door stopped her. Before she could say another word, it was thrown open and there stood the girl, Rebecca.

'Master says his visitor is here.'

'Rebecca! Must you fling open doors so violently?' said Mrs

Curtis in a sharp voice.

'But the master said to make haste.'

'Then make haste and get you back downstairs, my good girl.'

The girl departed and Fanny quickly dressed in a simple gown of linden-green cotton. Together they went downstairs in silence and Fanny imagined the ghostly forms of Mrs Curtis's nine children following them; their footsteps, their gay childish laughter, their prattle, all mute to her ears. How happy they must be if they are all together, brothers and sisters united eternally, she thought. But yet another part of her, that rational mind well-schooled against superstition by her father, argued that it could not be the case. It was only an illusion built upon loss and yearning. I will not dash her hopes nor break them as other false idols are broken, she thought. Instead I will indulge her and win her confidence, for she is good and has suffered.

Mrs Curtis delivered her into the library where Mr Baxter was busying himself in the setting up of an easel.

'Ah, here she is!' cried Matthew. 'Come, Fanny, make yourself comfortable on the sofa, for I fear this shall quite swallow up the morning as Baxter is diligent in his labour.'

Baxter seemed to notice nothing, so intent and frowning was he upon a large wooden box, glass bottles and several bladders of paint. A sheet of canvas had been placed over the rug under his easel and he had donned a long apron and white cap.

For the picture, Matthew was to stand by the window, a small volume of poetry held aloft in one hand so as to catch the light while he read.

'Like so?' he asked.

'No, lower the book a little and turn your head.'

'But I cannot read it now.'

'Never mind that. It is the illusion that counts, not the verity, and if your face is sunk in shadow the entire exercise shall be for naught.'

'Will this do?'

'Better. But wait. I should, I think, be closer.'

So saying, he set aside the box and the glass bottles, the many brushes, the easel and palette, and drew the square of canvas forward by inches, then set everything in place again.

'No. It will not do.'

'No?'

This time it was Matthew who was induced to move. The window seat was tried. The book with its black cloth cover was exchanged for one bound in burgundy Morocco. This too was dismissed. As was a blank sheet of paper folded to look as if it were a letter lately arrived.

It was only when Matthew, wearying of his task, rang the bell for tea, that Baxter at last relaxed and looked about him.

'Fanny, my dear, I hardly noticed you!' He looked at her for a moment in that very close and intent way of his, which she understood to be his artist's scrutiny.

'Why, Fanny, you look very well. That dress is most becoming; its woodland hue suits your pale skin and enhances the elusive auburn lights in your hair. Look Matthew, see how well your ward looks. She has almost the appearance of a forest sprite. Or perhaps the Lorelei from German myth.'

Matthew, lacking the extravagant vision of his friend, only said, 'Yes. The gown suits her.'

'I think I am thwarted in my choice of subject, for you, dearest friend, project stability and a reassuring mellowness in your frame, while here before me in our dear young lady, I perceive the other-worldly.'

'Oh Baxter, stop, do. The poor creature is blushing. Besides which, I think your fee was agreed upon the taking of my image.'

'Yes, yes.'

'My mother should be alarmed to receive, not a portrait of her son, but a fanciful rendition of a fairy sprite.'

'Quite so, but perhaps one day, if Fanny will permit it, I shall make her image.'

'Is that wise, Baxter, given that her position is one of seclusion and retreat?'

'Then I shall paint her in the very disguise of myth. She shall become Ariel or Ophelia, or, better still, Imogen from Cymbeline. Indeed, now I think of it, as that play is set in Wales it is very apt.'

'Would you like that, Fanny? To be painted by Baxter?'

'I do not think I can refuse, beholden as I am to both of you.'

This was said very meekly.

'Nay, Fanny, if you do not wish it, he will refrain. Say now. Be bold my dear, it shall not perturb me.'

'I do not mind, but do not think me suitable for such a subject.'

'That is for me to decide,' said Baxter.

The matter was resolved and after tea was taken, the morning hours were passed in near motionless contemplation. Baxter, being the most active, mixed his various concoctions, smoothed paint on to canvas, dabbed at his palette and wiped his brushes on a number of colourful and paint-spotted rags. Matthew, relieved of both books and paper, sat in a relaxed and very natural-seeming attitude, his ankles crossed, one hand resting on the chair arm, the other loose upon his thigh. His head was resting on a cushion and his countenance expressed an easy nature and untroubled heart. Fanny sat very quietly, speaking only when Matthew engaged her in conversation.

'Do you read novels, Fanny? Or is verse more to your liking?' This was said by Matthew through almost immobile lips and without a glance at the person he addressed, which Fanny found comical, though she tried not show it.

'I am fond of both.'

'Then recount for me your favourites. Give me their titles and authors, a brief résumé of their substance and their merits. I should be entertained to know what you have read.'

'Very little, sir,' Fanny said modestly. 'Though I have read the Waverley novels, and *Robinson Crusoe*, and a little Pope and Dryden. Also Richardson.'

'What of the modern poets? Have you read any Wordsworth?'

'A little, sir.'

'For myself, I…'

'You moved!' came Baxter's cry of protest. Then in a quieter voice, 'Perhaps Fanny will be so good as to read from one of the many volumes we are seemingly blind and deaf to.'

'Shall I?' Fanny asked. 'But what shall I read?'

'Choose whatever you wish, though pray not anything too dull or worthy.'

Fanny chanced upon a beloved volume from her childhood, the work of that English mystic, William Blake. Turning the pages, she eagerly sought her favourite, 'The Chimney Sweeper'. She began to read its first verse aloud.

> When my mother died I was very young,
> And my father sold me while yet my tongue
> Could scarcely cry " 'weep! 'weep! 'weep! "weep!"

'Oh no!' was the pained cry from both her companions.

'Not that! It is too sad. Today we are determined to be merry,' chided Baxter.

'You, dear Fanny, you are yet too weakened by melancholy to withstand those sentiments, however worthy. Come, find something that shall lighten our hearts!' said Matthew.

Fanny wondered at this, asking herself whether darkness clung to darkness, melancholy to melancholy? She had thought that any work which promoted moral feelings worked on the soul to strive for justice and the betterment of mankind, but now, she reasoned, for such as that, a price was paid. Most especially when the person on whom these sentimental words act is without any means to better the circumstances of even one poor child.

'Look, Fanny, there on that shelf is Gulliver. Let us travel again to Lilliput.'

She found the book and commenced reading:

'My father had a small estate in Nottinghamshire: I was the third of five sons...'

So the morning passed pleasantly, with three voyagers upon rough seas and on strange shores, the only sounds in the room being Fanny's lilting voice and Baxter's stirring and scraping and rattling. Outside the mist began to dissipate, until at last, at nearly noon, the sun broke through, sending cool light into the room and casting out all gloom.

SPECTRES

A fortnight went by, during which time Baxter did not pay a single visit. Perhaps his absence had a positive side, for about this time Matthew and Fanny began to take warm pleasure in one another's company and in these happy circumstances, Fanny began at last to emerge from her shell.

'I think I shall begin to call you sister,' Matthew said one day as they stood looking out at the mist which hung over the garden and hid almost all but the tip of the old oak tree.

'Then I shall call you brother,' she said, and had a strong sense that just such a scene had been played out before, that she had said those words to another man, exactly as now. Yes, she remembered, it had been Percy Shelley. He'd declared his everlasting fraternity and she, with an over-brimming heart, had promised to love and support him as a sister. But then the sight of Shelley caused her to quake and tremble with unsisterly emotion; his effect on her rang from the tips of her toes to the top of her skull like a struck bell. Her feelings for Matthew were, she believed, both innocent and warm. If she had at first mistrusted him, now she only wanted to please him. He wished for her happiness, therefore she would pretend happiness.

'Well then, how will we entertain ourselves this fine morning, dear sister?'

'You call it fine? It continues foul.'

'Nay. The morning is innocent, if a little damp, but we have much to be grateful for, do we not? We have a roof over our heads, a good fire in the grate, there is food for our sustenance and better yet we have conversation and companionship. What more could we want? A warming sun and a blue canopy of sky might be desirable, yet we cannot and should not yearn for what we do not have and allow ourselves to be sunk in misery. The weather will change. Then we will complain that it is too hot and the sun burns our skin!'

'Yet the weather this last year has been strange, has it not?'

'It has. I have read reports that say it is the worst in living memory, that the world has tilted on its axis or that some far-off star has untethered itself. I have also heard tell of the second coming, of End Times and Apocalypse. Of punishment for mankind's many sins.'

Fanny sighed.

'But, my dear,' he added, turning to look at her. 'This is idle speculation. We shall stop our ears to such gloomy tidings!'

'Just as all those who scoffed at Noah did?'

'Ah, Fanny, would it please you if I ordered the building of an ark, then? There are shipbuilders and sailors aplenty in this town. I will hire the services of Captain Lewis who sailed with Nelson. He was a boyhood friend of my father and still yearns for adventure.'

'Pray, do not tease me.'

'Fanny, I did not mean to. Only to exaggerate what is merely a passing season and thus make light of it.'

A knock at the door disturbed their disquisition and Rebecca came in.

'Mrs Curtis says there is cold tongue and Caerphilly cheese ready, but will you want soup also?'

'Does Mrs Curtis suggest soup?'

'Huh?'

'Rebecca, you must say "I beg your pardon" if you do not understand.'

The girl shuffled restlessly and looked down at her feet. She was wearing the red shoes and it seemed that there was something mesmerizing about their colour, especially when she moved: a dashing, blinking splash of red, like a butterfly glimpsed in a wheat field. Finally, she repeated the words, trying them on her tongue and pulling a face as if they were an alien fruit.

'That's better. Now tell Mrs Curtis that a hot soup shall be welcome, but we can also do without.'

'Is that yes, then, sir?'

'It is neither yes nor no. Let Mrs Curtis decide.'

'But she cannot. Otherwise why has she sent me?'

'Tell her no, then,' Fanny said. 'Will that do?'

It seemed that a sharp tone had slipped into Fanny's voice and the girl plainly heard it, for her eyes widened upon Fanny in a flash of anger. Matthew, not noticing, merely said, in the mildest of expressions, 'Yes. We can do without soup. Off you go.'

She turned very prettily on her heels and disappeared through the door, the red shoes like the fast moving spots of crimson on a butterfly's wing. The girl made Fanny uneasy, for she knew very well that those who are powerless search for a victim nearly as powerless as themselves, and while Fanny was a guest of the master and lived under his protection, her true condition was that of a nobody.

'Shall we play Piquet? Or...?'

Another knock at the door, this time very discreet, as if done in secret.

'Yes?'

The door opened inch by inch with extreme stealth.

'What on earth?' said Matthew in a whisper.

The door continued to swing slowly wider until at last the hall could be seen beyond it, but no person stood upon the threshold.

'What... can it be that the wind has...'

At this a human sound went up, 'Whooo who-oo!'

The noise aped the wind yet no wind comes from but one direction and no wind seems to carry in its wake a laugh.

'Ha ha!' Baxter sprang into view.

'You devil, you!' cried Matthew. 'Why did not the servants announce you?'

'Ah. I am the invisible man. Only those I choose to reveal myself to see me!'

'Well, it is very good that you are come, Baxter, but why did my servant not show you in?'

'The front door was ajar and so I took the liberty to enter.'

'That is very bad.'

'Then I apologise.'

'Nay. You need not, I am glad you are come, but my servants must be more circumspect. I shall speak to them.'

'I have brought something that should cheer you. Here it is.' So saying Baxter brought a package from behind his back. It was wrapped in brown paper, but its shape betrayed its contents.

'The painting? It is finished?'

Matthew carried the package to the window and unwrapped it with unsuppressed eagerness.

'Oh, it is a very likeness! What do you think, Fanny, is it like?'

'May I hold it?' Fanny said. She had stationed herself on a cushion in the window seat and the painting was given very tenderly into her hands. While she absorbed herself in looking at the picture, Matthew rang the bell, then went into the hall as he had some sharp words to impart to the first servant to answer.

Baxter watched warmly as Fanny inspected his work. Her eyes went from one corner of the image to another, going back again and again to Matthew's face. The portrait showed all the kindness and lively intelligence Matthew possessed, yet there was also dignity and a life-like presence.

'Do you like it, Frances?'

She nodded and after looking up momentarily, returned her gaze to the picture.

'Has anyone ever taken your likeness?' Baxter asked.

She shook her head.

'And would you object if I did?'

Again, she shook her head.

'You may refuse. I allow that. I would not be offended. You are not bound by your circumstances to do ought but regain your strength; both mental and physical. I do not wish to impose upon your good nature nor take advantage of your sense of indebtedness.'

Baxter, in the course of this speech, moved closer to Fanny and laid his hand gently on her shoulder. When he had done speaking she looked up and met his eyes. She was in the habit of never looking at anyone frankly; he was therefore surprised by the luminous green eyes that returned his steady gaze.

'Who are you really, Frances?' he asked, forgetting for a moment the fragility of the young woman and everything he and Matthew had agreed in regard to her care.

'I am no-one,' she said, and he saw that the lustre of her eyes increased as her tears began to brim.

'No,' he began to say, but Matthew bustled noisily into the room along with Mrs Curtis.

'See here, now. There is Mr Baxter. He found the door unsecured and crept in unnoticed. What if he were not the good-natured fellow he is, but a vagabond, a thief? What if a band of brigands had crept into our midst and we should find ourselves murdered?'

'I shall see about this. My guess is that it was the work of that silly girl, Rebecca. I set her the task of shining the knocker and the latches, then of washing the step. I daresay she left it ajar only a moment while she fetched water.'

'But, Mrs Curtis, in only a moment a throat can be cut and all manner of damage done! I have heard reports of disenfranchised sailors and soldiers, those who fought Napoleon and triumphed, who on returning home find they have lost sweethearts, lost work, lost families. They have nothing. Some have naturally sought the company of old compatriots and go from place to place seeking honest work but where there is none, these fellows turn to theft, and worse.'

'Yes, sir, very true. Now, will you be wanting tea?'

Fanny almost laughed to hear with what drollery old Mrs Curtis returned Matthew's premonitions of murder and Baxter seemed to detect this, as when she happened to glance at him, his face was marked by a wry smile.

'Now then, let me see again that portrait and consider where I shall hang it,' Matthew said and Fanny got up, glad of the distraction.

Different parts of the room were tried by means of one holding the painting aloft against the north wall or in the alcove, while the others gave voice to their approval or objections. At last it was decided that the picture should hang above the fireplace until it could be given to Matthew's mother when she returned from her rest cure in Bournemouth.

As if to change the topic from the intense concentration on his own image, Matthew said, 'Fanny has been writing a story. How goes it, my dear? When shall you share with us its delights?'

'Ah,' added Baxter. 'A story, you say? What is it about?'

'It is… that is to say… it is…' She sank back into silence, wishing she had never said a word about her story, for now she had put it into the world, it seemed a very sorry half-formed thing.

The two men looked upon her with such happy expectation that it seemed almost a sin not to find some recompensing description of her endeavour. 'Oh. It needs work. Even though it be a simple thing, merely a tale for children, it yet demands much thought.'

'Well said, Fanny,' said Baxter. 'That is an apt and modest answer. Nothing worthwhile can be made in the winking of an eye. I have been about my own great project these last six months. Not constantly, I own, but even when I am not working, I am working. Which is to say, the creative mind is like the water mill: even when there is no corn to grind, the wheel still turns.'

'And even when it is night the sun shines just as brightly on another portion of the globe.' Matthew said.

'Then do you find some work is done even while you sleep? In dreams, I mean,' Fanny asked in earnest.

Baxter laughed. 'Nay, not quite, more's the pity, but I have gone to bed at night puzzling over some problem or another and awoken with its solution. So yes, perhaps, tis so.'

'My sister…' Fanny began, but checked herself, for she was on the verge of enumerating the details of her sister's letters, those in particular that recounted an evening – a very stormy evening – spent at the Villa Diodati with those scandalous personages Lord Byron and Percy Bysshe Shelley. Mary had written to Fanny telling her how, trapped indoors by the foul weather and driven to distraction with boredom, they had devised the sport of each writing a ghoulish tale. Mary said she could not wring out a single idea worth writing up that evening, but that night, she had been visited by a dreadful nightmare and ere she found her story.

Fanny knew she must be silent on such topics even as she longed to speak of them. She was proud of her bold and clever younger sister, nearly the only true blood relative she had in the world, yet she was also aware of how the miasma of contamination which stemmed from her sister's elopement with a married man had ruined her own chances of even very modest independence and happiness. If this kind man who had given her shelter should know whose daughter she was, and whose sister, he should make great haste to cast her out before he too was enveloped by scandal and gossip.

'Your sister?' Baxter asked.

'My sister recommends warm milk with a teaspoon of brandy before bed for a good night's sleep,' said Fanny with an altogether different and entirely imaginary sister in mind, one who would swoon were she even to hear the name Byron, and whose passions were no stronger than a liking for a pullet's egg lightly boiled.

'Very sensible,' Baxter said and looked weary at the thought of such a dull lady.

Matthew glanced questioningly at Fanny, as if he detected an evasion on her part, but he was too much the gentleman to challenge her, and quickly changed the subject of their conversation. He could not know that the new direction of their talk should awaken further associations of past scandal for Fanny.

'So, Baxter, I have long wondered about this: how came you by your skill? Was it inbred or brought about by another's influence?'

'Both, for I was born into The Potteries, my father being a decorator of porcelain at Worcester, then later I was admitted to the Royal Academy School in London where I was taught by none other than the great Henry Fuseli.'

Fanny gave a sharp intake of breath when she heard this name. Noticing this, Baxter turned to her and asked, 'Are you familiar with that particular man of genius?'

'No, I think not. The name seemed to strike a chord; that is all.'

'You may have seen his many paintings, those illustrating scenes from Shakespeare perhaps? Or the engravings of the same – for example, Titania and Bottom, which shows the pair surrounded by a host of weird and unearthly creatures, fairies, sprites, goblins and elfin folk?'

'Yes. Perhaps,' Fanny said with little conviction. But even with this answer, he continued to look at her as if he expected further explanation. She could not admit that her mother had once been infatuated with the genius from Switzerland, had shamelessly pursued him, despite the fact he was married, or so William Godwin said.

She got up and hastened to the tea things which Mrs Curtis had brought. 'Let me serve the tea,' she said in a bright, urgent exclamation.

'It should steep a while yet,' Matthew answered 'and then it will not be so hot.'

'Oh, it has cooled already,' she said and placed the palm of her hand against the pot. A foolish thing to do and she drew back her fingers with a gasp.

'Oh, Fanny, are you scalded?'

Her hand was reddened and throbbed a little but no harm was done, yet she used this as an excuse to sit quietly and listen to their talk. Baxter gave a long disquisition on the science of glazing, of firing temperatures and clay. Fanny thought that she would like to visit the pottery on the banks of the river, to watch the artisans unload the kiln, to see how common earth was transformed into numerous objects of practicality or delicate beauty. Listening intently, she closed her eyes to better imagine the scene and quite soon, not meaning to, she dozed off.

The two men, noticing this, moved to a spot near the door to converse in low tones.

'She remembers nothing of the night of the inn?' Baxter said.

'So it seems.'

'And imagines we do not know who her connections are? What do we gain by the pretence of ignorance? Will not the upkeep of a false self add yet more wearisome trouble to an already troubled mind?'

'She labours under the impression that all association with her family draws prejudice upon her, that she is judged not by her own actions, but theirs. And consider, Baxter, her mother's reputation, and those of her real father, also Godwin's and her sisters'. Indeed, her sister's foolishness in running away with Shelley and the other's rumoured involvement with Lord Byron has scandalized all of Europe. Did you read, by the by, Godwin's account of her mother's life – her love affairs, the suicide attempts, the false marriage, the begetting of a bastard daughter, not to mention her adventures with the architects of revolution in France?'

'I have heard the rumours and also read what has been written in the papers, but not the biography.'

'The scandal has ensnared our poor young lady in a web of intrigue she cannot escape. It drove her to the desperate fate we plucked her from. Let us continue in pretence of ignorance until she is more ready to trust us.'

THE SHAKESPEARE CUP

Unnoticed by the two men, just beyond the door, pausing with an empty cinder bucket and a rag, stood the young maidservant, Rebecca. She had been eavesdropping on their conversation for some minutes. She glanced at her pretty red shoes as she listened and found they still pleased her greatly. She had quickly forgotten the person who had been the author of her master's liberality. For who was it that had taken notice of her outgrown old shoes that pinched her toes and rubbed her heels? None, but the mysterious house guest lately come among them. The rough-faced young lady who was said to be the master's cousin, then his ward, then the daughter of a dear friend, then too, the other man's cousin or his wife's younger sister.

She had been told that the lady's name was Jane, then Anne, until finally it settled on Fanny or Frances.

Round and round went the lies and Rebecca was called saucy if she questioned Mrs Curtis. But a lady does not arrive in the middle of the night with no possessions, not even a dress or a cloak and bonnet to her name. Clad only in a rough-made petticoat that was patched and repaired, its fabric worn through in places. Mrs Curtis had afterward burned that, though this was never her way before, nor any sensible person's way, for rags were valuable for any number of purposes. You only burned such garments if there was the suspicion of disease.

At thirteen years old Rebecca knew about the diseases that certain women of the town caught from sailors. Some caught babies and some caught the pox, some caught both. One she knew, who had been pretty in her day, had lost a part of her nose to the disease and she wore a contrived veil to hide it, poor thing. Yet once Rebecca had seen a man rip the covering from the poor woman's face on The Strand. He had done it in jest and drunkenness, thinking her shy, demanding a kiss from her. Oh, he was sorry when he looked upon her; he ran from her like a frightened child, stumbling and wailing. Rebecca, who had been a girl of no more than seven at that time, had chased after the veil when it caught on the wind and then taken it back to the woman, so she was able to study her damaged face at close quarters. Terrible it was, but Rebecca had seen worse things.

Some misfortunes are punishment for sin, the preacher told her, but some – those diseases and sicknesses that nearly all children get before they are grown – are a warning, a wringing out of a young soul before it becomes too avid for the world. Many little ones die, them that are born of sin and them that are pure.

Rebecca overheard the tale of the young lady in fragments, for the master must have cupped his mouth at some moments, or lowered his voice even more at others. Yet she heard enough and thought how, on her next free afternoon, she would go to her brother's house and recount the tale for him. Her aim was that her brother should release her from service and let her bide with him in the lodging house he kept.

Rebecca's brother kept a house on The Strand and she had been staying there with him on the day she saw the woman with the disfigured face. Her mother was confined and the expected baby was breech, hence it was thought unlikely either mother or baby would survive and Rebecca was put out of the way. It had seemed inevitable that she would stay there and be raised by her brother and his wife, but her mother and the new child, a boy, lived – so back home she was sent to help with the house and the baby and be held in check for naught but the domestic drudgery of a very poor household.

She had tasted freedom in her brother's house and seen life as a great circus of comings and goings, of Lascars and Spaniards and sailors from Africa. Laughter was what she remembered chiefly, and the playing of fiddles and accordions and tin pipes, dancing and drinking and card playing, and coins given to her when she fetched them ale or vittles or sang for them. Many said that she sang very prettily. One gave her a beautiful shell from Surinam, another a pretty ribbon, yet another the amputated milk-white hand of a German china doll.

Ever after she pined for that golden time – though all tried to persuade her that it was a bawdy house, a den of thieves and vagabonds who would cut your throat as soon as wish you a good day. Perhaps it was so, but amongst them she was a princess and never knew anything but kindness there.

Rebecca thought all that morning of how she could use what she had heard about the lately-arrived young lady, but could not come up with a proper scheme except for one of falsehood and spite.

CYMBELINE

'Fanny, Baxter has written. He wishes to use you as the model for the scene from Cymbeline he is to paint on the side of his Shakespeare cup. Are you not flattered?'

'Flattered? No, not I.'

'Then you will not help him?'

'Certainly, I will do it. If you think it is right.'

'Oh, Fanny. It is not for me to persuade you. Or order you. If it should make you unhappy then you may refuse.'

Fanny said nothing but pondered the matter, lost in thought for a minute or so.

Matthew waited. His expression was kind, his concern for her undaunted. How very kind he is, she thought.

'If it pleases you then I will. If I can be of service to him, then I shall do it, but for myself it has never been my desire to be painted or, as you say, "flattered".'

'Very well. That was only my misconception. I thought it the dream of all young ladies to be admired and...' Matthew caught sight of her face and bit back his words.

She returned his gaze steadily. It had been her habit to look away, to drop her gaze to the ground, to make a pretence of interest elsewhere, giving him the very strong impression that she was shy. Now he saw no shyness and not an ounce of false modesty.

'I apologise. I see that you are unlike the rest of your sex – hardship has perhaps made of you different stuff.'

'We are none of us exact replicas of one another. Women are

not, though they may seem to be, stitched together with every aspect of body and mind which pleases man. If we are weak or unlearned, it is only because we are unable to exercise either mind or body. If we seem to lack man's ability to rationalize and think, then it is only that no-one trains us to do it, nor does the world ask for our opinion. And, sir, if we do dare to speak out, we are silenced or laughed at.'

Matthew said: 'I only...'

'Yes, yes, tell him I am at his service,' she quickly said, her voice softening, 'and could I, if it be possible, borrow your Shakespeare? I have forgotten the particulars of that play.'

But Shakespeare could not be found; the library was in disarray due to its being redecorated the year before and the men tasked with the removal and restoration of its shelves had done it willy-nilly. However, Lamb's *Tales from Shakespeare* came to hand very easily and it was this volume, so very familiar to her, that was passed into Fanny's hands. She might have said, 'I have known the brother and sister who wrote this since I was a girl' or told the even darker tale of its authors' circumstances by saying 'Mary Lamb killed her mother with a kitchen knife, but all I knew of her was sweetness and touching delicacy, for she was always kind to me.'

But Fanny said nothing, only murmured 'thank you' and took up her place at the window seat to read the story, very simply outlined by the Lambs, of Cymbeline. How much she saw of her own story in it can only be guessed. That Imogen had a cruel stepmother was one thing she had in common and also that she had travelled to Wales and there took a draught which gave the appearance of death. Two men discovered Imogen, though they did not revive her but strewed her body with flowers.

When she read it through, she recognised the story she had read when very young, but her child's mind had discounted some parts and emphasised others. She had been thrilled by the adventure of dressing as a boy and running away to a vast forest in Wales, of finding a home in a cave. The pain and fear and hunger were part of the adventure, for to suffer in such circumstances was to truly live.

Did Baxter see the mirroring of her own story in Cymbeline? That she had taken a poisonous draft which rendered her unconscious and on the brink of death was clear. That she had travelled to a sea port in Wales was also an echo of Shakespeare's tale, but Imogen was beautiful and she was not. And Imogen was the daughter of a king and she, Fanny, was no-one. There would be no restoration of status, no happy homecoming for Fanny. A return meant only the restoration to worry, to domestic drudgery, to begging letters and appeasement, to spiteful speeches and hard looks from Mrs Clairmont.

The call to adventure and love had been taken up by Mary and that false sister Claire. They had escaped, they had given themselves to great men. They had experienced those parts of a female experience; namely love in its physical form which she had not and never would – for no-one wants a no-one.

While she read, she had nearly forgotten Matthew's presence in the room. He'd made himself comfortable in the winged armchair by the fire and also taken up a book. Now, when he rose to stand near the bookcase, she was once again aware of him, and raised her head to see that he was looking at her.

'So, does the story meet with your favour? Will you sit for Baxter, take up the attitude of the character?'

'He has not said which character I am to represent, though I think I can guess.'

'Oh, there is only one female character of any import in the play and that is Imogen.'

'The woman who runs away to Wales and drinks a deathly draft? Who is found by two men and then awakes from what seemed to be eternal sleep?'

'Yes, that is it!' He spoke with innocent happiness.

'Does that tale not sound familiar?'

'In what degree?'

'In its relationship to me.'

'To you?' At first he was puzzled by this, for time and distance had fixed Shakespeare's tale at an almost mythic remove so that it could not be fitted into the apparatus of modern life and modern people. The poisonous potion was vague and historic; it could not be bought by the grain from the apothecary, it did not come in a glass bottle labeled 'Laudanum' or 'Godfrey's Cordial'. Or at least these similarities had not immediately struck Matthew, who had almost forgotten the particularities of that terrible night at the Mackworth and how Fanny had come to live under his protection. Then it dawned on him and he struggled with his words. 'Oh. Goodness. My dear... I had not seen it that way. I doubt whether Baxter had either. I should imagine he merely saw the opportunity to illustrate aspects of the native landscape.'

'It matters not,' said Fanny, reassured by this stammering reaction and lack of guile. 'The best art should mirror life, should it not? Or spring from it to some degree?'

'Does it offend you?'

'No, but then I have long been better trained in offence than flattery.'

'That does not mean you should accept the offence or always turn the other cheek. If you do not wish to be portrayed as Imogen then say so. I will refuse him if you don't have the strength to. Only bid me what you will.'

This was reassuring; she had grown to trust Matthew – he had a straightforward approach to life. Nothing was hidden. Either that or he hid his true self masterfully. She saw Matthew day after day, saw the books he read, saw how he treated all those he came into contact with, whether a gentleman or a stable boy, with the same simple kindness.

'I will do it,' she said at last, 'and gladly.'

In the same letter Baxter had asked Matthew to meet him for supper. They had yet to arrange the philosophical fellowship which had been the aim of that night when they rescued Fanny. That it had fallen by the wayside was unsurprising; that its appeal was now tarnished was understandable. As in many things Matthew was carried away by the enthusiasm of others.

If he had a fault that was it. He swayed as a tree is swayed in rough winds, yet for the most part, stayed rooted in one spot.

Fanny had retired to her room early that evening as she often did, claiming a need for solitary contemplation. Once Matthew was assured that she suffered under no storm of mind or loneliness, he left her to her own devices, mounted his horse and rode through the evening mists to meet Baxter.

He arrived at the tavern at a quarter to eight and led his horse into the stable where an old groomsman, seeing the animal was quite wet from the relentless drizzle, clucked his disapproval.

'Now my beauty, old Tom will dry you off. There now, hold still.'

The old fellow got some blankets and began to rub the horse down. He did not look at Matthew nor address a single word to him. Even when Matthew thrust a few coins into his hand, he merely dropped them into his apron pocket and continued to croon to the horse. He gathered a handful of oats and fed them to the animal, running a calloused hand over his muzzle.

Matthew left the stable and crossed the yard, going in through the back entrance of the premises. He was feeling damp, for the drizzle, while it had seemed light, had clung to his clothes and hair, insinuating itself until it had almost soaked him through.

It was not a tavern he was familiar with, though he had passed it often enough. He had often taken it to be very small for the front that lined the street was indeed no wider than four yards. He found himself in a long winding passageway lined with numerous rooms. Making his way along it, he looked into each snug and parlour for his friend's familiar face. Some rooms were empty and their fires had not been lit, still others swelled with bodies and heat and noise. A cloud of sweetly-scented tobacco smoke hung in the air, though it hardly disguised the heavy miasma of human sweat. Evident too were the pungent hops that flavoured the bitter ale served there. Halfway down, the hall split into two passages, each as dark and narrow as the other; no light spilled from open doors in either. This, he thought, must be the route to the private apartments of the proprietor and his family, though no sign guided the unwary visitor or protected those who dwelt beyond the closed doors from the rude intrusion of any stranger.

Why Baxter had chosen this of all the establishments in the town he did not know and, retracing his steps, was beginning to ask himself if a mistake had not been made.

LIGHT AND SHADE

Fanny opened the door to her room and stood at the threshold looking in. It looked unfamiliar in the firelight, empty of any object that was hers. But nothing *was* hers, no object had been set in place at her request or for her pleasure or convenience; no item in the cupboard, no piece of clothing, even the most intimate, was really hers. No picture was chosen by her, nor had any grown familiar by looking down upon her since childhood. There were no embroidery silks or ribbons or buttons that had once been her mother's, no precious letter from a friend or sister, no pressed flowers that she had picked on a long-ago spring morning and preserved between the pages of a book. There was nothing, it seemed, to anchor her to memory, nothing to claim her, not even a chipped cup or a broken toy.

Lying on the writing slope were the papers, mostly blank, where she had tried to write her story for children. There were a handful of sentences only, each seemingly wrenched like thorns from her bloody fingers, yet these did not give relief once they'd been removed, nor did they flourish on the page, growing roots and stems, spreading like a rambling rose and sending forth beautiful blowsy flowers.

Hearing a noise in the hall downstairs, Fanny stepped quickly into the room and closed the door behind her. Steps came up the stairs and along the passage. Brisk steps at first, but as they drew closer, they slowed and became more deliberate. They were feet that brushed lightly over the floor as they moved; they evaded detection, had the stealth of a cat. Outside her room, they seemed to stop and listen.

Holding her breath, Fanny knelt on the rug and, lowering her head, peeped under the door. The gap was less than a quarter of an inch, but the candle held by the person beyond the door spilled its light downward to reveal feet clad in red shoes.

Fanny stood up and drew quietly back into a corner of the room. The girl might be about to knock on the door. She might have been sent by Mrs Curtis to check on Fanny and to enquire if anything was desired. Or she might have her own motive, a childish curiosity about Fanny, or something more sinister. There was a simple way to discover what it was.

'Yes?' Fanny called and stepped with a definite and noisy tread towards the door. She grasped the latch which rattled a warning preliminary to the mechanism opening and heard the feet bearing the intruder away at a pace.

She opened the door a crack and said, 'Who's there?' Then listened to the retreating feet, soft, soft, down the stairs and then the distant creak of a door opening somewhere.

Then silence.

What did it mean? Nothing good, she could be sure. But the girl was young, a child really, with a child's curiosity and naughtiness. But such a child can see and do things she ought not and she can tell tales, carry stories out of her master's house and into the world where, embroidered and distorted by gossip, they become dangerous.

Fanny went to the fireside and, taking up the poker, disturbed the coals so that they flared up, throwing more light into the room. She sat at the desk and lighting the lamp looked over the pages she had left there. That girl may have read these, she thought. I might have written something else here, something far more dangerous – a letter to my sister in Bath or to my father in London. Those letters were as real in Fanny's mind as if she had actually penned them, for she had tried them out in her mind many times: Dear Mary, You will be shocked to receive this letter … Dear Father, I had meant to die, but was discovered. I am amongst kind people who have taken me in and do their utmost for my well-being. Do not mourn me; I am not dead, but do not wish to be discovered. Therefore, I offer no means of reply, no address and can see you nevermore. Adieu!

In other versions of these as yet unwritten letters, she gave a full account; her journey on the mail coach from London to Bath to Swansea, the name of the inn, a description of the chamber she'd been given, the sad note she had penned, the way she'd sat for a long time with the bottle of laudanum resting in the palm of her hand. Such an innocent-looking bottle, the contents apparently as bland as milk and yet with the power to obliterate the spark of life which burned so brightly, so uselessly within her.

All of that she might have written. Should have written, except she had no sense of her value to those she loved. William Godwin was not her natural father; there had been a degree of affection from him but not real love. Every day she had seen the darting glances, the warm admiration, the loving caresses that were Mary's due. Seeing these signs of true filial devotion day after day, Fanny had increasingly felt their want. Nothing she did could win that same love – not her goodness, her usefulness, her attempted joy nor her all too frequent tears. Indeed, the latter brought only his scorn, his impatience – her sorrow was merely the noise of yowling cats in the night, a disturbance to his peace, an irritation. Her tears, in his view, had no source and were therefore affectations. Let Mary prick her finger or knock her head and then her lamentations must be soothed, she must be comforted and bandaged and warmed by the fire. Not so for Fanny. Therefore, she had not written to Godwin to reclaim her former life, springing from her tomb like a Lazarus, a miraculously returning prodigal daughter. She had instead made silence and secrecy her watchwords, but now there was someone who was watching and listening with hidden intent. An enemy at the gate.

She picked up her quill and beneath the last abandoned sentence of her story wrote:

> But Summerland was haunted by a darker force, one that was invisible and barely acknowledged. It came at night wearing winged slippers, but as it crossed the boundaries between life and death to reach that happy land, the slippers

were stained scarlet with the blood of all those who had before tried to pass into the kingdom with ill intent. All who lived in Summerland were warned to avoid those strangers whose feet are clad in crimson.

She left the page exposed on the desk, extinguished the candles one by one, and made the fire safe, then she got into bed and, believing she had slain a serpent, fell asleep as easily as if she were once more a small child, rocked in the loving arms of her mother.

Yet unbeknownst to Fanny, of this crime of reading her tale, the servant Rebecca was innocent. But the moral vigour of this innocence was not founded on goodness, but rather on the simple fact that Rebecca had never been taught to read.

Meanwhile, other evils were unravelling – they unfurled themselves like scarlet ribbons, each one becoming a path that led one or other of our unhappy subjects astray. The path to righteousness was ever bent, and for those with lives already troubled or trampled in one way or another, it was a narrow switchback, twisting through brambles, breaking and crumbling above perilous cliffs. Snakes moved through untended grasses while berries, brightly-coloured and gleaming, glinted from the undergrowth to tempt the unwary man.

Fanny quickly forgot about the words she had added to her story. She had been tired when she wrote them and her mind was knocked into a moment of high excitement by the discovery of a spy creeping along the passage outside her chamber. Her life, from its very inception, had been one of tangled impressions, of rapid change and elaborate storytelling and flights of imagination that were the mark of those men and women who were the domestic companions of her home. The regular habits of a simpler family who dwelt in a single and steady home with an unchanging cast of characters: mother, father, a village priest in a stone-built church, hardworking neighbours, the butcher, the baker, the candlestick maker, might have made her childhood dull, but it would have anchored her to a more reliable world – alas, these regular comforts she had never known. Whatever was the case, Fanny, three days after the event,

had forgotten writing the words about a darker force in Summerland and when she idly looked upon the sheet where she had
scribbled the new passage by candlelight with a trembling hand, she
could not recognise either the handwriting or the words as her own.

WILD NIGHT

Meanwhile, Matthew stood in the winding passageway of the tavern, wondering if a mistake had been made – either by him misreading Baxter's note or, more likely, Baxter's having confused the name of two taverns – writing down The Mitre when he was thinking of The Heart of Oak or indeed The Mackworth. Yet neither had been back to The Mackworth, nor had they spoken of it. Each, or so Matthew thought, feared that someone there might recognise them as the two men who were there that terrible night when the dead woman was found. Yet so far their actions had not been discovered. They had revived Fanny and rescued her. They had put another woman's body in her place, the poor drowned creature they had spirited away. No-one had seen this corpse and said it was *not* the young woman who had arrived on the Bristol Mail a few hours before. Yet they believed that some memory might be stirred by the sight of himself and Baxter.

In the midst of such thoughts, Matthew heard the distinct sound of Baxter's voice, which was a deep, almost rumbling baritone. It seemed extraordinary that his voice should rise out of all the other noises in that place, but rise it did, as clear and loud as a bell.

'You dare, do you?' Matthew heard Baxter cry. 'You dare to threaten me?'

Following the source of the sound, Matthew headed to the open doorway at the top of the passageway. This had been the busiest room when he first glanced in, with a press of bodies nearly spilling from it, and so he had not even tried to gain entry. But now Matthew elbowed his way through the crowd until, at last, he came to a sort of clearing. It was evident that people had moved back from the place where a confrontation was unfolding. Here too was the reason he had heard Baxter so distinctly, for people had arrested their own conversation in order to pay proper attention to the dispute. Indeed, the crowds looked on with great pleasure, for what better entertainment could there be but a quarrel between an English gentleman and the keeper of the local brothel and handler of various pawned, stolen and ransomed goods? The latter, a young man of average height whose frame was wiry and muscled, was nonetheless incapacitated by drink, a compensating factor that probably saved Baxter, who was older, shorter and less skilled in the fine art of brawling.

The young man had raised his fists and adopted the pugilist's stance with both his legs flexed at the knee, ready to both dance out of range and strike blows at his opponent. Baxter faced him with his arms held loosely flexed and open hands hanging down, seemingly relaxed and useless.

The young man tried to jab at Baxter, who stepped back smartly, avoiding the blow.

'Oh, you dare, do you!' Baxter shouted again and springing forward slapped the man resoundingly across his left cheek. In reply the younger man swung his fist, but the momentum of it unbalanced him and he swayed forward and down as Baxter elegantly, as if he were dancing a quadrille, once again stepped sideward.

The crowd roared with merriment and, mistaking this for encouragement, the young man swung again at Baxter, this time crashing into a table from where, unbalanced, he collapsed in a tangle onto the floor. Promptly, a bystander, perhaps thinking the young man was in need of revival, emptied a pot of beer over his head. A tremendous howl went up from the crowd as the young man spluttered and growled and tried unsuccessfully to raise himself up. Then a group of three grim-looking men, presumably the younger man's compatriots, moved in decisively and hoisted him unceremoniously to his feet, then carried him cursing and flailing out of the room.

Baxter, looking around with satisfaction, suddenly recognised his friend amongst the crowd and hurried forward to greet him.

'Did you see?' he asked. 'Did you see how I dealt with that lout? A man's anger can be turned upon itself. I did not strike him, though I was sorely provoked. Did you see?'

'I saw the end but not the beginning. What on earth happened?'

'Oh, that fool objected to my sitting in what he said was his chair. I said, "But I have warmed this seat a good half hour and if it were yours then I should have felt your heat!" So, he said some very crude words not worth repeating and I said he should go to the Devil and he said he was the Devil and he would very soon give me a taste of Hell. Then he raised his fists and so I stood up from the chair as I did not want him overturning me. He was very drunk and I not at all. But I did not strike him, much as he deserved it.'

'I saw you strike him.'

'No, not me.' Baxter was nearly breathless with excitement.

'Yes, you did. I saw. You struck him with the flat of your hand.'

'Nay, but that was only to bring him to his senses, not to do harm. Is there not a difference? I think there is.'

An old fellow standing near, hearing Baxter's words, said, 'Do no harm? Do no harm! To slap a man is an insult worse than any for a man such as he. If I were you I'd pray he's too drunk to remember your face, but others here aren't and they have long memories and a code of brotherhood. You have won the battle, sir, but not the war; it may be to your purpose to leave now before his troops are mustered.'

Baxter's face changed rapidly at this news. For the old man's words had more than a ring of truth to them.

'Let us go elsewhere,' Matthew said. 'I like it little here.'

So they went, elbowing their way through the crowd once more, some of the men clapping Baxter on the back or shaking his hand for his 'fine deed in taking that rascal down a peg or two', others scowling and muttering oaths. Down the winding passage they went and across the yard to the stables. There in the lamplight was the grizzled old hostler and beside him another younger man holding a black Welsh Cob by the reins. The two were talking in low, confidential tones. When they noticed Matthew and Baxter they quickly stopped talking and the stranger looked very hard at Baxter.

'I shall take the horse now,' said Matthew, and although he had only left the horse for ten minutes or so, and already tipped the old man, he offered him a farthing for his trouble.

With a sour face the old man removed the blanket from the horse and mouthing silent words replaced the saddle.

'That's a piteous price for an old man's trouble!' said the stranger.

'I paid him before,' Matthew said.

'So you say,' said the man.

Matthew looked at the old man seeking confirmation of this fact. 'You are satisfied, are you not?'

But the old curmudgeon did not reply, merely shook his head.

'I paid him, you have my word for it,' Matthew said, taking the reins and leading the horse out.

'Your word?' the man called after him. 'Your word is but a piss in an ocean, easily spent and all too soon diluted!'

Giving no reply to this insult as he walked away, leading the horse, Matthew said in an undertone, 'I fear we have made enemies this night.'

Baxter shook his head, though whether it was from regret or denial was unclear.

When they reached the main road, and had put some distance between the tavern and themselves, Matthew spoke plainly to Baxter.

'Why did you choose such a place for our meeting? It is well known as a rough den.'

'I had a mind to find some characters.'

'Good God, you succeeded there!'

'Not really. I'd hoped to engage some characters to sit for me. A good model is needed for the scene I planned for my Shakespeare cup.'

'Then you have found a veritable nest of Calibans and Iagos and mightily enraged the servants of the Capulets! Thank heaven there was no trio of weird sisters to seduce you!'

'True, but there was no harm done. All will be forgotten by morning. Indeed, I often wish there were a way of fixing scenes like that of an instant! They do not remain on the inner eye but for a second. Capturing movement is the most elusive skill. Then, too, there are those particular facial expressions that are so fleeting – they are there, then gone, and if one tries to fix such a look, whether a laugh or a flash of anger, it very quickly becomes slack or artificial. I know – I have tried this in the looking glass and all I get is that sort of grimace of concentration such as every self-portrait wears.'

'Does not the Dutch painter Hals do some expressions very well?'

'Yes. That's true. Rembrandt is also a master who could make something very lifelike, but there is still something fixed, something solid and immovable.'

'But that is the very heart of painting, is it not? To fix a moment, a face in time? To hold it steady so that it can be looked upon, studied?'

'No, that is not the very heart of painting!' His voice was curt. 'That is merely the machinery of painting – its heart is to create a story; that is why history painting is the most sublime. It incorporates illustrations from the Bible, Shakespeare and the Classics as well as vivid scenes from history. Have you seen the work of the French master, David? I have only seen an engraving, but The Oath of the Horatii is a masterpiece. As is his Death of Marat, which is a new form of history painting entirely.'

Matthew nodded gravely. He was woefully ignorant. He knew his shortcomings very well. Compared to the worldly Baxter he was a mere infant. He sighed loudly, not quite meaning to.

'You are weary and I lecture you as if we were not out on a gloomy and damp road, but by a warm fireside.'

'My sigh was in recognition of my ignorance, not your words. But you are right, I am weary.'

'And I am not; my blood runs hot! That is passion, the pure energy of anger!' Baxter ended this speech with a low growl. Matthew, alarmed, looked at his friend. Baxter had distorted his mild face into that of a monster with bared teeth and a rumpled nose. Seeing Matthew's expression of alarm, Baxter laughed and the sound echoed and re-echoed on the walls and cobblestones of the street, startling the horse.

The two men quickly found another inn, this one quite empty, its gentility meant to attract a better class of citizen than the hoi polloi of the Mitre. This endeavour on the part of the proprietor succeeded very well in the earlier part of the day, but by nine o'clock the goodly people had returned home for prayers and warm milk and parsimonious sleep, so the two friends were the last and only customers. Baxter still frothed with energy and, declaring he was starved, ordered cheese and bread and port for both of them.

'I will have nightmares,' Matthew said, but he nonetheless broke off a chunk of the white crumbly cheese and ate it.

'Caerphilly, which this is, is a young cheese, therefore your dreams will be innocent. There will be naught but milky virgins and angels and lambs. Try Stilton or a strong Cheddar if it's nightmares you are after!'

'Is that true?' Matthew innocently asked and by way of reply, Baxter slapped the table and laughed.

Since the episode in the Mitre, Matthew had been in that state of mind where known facts and early sympathies were being rapidly reassessed. He had, up to then, convinced that Baxter was a man to be admired and trusted. He'd judged him noble, clever and learned – a true friend – but now the clear glass through which he beheld his companion was growing clouded, its purity in doubt.

It was therefore with relief when, an hour before midnight, he parted company with Baxter and unsteadily mounted his horse for the journey home to Sketty.

THE GARDEN OF EARTHLY DELIGHTS

The drizzle had stopped, but the moon and stars still withheld the full beam of their light behind a thin gauze of cloud. It was not entirely dark, but the world was reduced to grey masses of objects: trees, cottages, hedgerows, the muddy road lined with white-painted stones, and beyond that the farms. One field was inhabited by two pale horses who might have been ghosts if creatures other than humans possessed the restless spirit which sought resolution for a problem unaddressed in this earthly realm. Matthew glimpsed these fearfully at first, then immediately relaxed, feeling foolish. The night had taken its toll upon him.

Matthew dismounted from his horse and led her around the back of the house to the stables. He rubbed her down and threw a blanket over her. He was troubled by the many incidents of the night and turned them over and over in his mind. These he added to other events and the stain of them leached into and polluted all.

None could be more troubling than that night when they had discovered Fanny close to death and revived her. What was that but the work of any good Samaritan? Nothing to be ashamed of there, he thought. No, it was the other deeds of that night. Those done at Baxter's instigation. With himself acting as accomplice, he'd been mute and acquiescent, the schoolboy who hangs at the back of the crowd and watches the wrongdoing of his fellows and does not act either for or against their sin.

And what a sin it had been! They had replaced the barely living woman with one newly dead. He, Matthew, had been at Baxter's side throughout; he had helped, he had held the half-dead woman in his arms as Baxter removed her undergarments. He had lifted the corpse of the other woman and laid her upon the bed in Fanny's room in the Mackworth. He had lied to Mrs Curtis. Yet at the time it had been as if he were the mere spectator, an innocent member of the audience called onstage to work under the mesmerist's control.

It had seemed so right and so noble at the time – their aim had been to subvert injustice and the law in order to achieve a higher moral justice – to give this unfortunate gentlewoman a second chance. Her suicide note made clear her state of mind. She believed herself to be a burden. Could she be made anew?

But what if Baxter had an unspoken aim? If his seeming goodness were a mask, then what lay beneath? What if instead of nobility there was corruption? As a man of science, Baxter had learned to distance himself from sentiment. Just as the lepidopterist kills the butterfly in order to preserve and study it, and the anatomist flays a human corpse to see the workings of muscle and artery and organs, so Baxter had captured Fanny to see what a young and melancholy woman stripped of her identity would become. And, it dawned on him, he too was both implicated and tested by Baxter. Matthew was as much a part and subject of the great experiment as Fanny.

'No, it cannot be.' He whispered these words aloud as he bolted the stable door and, shaking his head as if to throw off this terrible idea, took the path over the wet lawn to the back of the house.

A noise startled him, stopping him in his tracks. He listened, wondering at the sound. It had been a single dull crack followed by a soft dry rustling – only an animal moving through the trees: a badger or deer or stray dog. Or it might have no living agency at all, being a dead branch falling from a tree. But then, just as he was about to go on his way, he heard what was unmistakably a whisper. Or rather two whispers, one male and one female. 'No,' said the female voice. 'Yes' answered the male.

'And I said no.'

This last was followed by an increase in the rustling noise. Only a few yards away Matthew saw a female form pop out of the shrubbery and onto the lawn; yet like some creature attached by a tether,

her pale arm was extended and caught in the black mass of the undergrowth. She tugged again. In a giggling hiss, she said 'No. Oh, no,' and turned her gaze towards the house as if to check that she had not been seen.

It was the servant, Rebecca. Just as he recognised her, she pulled violently at what held her. The effect was that her male companion, despite his greater strength, was pulled from the bushes and into her arms. He took advantage of this and grasped her in a tight embrace, which she struggled against, all the while giggling enticingly.

Matthew, feeling every bit as exposed and in danger of discovery as these two might, took a step backwards in order to conceal himself behind the rhododendron. He stepped upon something that gave a sharp cracking sound and looked down to see what was underfoot – a razor shell, of which there were a great many in the flower beds. When he looked up again, the man had gone and Rebecca was making her way across the lawn into the house. As she neared the door, it swung open as if by magic. He guessed that someone inside the house had been waiting and watching, opening the door to allow her to slip inside without rousing the household. There was no magic, only intrigue.

He was less surprised to discover that a young servant should be breaking the rules of the household by sneaking out after hours to meet her beau than by the idea that she had an accomplice inside the house, for there was none but Mrs Curtis to play such a role. And Mrs Curtis ran a tight ship. He did not even consider the deed could be done by the listless Fanny; why would she?

He remembered the man Baxter had fought with and humiliated in The Mitre. He should not like to make enemies as Baxter had done. Yet was he implicated alongside his friend? All too well he remembered those words from Shakespeare his father had counselled him with when he plotted revenge on his schoolmates: 'thy brain is more busy than the labouring spider who weaves tedious snares to trap his enemies'. Yes, it was an apt saying, though he had sighed and rolled his eyes to hear it time and again, but repetition had fixed the words in his memory. Yet he had no enemies. No tedious snares wove through his imagination. If there was danger, it was outside him. Much as he looked, or tried to look, kindly on all mankind, this did not mean the kindness was returned. Who knew who looked on him as an enemy?

Bands of men, hardened by their years fighting Napoleon, alienated from their families and friends, maimed in body and unable to take up the tailor's needle or plough or pickaxe with which they had formerly earned their bread, roamed the country getting by force what was their due. They were desperate and angry, full of hatred for those who should have honoured them for their service.

Such men would cut your throat and laugh as your life's blood spilled hot and red in the street.

Inside the house were his father's blunderbuss, sword and long hunting rifle, but these were locked away and the key was stowed in the desk, among such a strew of papers and sealing wax and bills and string that it could not be easily found.

He stood shivering in the shadows with growing dread. What should he do? Run to a neighbour to beg shelter until dawn? But what if Mrs Curtis was held by them and terrorised? And what, he remembered – how could he have forgotten? – what of Fanny? That poor, frail creature might be violated and destroyed in the process. While he, shameful creature, cowered trembling in the shrubbery.

He listened for any sound that might suggest his worst fears, but there was nothing save for the sharp cry of a fox. Matthew's head began to ache. There it was, the excess of the night draining away, the port and ale, the last cheering brandy, all now churning in his stomach. Desperate for bed or death, which ever awaited him indoors, he crept around the side of the house meaning to enter by the same door Rebecca had used, but on reaching he discovered it was locked once more.

Stumbling, weary and angry, he retraced his steps, unlocked the main door and entered. Lighting his way with a single candle, he passed through familiar rooms, peering into dark corners and each turn of the passageway before moving cautiously forward. The clock chimed the hour: twelve.

Only midnight; how could that be? On up the stairs he went, the shadows dancing and making prison bars of the stair balusters on the walls. Into his room, then after placing a chair against the door, into bed with the sheets pulled over his head. Mrs Curtis and

Fanny might be lying slain in the rooms just yards away, but he *would* sleep.

'If sleep shall come', he thought and half-dreaming, seemed to be upon a small rowing boat that rushed towards a waterfall, and for a moment, he was falling, falling.

A SNAKE

At a quarter to twelve, Fanny unlocked the back door and stood behind it, peeping out in order to see anyone who might approach. She had been told to do this by Rebecca. It reminded her of those nights when Mary and Claire asked her to stand watch or to carry private notes to a certain person, or once, to take a shilling from Mrs Clairmont's reticule.

In the darkness she had heard the voices, a man's and Rebecca's, but could see nothing until, many minutes later, a figure appeared, running soft-footed to the door. The red shoes looked black but she knew by the movement and the outline of the figure that it was Rebecca. She pushed the door open, letting it swing just wide enough for the girl to slip through.

She thought the girl would smile and thank her, and as her own errant sisters had done, would draw her further into the intrigue by telling her of her adventures. Instead, Rebecca brought her face very close to Fanny's and said in a hiss, 'Don't you tell! Don't dare! I have friends who would pay you a visit and make you sorry if you betrayed me.'

Fanny drew back. Rebecca closed the door behind her then blocked Fanny's way.

'What are you staring at?'

'Nothing.'

The girl was breathing hard. In the light from the candle her cheeks glowed red and her lips seemed wet and swollen.

Fanny turned and hurried upstairs. One word seemed to knock

about in her head like a trapped butterfly. Alone. Alone. Alone. Always and always alone.

Once in her room, she went to the window and stared out at the black unforgiving night. She opened the window and listened. A fox yelped. She thought about the she-fox on her lonely retreat across fields and through woods. Alone. The anguished scream of the fox, nearer now, seemed to answer. But the fox would go back to her den, back to her kits and her mate. The fox was not alone. The cry came again, high, urgent and sorrowful. Alone. If the state of being alone had a voice, that would be it. Or would it be that desperate whispered drumming of a butterfly under a glass as it tried to escape its prison? Tears began to roll down Fanny's face; she felt them fall from her chin. Sorry for yourself. Luxuriating in self-pity. That was what Papa had said. Oh, she had wished over and over to change herself. She had tried, as she had tried tonight. She had wanted to make Rebecca her friend, but the girl had threatened her. How could that be?

Matthew and Baxter might have brought her back from the very brink of death but nothing had changed. Baxter said to her time and again, 'You are free, my dear, you can begin anew. We have shut the door on your past sorrows, we have locked them away in a strong box, we have heaved the box overboard into the very heart of the ocean, where it sinks to a thousand fathoms. Oh, how I envy you that chance. It is rebirth. You will rise like the mythical Phoenix from the funeral pyre of your old life and be renewed!'

Fanny almost believed it when he stood before her, his glittering eyes bright and alive, and said such things. 'Is that not so?' he said and 'yes,' she answered, but then his words drifted, her reply drifted, his eyes in her memory darkened and shrank, and it seemed that he was taunting her. Even Matthew, the kindest and most amiable of men, could seem, when she considered her situation in darker moments, to have hidden motives which guided his every word and look.

If she were truly reborn then wouldn't she be another person? A very different person with a lighter heart and a stock of memories, which gave her courage and good resolve, which attracted others to her? And what of the external appearance; would that same dreary face rise in the looking glass, would that same rough and pock-marked skin still be her inheritance? Could not the fire that regenerated the Phoenix also burn away each layer of the past? Undo the marks of smallpox? Revive her poor dead mother? Stop the fever. Then, too, might it not stop Mary and Claire from running off in the night? Might they become as meek and obedient and patient as she was? No. It was impossible. They were ever as wilful and naughty as she was dutiful and dull. In whatever forge they were each cast, it was fixed. Immutable.

There was only one change she could make to her essential self, only one way of silencing that word – alone, alone, alone – and that was death.

It came to her that she could lean out of the window. Lean out and lean out yet farther. Standing on tip-toe, her hips against the low sill, her weight pushed into the airy night. Then, like all things in the world, when not counterbalanced or securely lashed down, she would overtip and the window would release her and the earth would claim her. No-one would ever know if her intent was innocent or otherwise.

'Poor girl to die of such a misfortune just as she was beginning to recover!'

She could hear Matthew say the words. She also thought that she detected a certain fatalistic relief in his eyes. Mrs Curtis would say, 'Oh, poor girl! Now she shall join the shades of my own lost darlings and be their most loving sister and nursemaid until that blessed day when I am restored to them.'

And Baxter would gnash his teeth for she would become an aborted experiment, the laboratory mouse that had escaped.

She opened the casement and leaned out timidly, uncertain of her intent. Her window stood over an overgrown lawn which was richly sown with chamomile and had not been cut because of the endless rain of the preceding summer and autumn. Her fall would be cushioned as if by a cloud. Besides which, the drop was only twelve feet or so. She might break her neck, but more likely an arm or leg. Then, burden that she was already, she foresaw a crippled life wherein her nuisance and debt to those who sought to help her would increase a hundredfold.

She was about to abandon the window when she saw a figure moving stealthily along in the shadow of the house. It was a man in a dark greatcoat with a brimmed hat that hid his face. There was something familiar about the figure, a sort of elegance even in that quick skulking movement. It was Matthew. Matthew, the master of the house, and yet how wondrous it was that he should creep like an intruder into the garden and move with such guilty unease! When he came to the door that led into the passage by the boot room, he turned and looked around him as if he believed he was pursued. It cannot be him, she thought, what reason would he have for creeping about like a villain? Then she saw his face clearly and had not a speck of doubt; it was the master.

Her thoughts of the second before faded away in an instant. All melancholy, all self-pity, all ideas of her own destruction became so many reeds in the wind. They bowed as one in the face of a darker power. His trouble, whatever it was, seemed like a lonely ship on a rough sea. She would be his Cordelia, his Portia, his Stella Maris. She was needed and could not betray him, not now. She had little doubt that trouble haunted him, but what form it took she could not guess.

She crept into bed that night wondering at his troubles and inventing a thousand and one ills which might threaten him. Then she thought of all the ways she would come to his assistance. She played out the minutiae of these in their various forms. Her favourite was the one where an intruder raised a knife to stab Matthew and she, with supernatural swiftness, stepped before him, crying, 'No!' The knife was plunged into her breast. The attacker's eyes filled with horror and sorrow to see what he had done. Matthew opened his mouth in a low and lamenting moan. She dropped to her knees clutching her bosom. Pretty streams of blood ran like ribbons through her fingers and flowed in bright streams over her white gown. She fell sideways and Matthew dropped to his knees beside her, catching her in his arms.

'My love,' whispered Matthew as his tears fell hot and fast. 'Do not leave me! Pray do not die. You are my heart, my life!'

But she could not be saved and Matthew, ever after, visited her lonely grave, placing white lilies on her tombstone. His grief never wavered. Summer became autumn, then winter. He trudged through snow to lay wreaths of green holly spackled red with berries over the icy earth that covered her. In spring he was there again with bunches of snowdrops, then daffodils, then in sweet June, wild roses.

She drifted off to sleep thinking this; the flowers, the scarlet blood, his cries of anguish, her last whispered words to him: 'Do not forget who loved you. Remember me.' His tears fell onto her face, onto her lips, tasting of salt.

That dreams of her own demise should rock her so gently to sleep was unexpected, but no miracle, except of her mind's making. Now she had a cause, she could live. Now she had to live, she had to rest. Sleep came softly and kissed her where she lay.

JONAS

Picture that old house barely illumined by the full moon behind its thin shroud. The roof here was grey with slates, but another part of the house, which jutted out like a long, low, hairy giant's arm, was thatched. At one end, the barley-twist chimneys were tall extravagances. At the other they were squat and functional. Behind its windows, all harmonised in sleep, were a single young man and a veritable harem of women, none of them a blood relative or wife. Each of them nearly strangers to one another, each bred of a different tribe, each filled with all the hope and desire and memory and despair, and schemes and dreams and plans that every human heart can hold. Yet each sleeper's dreams were often only for themselves and sadly, at times, in opposition to others' designs.

Jonas Jones stood on the breast of the hill watching the house and thinking about its inhabitants. There was Tom's sister Rebecca who he had just left in the garden. Then too, or so Rebecca said, there was an old crone and a mysterious young woman who was kept very secret. Acts the lady, said Rebecca, but a lady with no jewels, no trunk of clothes, no relatives, who creeps about and weeps and scribbles secret things when she is alone.

'Spells,' said Rebecca,

'They don't burn witches no more,' he'd said to Rebecca. 'But I'll make thee burn if you'll let me.' They were in the graveyard and he tried to lift her skirts when he said this. She knew what he meant and what he wanted. She pushed him away. 'I don't mind kissing and cuddling but I don't want no baby in my belly off of you, Jonah

Jones. Nor do you, as my brother would kill thee for my ruin!'

'Only on account of how he plans to sell thee to a gentleman that wants a pure maid to break in. Speaking of gents, tell me more about the young pup who owns the house. Does he lord it over you? Has he had you yet?'

'Let him try,' said Rebecca, straightening her skirt and looking admiringly at her shoes, though their bright colour was lost on this dark night and they were wet with dew.

'Is there a great coffer in there? Filled with silver and gold? Does he spend his time counting his riches? Does he have a set of keys that he keeps close?'

'Maybe.'

'If I had riches such as he, I'd marry you, I would.'

She broke into a smile, then turned from him, gazing at the gravestones that stood like so many hunched men, an army of the dead awaiting orders.

'I must go,' Rebecca said.

Jonas walked with her despite her protests. He trailed her all the way to Sketty Cross then through the field and the path in the woods and onto the edge of the garden. As she made to take her leave, he'd grasped her by the wrist and would not let go, until at last she caught him off balance and he fell into her arms in full view of her master's house.

If he could have, he would have taken her on the lawn there and then. Made her burn, made her scream as he broke her maidenhead, but that was just his lust raging in him and he could spend it later down on the Strand with a girl who'd do it for a couple of farthings.

With that happy thought in mind, he set off back in the direction of town walking at a fast pace so that by two o'clock he was there and spent.

A FERAL CAT

The weeks went by, the constant rain and grey skies of the year before were broken now and then by blessed sunshine. Food was still scarce; wheat and therefore bread was beyond the means of many people, and those in the cities suffered and starved. Yet life went on. Fanny seemed better. Instead of being sunk down, she fairly glittered with a sort of manic energy, seeming to cling to Matthew's side and worrying him with questions about his comings and goings, about every man who came to deliver food or hay or letters or came to repair the thatch or put up a fence.

Baxter did not appear for a few weeks, but he sent notes enquiring after their health and explaining, sometimes with the aid of drawings, the work he was undertaking. Chiefly, he mentioned the Shakespeare cup, and Matthew and Fanny were invited to say whether diagram A which showed a deep bowl on a flaring stem was more elegant than diagram B which had a shallow bowl and a shorter stem with a wider base. They debated this between themselves and usually disagreed, so their response was that both were of equal beauty and they were certain that Baxter would produce a sublime object either way. Then a series of roughly drawn sketches would arrive: here was a scene from Macbeth, here one of Prospero by the seashore, and here was a maiden wringing her hands with eyes upcast to the heavens. All quite perfect, they responded, but the next day more drawings came, showing Juliet lying on a tomb at the moment Romeo discovers her, yet another of Ophelia leaning against a willow and gazing into a brook. The next day there were more diagrams, each of them so alike that it was hard to see what distinguished one from the next.

'Well, Baxter is busy,' Matthew said. 'I'd hoped he would have been to see us by now. There was the drawing of you he requested – are you disappointed, my dear?'

'Only because I was unable to be useful to him. Did I put him off by my lack of enthusiasm?'

'I think not; he has the enthusiasm of a hundred men – perhaps too much. He seems to run at one object, then another, then to abandon both to run at a third.'

Fanny pictured Baxter as a diminutive Don Quixote charging first at a windmill, then a bull, then another windmill. She smiled to herself at the image.

'Shall we visit him at the pottery? Surprise him as he has so often surprised us? Would you like that, my dear? We have been cooped up too long, I think.'

But then, as if in answer, the wind suddenly gusted and seemed to slam a fist against the window, rattling the panes, then rushing away again. They both turned to look and saw the tree sway and bend as crows darted from one branch to another. Goosebumps rose on Fanny's arms and she pulled the Paisley shawl more closely around her. Yet she wasn't cold; rather it seemed as if some danger lay ahead.

'No,' she said and moved closer to the fire. 'We should not go to his place of work. Not without an invitation.'

'You're right. The weather prevents us anyway.' He rubbed his hands together, then paced from the fireside to the window and back again. 'We will see him soon enough, I'm sure. Or I could write to him, perhaps invite him to dine with us?'

Fanny agreed and Matthew wrote that afternoon, adding that they longed to hear about Baxter's progress with his Shakespeare cup. The wind continued fitfully, moaning low then whooshing and whining. Great clouds travelled swiftly across the ultramarine sky, some pure white, others a powdery grey, still others like soot-smeared snow. The fire ticked and creaked placidly, then flared up in sudden draughts.

'I thought it might rain,' Matthew said, his voice suddenly weary.

'You sound sorry it hasn't,' Fanny answered.

'No, it is only that the weather is so strange these days. I wish it would settle.'

Their desultory conversation was interrupted by a sharp rap at the door to the drawing room.

Matthew's face brightened. Clearly, of all people, the one he expected at that instant was the one that had occupied their thoughts for many a day. Leaping from his chair, Matthew strode across the room and flung the door open, crying, 'My dear, dear fellow …' but at the threshold stood not Baxter in his winter trews and riding boots and cloak, but Mrs Curtis with her neat white cap awry, her grey hair half-unpinned and one of her round cheeks blazing red, while the rest of her face was ashen.

'Oh, sir,' she wailed.

'Mrs Curtis, what is it?'

She began to speak, but her voice caught and she choked and hiccupped between sobs.

'Sit you down,' said Matthew and he guided her to the nearest chair. 'Get brandy.'

Fanny poured a measure and brought it to the old woman's lips. She sipped a little, but then shuddered and coughed all the more.

'There now, there,' said Matthew, his voice as gentle and lilting as his old nursemaid's once was. 'There, there. Peace. Breathe slow. That's it.'

The old woman lifted one hand to her cheek where it was reddened, as if to test it. The back of her hand and wrist were crisscrossed with thin red welts, and beads of blood rose in places.

'What have you done to your hand?' Fanny said.

'Oh, that little cat, that spiteful thing,' said Mrs Curtis. 'She's flown now, sir, and good riddance.'

'Cat?' said Matthew, for the old house cat had died a year before and now only the old half-tame Tomcat remained, banished from the house but doing good service as a ratter in the outbuildings and barn.

'That girl, I mean. That ungrateful wretch, Rebecca.'

Matthew took Mrs Curtis's hand in his and inspected it. 'She did this to you?'

'And pulled my hair and slapped my face and kicked and spat. All because I told her off. Oh, I thought she would nearly murder me!'

She took more brandy then, and Matthew fetched water and vinegar, and a piece of muslin that he dabbed very gently on her fingers and wrist.

'I knew she was a bad 'un,' Mrs Curtis said, 'but I thought she only needed guidance and a kind word. More fool me to not see what she was about.'

'And what was that?' asked Matthew.

'Badness. The worst badness a girl can get into, sir. Sneaking out every night. Going back to that dirty hovel on the Strand, no doubt. Dallying with all sorts.'

'And she is gone?'

'Gone and took the ham with her, sir.'

'The ham?'

'The hock, sir, that was cooling in the pantry. And other vittles too.'

'I see.'

'I caught her taking a bite of it and told her only pigs do that and she said I would know as I was an old sow myself. I said she should watch her tongue as there was things I knowed and would tell the master. So, she said she knew a fellow who would come into my chamber and cut out my tongue and roast it for her if she asked him to. I said that was evil talk and I turned away saying I was going to speak to you, sir, and she pushed me and slapped me and dug her nails into my flesh. Then she seizes my hair and bends me down to the floor nearly. I cried out, "My heart! My heart is stopped!" then I did pretend to faint and lay quite still. Then I heard her going about in the kitchen, opening cupboards and drawers, taking this and sniffing that, until at last she's done thieving and the door slams and she's gone. I saw the ham was stolen straight away, sir. Then I came here as you find me this moment past.'

'We shall report her to the magistrate.'

'Oh, sir, she's very young.'

'But Mrs Curtis, she left you as you seemed to be dying. One might call that murderous.'

'Yes, but her ways are not our ways. She knows no better. She is gone and all we've lost are a few morsels and a ham hock.'

'And a handful of your hair,' said Fanny who had noticed a bald patch near the old woman's ear.

'Oh, sir,' said Mrs Curtis and she fussed with her cap, pulling it straight and pushing the loose strands of hair under. The ruddy colour in her struck cheek had begun to fade though the impression of four fingers remained.

'She hasn't taken any keys, has she?' said Matthew.

'No, sir, they are all about me on my chain. Oh…' She stopped and looked frightened, 'Except for the back-door key which by day we leave in the lock.'

'Go and see if it is there, Fanny, and if it is turn it, then bolt the door.'

Fanny ran to the kitchen but although the door was shut, the big iron key was not inside the lock. She pulled the bolt across, feeling as she did that what she feared, what they all feared, was inside the house already.

'It isn't there!' she reported breathlessly. 'But I've bolted it.'

How can it be that the simple matter of a lost key, which after all is only a piece of metal cast in a mould, a very small and ordinary object, can so alter the atmosphere of what had been an unexceptional household? Without the theft of the key, all the inhabitants of that house, Mrs Curtis's cuts and bruises aside, would have let the matter of the bad and ungrateful servant drift into the past. Yet the key, doing its original duty, kept them locked in a prison of defenceless dread.

A RAGGED CROW

To add further disquiet to their anguished household, another matter arose. Matthew's old school friend, a man with ambitions to enter parliament, was embarking on the Grand Tour. His circumstances had been those of genteel poverty, lived out in rented rooms in the cheaper part of Bath, before he came into an unexpected inheritance. Some months before, he had written to Matthew saying he had a few books and papers and other personal effects he did not wish to lose and asked if Matthew could keep them for a year or so while he explored Europe. Matthew gave his consent, believing that these papers would be no more than the contents of a small trunk. Without further notice, and after Matthew had begun to forget his promise, a carter's truck came ambling along the lane and onto the drive. Two men climbed down and began unloading several wooden crates, then asked where they should put them. Matthew, somewhat taken aback, instructed the men to put them in the barn.

'Can't do that, sir. Master instructed that they be in "a room such as a study or library or drawing room", that being the proper place for valuable papers such as these.'

The men were directed to the library, where they unceremoniously emptied each crate onto the floor near the window seat.

'What are you doing?' Matthew cried, for although the piles of books and rolled bundles of newspapers had been neatly packed, once turned out, they slipped about and with each up-tipped crate became a mountainous heap. 'This is preposterous! Why can you not leave them in their boxes?'

'These are the company's shipping crates, sir. Can't do without them, sir.'

'But I might have willingly paid for them. What are they, a penny or two a crate?'

'About that I should think, but we do need them. So, good day to you, sir.'

Matthew and Fanny stood staring at the pile in disbelief.

'Well,' Matthew said after a second or so. 'I cannot think that my friend intended this. He is a good fellow but never was one to think ahead. Not in practical matters anyway. I don't know what to do.'

'Do?' said Fanny. 'Why, we should find shelves for them or at least make a more tidy pile. Perhaps we might also read them.'

'Read them? I had not thought to even so much as touch them, these being his particular personal possessions.'

'Well, if there are letters or diaries or other documents, we should not read them, of course. Those could be kept in a box. But these look to be ordinary books and newspapers. Surely there can be no harm in putting these into some sort of order, if only to secure them from harm, as I'm sure harm will be the result of leaving them as they are now.'

'Yes, yes. Of course, you're right, but the locksmith is due and I have other matters to attend to. I don't have the time.'

'I have time. Indeed, time is my enemy; it stands before me, a vast empty expanse with little to fill it. Besides which, this is work I am familiar with. I often assisted my father with the organisation of his books and papers in his library as well as the bookshop.'

Matthew frowned, for in her innocent words it seemed that Fanny had revealed something more of her past life, something she had hitherto concealed.

Mistaking his frown as due to concern for his errant friend's property, Fanny said, 'I shall be very careful, I promise you, and it would give me pleasure to do this. You have done so much for me, making our account very much out of balance.'

'Oh, Fanny, my dear, I do not measure such things. There is no account, only an enduring concern for your wellbeing and happiness.'

'Then let me put the case thus, dear Matthew: it will make me happy to undertake this task. I am a very willing miller's daughter and will spin this heap of straw into gold for you!'

Not understanding, he frowned.

'That is an old German story about a strange little man called Rumpelstiltskin. A girl is given an impossible task, but this is easy. Please allow me this indulgence.'

'If it makes you happy.'

At ten o'clock a journeyman arrived as expected to change the lock, but found he did not have a chisel with him and went away, having first secured payment for the work. He swore he would have to buy a new chisel and a rasp and could not do the work without them. Matthew gave him the money with little thought on the matter, but Mrs Curtis did not like the look of the man from the outset. He was wearing nankeen trousers and a badly patched pea coat and on one side of his face there was a mark like the black peppering stain of gunshot. He was no-one she had ever seen, Mrs Curtis said, not in the village or the town, and Matthew should not have paid him until the work was done.

'But we must have the lock changed – he will be back later, then we can rest assured of our wellbeing and safety.'

Fanny was in the library, sitting under the window seat with a tower of books at her feet. She was going through them steadily, noting their titles and the author on a piece of paper. Despite the upset of Rebecca leaving, her mind was taken up with the task in hand and as she worked, she seemed to hear her father's voice. 'Knowledge if not ordered falls into squalor.'

She knew her job was to efficiently organise the books, yet she could not help but let the books fall open in her hands, could not resist the temptation to let her eyes greedily devour random passages. Hours could easily pass in this pleasant pastime if Fanny did not, every so often, pull herself up sharply with a reminder of her promise to Matthew.

'The law is the publique conscience' she read in Hobbes' *Leviathan*, a book her father often mentioned. Then there was Milton, a very ragged copy, whose opening words she read with a long unassuaged thirst, for her father had suggested the book too religious and dark for Fanny's impressionable mind: 'Of Man's First Disobedience, and the Fruit...'

A shadow seemed to fall upon the page and something moved in the corner of her eye. She looked up. There, staring in at her from the window, was a man she had never seen before. He looked shocked at being seen, for he had come right up to the glass and cupped his hands around his face, the better to peer into the room. He was evidently not expecting to see a woman sitting just beneath the window. But when he saw her shocked expression mirroring his own surprise, his look became a twisted sneer. She saw with horror the black pitted disfigurement that marked one side of his face and seemed to distort his mouth. 'Devil,' she thought in that instant. Whatever he was, man or devil, he did not linger but hurried away with such speed that she almost believed he flew, his tattered coat a flurry of crow-black wings carrying him off.

Disbelieving her eyes, she leapt up and, drawing close to the glass, saw him running off at a loping canter. No flying demon sprung straight out of *Paradise Lost* then, but a mere man.

Only a man. Only one of the gardeners. Only a vagrant come to beg a crust of bread or a cup of water. That was all, yet her pulse seemed to grow languid and a coldness infused her entire being as if she had plunged into an icy mountain stream.

She left her station by the window and pulling the brightly patterned shawl from the chair she wrapped herself in it, then went in search of Matthew. He was in the breakfast room, still lingering over coffee and going through his correspondence.

'Fanny my dear, here is another letter from Baxter.'

'I saw a strange man in the garden.'

'Ah, that would be the smith. He came to fit a new lock, but would you believe it, had not a chisel or a plane.'

'He was peering into the house.'

'I daresay he was looking for me. Yet he cannot be back already. When did you see him?'

'Just a moment ago.'

'Ah...'

He seemed not to be listening, but cast his eyes on the letter he was holding as if irresistibly drawn to it. 'Baxter prays our indulgence, and promises, weather and all other matters permitting, to be with us tomorrow. He particularly asks that you wear the green gown as the

moment has arrived for him to make your likeness!' A smile of such
happy anticipation lit up Matthew's face that Fanny, aware of past
accusations of sending a storm cloud to darken the sunniest of
moments, held fast her tongue on further mention of the devil she had
just seen.

'What do you say?' Matthew said brightly, 'Are you not cheered?'

'Yes, yes,' Fanny exclaimed and faked the sort of laughing smile
her step-sister Claire had been so adept at. Yet, her eyes, unlike
Claire's sparkling brown ones, were dull and fixed and her cheeks
wore no pretty dimples.

He refolded Baxter's letter and picked up another, this one
evidently a bill of some sort, for his face took on the look of grim
determination that he often wore when figuring his accounts or
dealing with lawyers or Chancery. Still unsettled, Fanny found
herself turning towards the window, half expecting that this room's
privacy should also be violated and that she would find that
evil-looking man or another peeping in. The breakfast room faced
east so that its window could catch the early morning light.

The juniper bush that was planted near the window moved in
the wind. Fanny had the curious sense that the undulations of its
branches were a sign that it was alive and might uproot itself and
come tapping on the glass in order to communicate something very
important. A warning perhaps, based on the report of what it had
seen and its knowledge of future events. Like the trees of Birnam
Wood, this common shrub might move. Prophecy came in subtle,
coded forms; trees did not walk – not in reality. Yet no idea, no
intuition of threat should be dismissed. Did the juniper agitate its
limbs in that sly, slinking way because a man hid behind it shaking
its trunk? If so, was it done to frighten her?

'Fanny? Did you hear me?' Matthew was saying, his voice
coming to her as if from afar.

'No, I...'

'You were daydreaming!'

'Yes, but I was also thinking of Macbeth.'

'Macbeth? I do not think Baxter would want you for any of that
play's characters.'

'I wasn't thinking of Baxter. I was thinking about the prophesy.'

'Prophesy?'

Fanny was all too familiar with this scene; herself speaking while a man, once upon a time her father, William Godwin, now her saviour, Matthew, only half-listened to what she said, and therefore heard only loose strands, rendering them meaningless.

A STROKE

A loud rapping at the front door startled both of them. Neither stirred as it was Mrs Curtis's duty to greet visitors or, if instructed, to turn them away.

The house was such that its back entrance was hidden away by the various extensions and outbuildings, so that very often beggars, hawkers and commercial travellers called at the main door. These low persons were either dismissed or sent around to the servants' entrance as deemed appropriate by the steely faced Mrs Curtis. Some of these importuning strangers then met a very different Mrs Curtis at the back door, where she smilingly doled out water and broken vittles to the needy.

In the case that the visitor was a gentleman or lady, she invited them into the hall then went to the master to discover if he would see them. As no knock came at the door to the breakfast room, Matthew, quite naturally, did not stir from his place but only sighed in happy anticipation, for visitors were always a welcome distraction. A minute or so passed and then the knocking came again, more fervent and prolonged than before.

'Dear me,' said Matthew. He half-rose in a sort of bewilderment for he did not think it becoming to his status as master of the house to open the outer door.

'Shall I answer it?' Fanny asked.

'Oh, would you, dear Fanny?'

She went wonderingly to the door as Matthew, his interest piqued, stood in the hallway.

'My 'pologies, Madam. I would not have come to the front door but I got no answer at the trade door. I'm here to do some work on a lock that needs changing.'

Fanny took in the man's appearance. He was dressed in a long cambric apron, a great coat, cloth cap, hard-wearing canvas trousers and boots. In one hand, he carried a wooden box that was scored and scuffed and bore the carefully painted words, 'William Williams and Son, Locksmith.'

His manner spoke of his honesty and integrity, exactly those qualities which should recommend him to any employer given the nature of his work. No-one would want to employ the skulking rogue who had called earlier without the very tools on which his trade depended.

'Who is it?' said Matthew, coming out of the shadows.

'Pardon, sir. William Williams come to do your lock as was asked for. I did try the back door but could get no answer and as I've walked from Townhill to do this particularly, I didn't want to turn back.'

'And you have your chisel?'

'Yes, sir.'

'And your plane? Your rasp?'

'Indeed sir, I could not do without them.'

'And the other fellow, is he returned or can you do without him?'

'Other fellow? Oh, you mean my son. He's at school still.'

'No, the other man. Your journeyman, perhaps?'

'Don't have no journeyman. It's just me and I like it that way. Least 'til the boy's 'prenticed to it.'

'But another rough-looking man was here only an hour ago saying he was come to see to the lock.'

William Williams scratched his head and put the wooden chest on the ground at his feet. 'Well, I don't know who he be and don't vouch for him in any way. I'm the only locksmith in this parish and a good many others too. There's Hogg's over near the Hafod – did he say he was from there? Did someone in your household ask them for to come, then another send for me?' A new idea dawned on the honest man's face. 'Lawd, sir, has the job already been done? Have I wasted my time?'

'No, no. It hasn't been done, for the fool came without his tools.'

'No tools? Well, he must be *twp!*'

'And I'm certain that only one locksmith was sent for, as that honour was mine and mine alone.'

The two men stood facing one another; they were of a like age and height and their faces, straight-nosed and well-proportioned with fair skin and cleanly shaven chins, might have marked them out as cousins. Both seemed to awaken to a new idea at the same time.

'Why,' said William, 'I do believe that someone's after filching my trade! Though how they've done it I cannot think!'

Matthew did not answer, but thought of the night in the Mitre Tavern and how revenge was promised. Then too of the girl, Rebecca, her sudden violence and the theft of the key. He thought ruefully of the coins he had foolishly given the other man, but not wishing to look like a dupe, did not mention it.

'I don't know either, but the man looked a rogue while you are clearly an honest fellow. You shall have the work and I will pay you double to have it done by close of day if it be possible. And I will pay a bonus if you would check the fastness of all the windows and doors, and should these need changing or other alteration, then you shall have my custom there, too.'

While this happy conclusion was underway, Fanny had the sensation once more of that same disquiet she often felt. It seemed a premonition of something awful arriving, or worse, the emptiness of loss. This last had been her lodestone and pointed always to the departed. First, she'd lost her real and unnatural father, then her beloved mother, and lastly her dearest sister and less dear step-sister, who had run away without a care, and even more painfully, without her.

'Why sir, you are very good,' said William Williams and doffed his cap.

'But where is Mrs Curtis?' said Fanny, for a sudden realization had dawned on her.

Matthew seemed not to hear, as he was proposing that he walk the man around the back of the house to the door that needed a new lock.

'Matthew!' she said, but her voice was a downy feather lost in an avalanche of snow. Off the men set, heedless and busy. She shut the door after them and hurried through the hall and down the long passage that led to the kitchen. The door was wedged open as it always was, so that the heat of the range could escape and air circulate. Straight away, Fanny saw a pair of feet where they should not be. They were on the ground, the heels against the red tiled floor, toes skyward, one foot pointing east, the other west.

'Poor old feet' Mrs Curtis used to call them, and very poor they looked now, one shoeless, the other speckled with splashes of a thick creamy stuff, and neither moving. The legs to which they belonged, the 'poor old legs', disappeared between the door and the table.

Fanny kneeled by Mrs Curtis's side and touched her 'poor old face.' It was pale and seemed oddly distorted. She had expected it to feel as cold as the tiles beneath her, but it was still warm. Fanny put her ear to the old woman's chest and heard within, like a clock wound about with layers of dough, a beat, then a pause, then two fast beats, then another long pause. A broken clock, but one that still went, even if it no longer kept time.

She called the old woman's name, and gently pushed at her shoulder so that the body rolled and rippled but did not stir back into life.

She heard the two men's voices drawing near, talking of windows and glass, of locks and iron bars. As they grew louder she thought they must be right outside the kitchen. There was a broken earthenware bowl at Mrs Curtis's side, some of its mixture of flour and eggs still pooled within, while the rest had escaped, flying here and there in glossy splashes and droplets. Here was the story of the moments before, Fanny surmised: the old woman had been surprised by an intruder and dropped the bowl. Then he, or she, had done some violence to her, knocking her out. That man she had seen, the one at the window with the scarred face – he had been the assailant, he had done the evil deed, and now he had fled to God knew where.

'And here is the one with the lost key,' said Matthew opening the door into the kitchen, his voice no longer muffled but loud like that of an actor as he first walks on stage and projects his voice into the auditorium.

Fanny leapt to her feet and cried in alarm, 'Mrs Curtis is struck down! Get the doctor!'

All would have been chaos then, for neither Fanny nor Matthew had the knowledge or calm presence of mind to do that which was most sensible and most needed, but providence had sent them William Williams and he, his humble background notwithstanding, took charge.

He and Matthew lifted Mrs Curtis into a chair. She blinked and opened her eyes, but her mouth gaped wretchedly.

'What is your name?' the locksmith asked her, but she only twisted her mouth upon silence.

'Can you hear me?' he cried and took both her hands in his. 'Squeeze my hand if you can hear me.'

Fanny saw that Mrs Curtis gave some sort of sign, though it was weak, as her fingers, once so quick and adept, seemed to move with a frail answering pulse.

'I'll get brandy,' Matthew said.

'No. She may choke. Bring blankets.'

'What shall I do?' asked Fanny.

'Rub her feet and hands; she's cold and her blood is sluggish.'

Fanny did as she was told, kneeling before the old woman and chafing first her feet, then her hands. 'It must have been that man,' Fanny said. 'I knew he looked evil.'

The locksmith looked at Fanny and shook his head. He untied the old woman's bonnet and her fine white hair fell about her neck. Some colour came into her plump cheeks.

'Talk to her,' William Williams said. 'Talk about familiar things, say her name and the names of those she knows intimately. Talk of the house, the weather, anything to bring her back to herself.'

Fanny talked. Oh, how she talked! Never had such a stream of words and associations and nonsense and rhymes and names and endearments flowed from her lips. She spoke of Mrs Curtis's children, plucking from memory their names which were: Eliza and Susan and Beth, Polly, Grace and Kitty. Fanny thought that if ever there was a moment for the shades of Mrs Curtis's departed children to come to her, this was it.

Matthew set off on horseback to fetch the nearest doctor.

Mrs Curtis seemed to recover a little and lifted her left hand and again tried to speak, but her voice and her mouth were so distorted that no sensible sounds came forth, only a drowning, gurgling, noise. 'Garh. Guh.'

'That's right,' said William Williams, as if he understood. 'Don't fret, my good woman; we're here to make you better.'

Fanny looked at him wonderingly. He seemed so capable, so calm and understanding.

He saw her look and in a quiet voice said, 'My grandmother and my mother both had fits such as this. So, I am doing what was bidden of me then by a doctor. It does no harm and may do good.' Then in a louder voice for the benefit of the old woman, he added, 'We shall have you well very soon, but in the meantime, rest!'

He then touched the back of his hand to her cheek and checked her feet and fingers.

'She's warmer now. That's good. Hold her hand and keep talking. I'll be back.'

He slipped out the way he had come and a few minutes later reappeared with his work chest. Pausing only to smile and nod at Fanny, he commenced levering and tapping, removing the old lock and fixing in place the new one. It was done by the time Matthew arrived with the doctor.

AN ALBATROSS

The next day, William Williams returned, and it being a Saturday, he brought his son and namesake to help him. The boy, who went by Billy, was a very serious little fellow of eight or nine, with white hair and bright blue eyes. He followed at his father's heels, solemnly watching all he did and handing him such tools as were needed.

Fanny, being used to many aspects of running a house on a budget, fried leftover bacon, cabbage and potatoes for the men and the boy, which they ate with manly relish. Soon after, Baxter, who they had quite forgotten was expected, showed up as the locksmith was going over the house with Matthew. Bolts were added or secured where they had worked themselves loose. The mechanism on the front door needed changing, too, as it was a very common type that many keys could unlock. Baxter came upon the group when he arrived and seeing as there was nothing else for him to do, got out his pencil and a small leather-bound sketchbook to make drawings of William Williams and young Billy as they worked. Behind the father and son, he sketched Matthew, who stood about looking on, worry creasing his smooth brow, his body taut with agitation.

Fanny sat with Mrs Curtis in the library. Being unable to mount the stairs, the old woman had been put to recover on the large sofa there. She had taken a little water and some bread soaked in milk and seemed greatly improved but was still unable to speak properly. Most of the time she dozed.

Fanny, although restless, felt she could not recommence her work of putting Matthew's friend's books and papers in order for fear of disturbing her charge. After a very long time of doing naught but gaze at Mrs Curtis, whose face seemed tipped sideways, the mouth and eyes on one side sliding down limply, Fanny got up from the chair and picked up one of the newspapers. It was *The Times* from December of the previous year.

She turned the pages idly, feeling far removed from the world the paper described, beyond Europe, beyond America and Africa; on dry land, but somehow cast adrift. Her new situation, her new identity – the tabula rasa Baxter had spoken of so excitedly – made her feel disconnected. Furthermore, with Mrs Curtis incapacitated, it would be no time before Matthew deemed it necessary for Fanny to leave his house. A young single woman under his roof with no chaperone could ruin his reputation, no matter how innocent. This she knew all too well. It was a contamination as destructive as any disease. Unfair as it was, irrational even, it was she who carried the burden of her half-sisters' elopement, her mother's many indiscretions, as surely as if it was she who had offered herself to the painter Fuseli, or run away with Shelley or thrown herself at Lord Byron. She was like the man who shot the albatross in dear Coleridge's poem. 'Alone, alone, all, all alone' – lost in the doldrums of no future and no past.

She remembered, as if it were some half-forgotten dream, that evening when she and Mary, both of them in their cambric night-gowns, had hidden behind the sofa as Coleridge recited his nightmarish tale of the ancient mariner. Mary had snuggled close, then closer still, and at one point had twisted her face up to gaze for reassurance at her big sister. Fanny had stroked a loose hair from her darling sister's brow then looked from Mary to their mother's portrait. Mary Wollstonecraft was looking away from the spot where Coleridge's voice was coming from, yet her calm face, so still, always so still, seemed to hear his words. Fanny knew it was her duty to care for and love little Mary, yet Mary won ample love from every-one. More than enough – as if one can ever get too much love and regard – while Fanny's quota always fell short. There was never quite enough love to make the walls of her bedroom seem solid, or for the rattling window glass to hold fast against the rain and howl-ing wind, the sudden shouts of alarm, the drunken laughter and other sounds of the city streets.

Alone. Alone. She must once, when she was barely able to walk, perhaps during that long journey with her mother and Margarette to Scandinavia, have done some evil. There must have been something, some ill deed that damned her infant self for eternity.

What was it that her step-brother Charles had said? 'It is sure to rain on Fanny's birthday!' They had all laughed and rolled their eyes while she sat amongst them blushing with fury.

'Dark thoughts,' she reminded herself, 'Banish them. Stay busy. Think of other things.'

She opened the paper and noticed pencilled remarks in the margins. 'Not Mrs Smith! But Harriet Shelley!' She gasped, feeling in the intimate urgency of the handwritten words a message meant solely for her eyes. Yet how could that be?

She read the story that was circled beside it. She learned that 'Harriet Smith' had been found drowned in the Serpentine, that she had been missing for six weeks and that 'a want of honour in her own conduct is supposed to have led to this fatal catastrophe'. Those last thinly veiled words in the report could only mean that Harriet had been with child, very obviously in the late stages when it could not be concealed.

Smith had been one of the names for her that Baxter had proposed. 'Miss Smith' was everyone and no-one. 'Or Miss Nemo,' he'd said, warming to the plan.

'Nemo?' she'd said.

'Yes. Yes!' Swelling with enthusiasm, he said, 'Nemo is Latin for no-one. Quite, quite perfect for our woman of mystery, our empty slate!' He was laughing with delight. Though not unkindly.

A noise from the makeshift bed interrupted her thoughts, that strange and urgent gurgling sound which had replaced old Mrs Curtis's gentle and lilting voice, 'Garh – rah. Gar...'

'I'm here,' Fanny whispered, going closer to the bed. Mrs Curtis blinked unevenly and a movement at one corner of her mouth suggested a half-begotten smile. Fanny, despite the revelation and dark thoughts of seconds before, managed to smile. The old woman, seemingly satisfied by this, closed her eyes again and her breathing slowed.

Fanny went back to the newspaper, folded it and placed it underneath three or four others in the pile.

Harriet Shelley dead? Poor sweet Harriet, her own dear echo of a soul deserted in the name of love. Mary's reckless heart had swollen with greed and struck dead two other hearts, first Fanny's, though it still beat, terrible and irrepressible in her chest, then Harriet's. Or not two hearts, but three, for within Harriet's womb there was also her unborn baby's heart. Boy or girl, who knew, but Fanny felt it to be a female soul.

Echo and re-echo of remembrance struck her, waves upon eternal shores; lake or sea or mighty river, where a woman waited by the water's edge, her body swollen with the budding life inside while before her stood the arms of death. If her own mother had succeeded in drowning herself that day twenty-four years ago, she, Fanny, might have passed into lasting bliss and innocence. No words would she ever hear apart from the murmured sounds she might have perceived from inside the blood-red womb. No sight of her beloved mother, no glimpse of an azure sky or sheltering tree, no bird soaring high, no beauty, no city, no sorrowful beggar or crippled child, no mutilated soldier home from the wars against Napoleon, no hateful chores, no half-glimpsed joy. No tears.

No wretched, ragged, unstoppable tears. No perpetual melancholy.

Poor Harriet.

Poor, poor Harriet. If Shelley had ever loved her then how could he leave her? If only from common humanity and sympathy he should have protected her, body and soul. And the child she carried? Was it his? They must know, she thought, considering how this news would have fallen on the two reckless lovers Mary and Percy. Did they sorrow?

No, they did not, she decided, for Shelley would now be free to marry Mary. What luck, Fanny thought bitterly, what joy might spring from tragedy.

Did they even know of her fate? The newspaper account only named Harriet Smith. Just as the account of her own death did not name her.

It had rarely crossed her mind to consider the effect of her own loss on Godwin's household at Skinner Street. She seemed to see Papa's worried brow crease in sorrow and heard him sigh. Yet she distorted even that thought and imagined his sigh as a sound that signified relief rather than real sorrow. Gone was the troubled girl who was not any blood relative of his. It was one less mouth to feed, one less body to clothe, one less mind to clutter his.

DESERTION

All about her she felt the sorrow and pain of others. Disaster seemed to fall on those she loved; it sent her real father, Gilbert Imlay, running for his life. It killed her mother. She was naught but a drain upon Papa who, because he was very good, had tried his best with her for her mother's sake. But Mary and Claire had run away. Did they even think of taking her? No. And what if they had? She would have said no. She might also have warned Papa of their plan. Yes, she was sure she would have. Then he and Mrs Clairmont would have stopped them and now, she was certain, Shelley would be living happily once more with Harriet. Mary would be heartbroken for a time and Claire would hate Fanny forever and ever because that was what Claire was like. All passion, all immediacy, all boldness and hang the danger!

Fanny tried to be good. To harm no-one by word or deed. She had been kind to Rebecca, noticing how the poor girl's feet must have pinched, yet Fanny's reward was hatred. She had been good, or so she hoped, to Mrs Curtis, yet her very presence in the house must have increased her workload and now here she lay on the brink of death.

And Matthew, how would he be punished for letting her into his house? What dread thing would befall him? And Baxter too, who was strange at times, but an artist and scientist must have his foibles.

I bring misery on all, was her conclusion.

A voice intruded upon these dark thoughts.

'Fanny!' There was Matthew at the library door, silently

beckoning. She went to him, reluctant to leave her sleeping patient.

'Good news, my dear Fanny. The girl is returned. All was a misunderstanding. She is most concerned to see to Mrs Curtis's needs and to stand in her place! Is this not a happy thing?'

Happy? The word had no meaning at that moment. Yet he, Matthew, looked happy, so she made the pretence of a smile, then turned away so he would not see her face, for she could not maintain the pretence.

'Ah, here she is now!'

Fanny heard a light step and, keeping her head bent, saw the approaching feet in the familiar red slippers. The shoes were a little discoloured now and scuffed. Fanny noted this and considered it a sign of the girl's ruin and duplicity, but it gave her no pleasure.

What did it mean that this girl had come back? Now that she had tasted the cold reality of no work and little food, was she ready to be good and obedient? This girl was young enough to change, to learn from her mistakes. Let it be so, thought Fanny, and this being the case I can now leave with some balm for my conscience. All will be as before, my time here was but a brief sojourn, soon forgotten by them.

'There, there,' Matthew said to Rebecca. 'Away to your work. Mrs Curtis is resting, but you shall sit with her tonight.'

'Yes, sir,' said the girl and the feet retreated, red flashes turning grey in the shadows.

'Did she return the key?' Fanny asked when the girl was out of earshot.

'Yes, though it is useless now that we have a new lock.'

'True,' said Fanny, though she found Matthew too forgiving on this point. Did he doubt the seriousness of her attacking Mrs Curtis? Did he think that being young and female her blows inflicted no pain? Or that such incidents amongst the lower orders might be as common as cat fights?

'Matthew, are you quite sure she is repentant? That she can be trusted to treat Mrs Curtis with kindness now that the poor woman is quite defenceless? I am sure that Mrs Curtis should not want the girl in the house.'

'I too might have doubted it, but her priest wrote to me. She had been to him day upon day begging forgiveness and promising only humility and piousness. He said she is quite changed.'

'Do you know this priest?'

'No, but it was a very good letter, most learned; he is clearly a respectable and amiable gentleman.'

Fanny considered this very poor proof of Rebecca's changed character. A piece of prose, even one that is well-composed, might be nothing but a fiction. Yet how could she say this to Matthew without insult?

DAUGHTERS OF EVE

Fanny brooded upon many matters and tried, when possible, to serve these twin ideas: one, that men were inherently evil and secondly, this being the conclusion of the first, that women were their victims. She thought again of poor Harriet who had borne Percy Shelley two children only to be abandoned by him. Harriet had then fallen prey, no doubt, to another man. The words in *The Times* made this clear, for 'a want of honour in her own conduct led to the fatal catastrophe.' Her own conduct! What of that of her husband? Poor, wretched Harriet! Poor daughters of Eve.

Yet creeping into her mind came another recollection; indeed, it happened so recently that as yet, as a memory it was unfixed and so it floated, an uncertain cloud that might yet swell and darken until it became a storm. This memory was of Rebecca's return. Was it truly, as Matthew believed, a prodigal return, the supplicant full of genuine regret, a changed woman, full of Christian penitence and ready to do all in her power to heal past sins? Thus far Rebecca had given every sign that this was the case. When Matthew had taken the girl to see Mrs Curtis, she had fallen to her knees and kissing the old woman's hand had wept and wailed and covered her own face with her hands.

'Poor child,' said Matthew. 'See how her heart is almost broken.'

Fanny looked, but saw no tears fall from the cupped hands.

'Get her a little water, she is quite beside herself.'

Fanny did as she was asked and the girl, her face quite hidden until then, was forced to look up in order to take the proffered glass.

Her eyes, although reddened, for she had been rubbing them furiously as though to stem tears, were quite dry.

As dry and cold as the marble eyes of a Greek statue.

Mrs Curtis hardly stirred as the girl's handwringing and wailing went on, but lay very still and silent. More still and more silent than she had been while asleep. Fanny suspected that the old woman, even in the condition to which she had been reduced, had heard Rebecca and feigned sleep rather than cast a glance at the false girl.

'Poor girl,' said Fanny. 'It is too much for her. She will make herself ill. Take her out of the sick room, Matthew; let her rest in her chamber for the remainder of the day. Then she will recover.'

'Yes. Of course. Come now, Rebecca, do as your mistress says and away to rest yourself.'

Once she was gone, Mrs Curtis miraculously stirred herself and moaned. She blinked and, finding Fanny gazing on her, smiled in her new lopsided way.

'She is gone to her room,' Fanny said and the old woman tried to speak, but failing, weakly turned her head from side to side. Exhausted sleep fell upon her again and her breathing was loud and at times she snored.

Fanny gestured to Matthew to walk with her to the window, then said in a whisper, 'The girl is too upset to care for our patient. You must tell her she is not to enter this room. I can continue as before; there are many other tasks the girl can undertake which will be of service. She can clean the house and prepare vegetables and do any number of things, but not this.'

He nodded gravely, then touched Fanny's hand, conveying a gentle warmth. 'You are very good,' he said and left the room.

So here was Fanny's dilemma: if all men were evil, how did Matthew hide it so well? And what of evil women? Was it in woman's nature to be cruel? Yes, came the answer. Might they be violent? Yes, again. Deceptive? Scheming? Able to feign innocence and shed false tears? Without doubt.

The girl might be the dupe of that man Fanny had seen her with in the garden. She might yet be seduced by him and then should nature bless their unholy union with a child he would no doubt leave her. After that she might not suffer the shame that her betters did, but penniless with a starving baby at her empty breast, how could she survive? She should fall into a worse condition, succumb to drunkenness and prostitution. Such women were everywhere. They were often diseased and brutalised. Give them a cup of gin and they might laugh and dance and sing their sad ditties, but morning dawned colder than ever upon them. If they shivered back to life it was only for another day the same as the last, until ere long they woke no more.

The preachers foretold their doom, yet did those women listen? No, the words were just noise unto their ears and there were other sounds far more enticing: the music of the sailor's accordion or the hurdy gurdy man's jangling music or that of the Scottish fiddle player.

The next day, unnoticed by anyone, a wounded dog crept into the garden and dragged itself over the lawn and onto the flagstones beneath the windows at the back of the house. It made no sound, or at least none loud enough for any of the inhabitants to hear. But all too soon its blood and death scent signalled to carrion crows and they gathered nearby.

All that was noticed at first was the cawing and the black-winged scuffle. Fanny watched for a time, seeing omens of death yet not realising that their presence signified not a premonition but the real presence of death.

Going closer to the window and looking down into the garden, she saw in the crows' midst the greasy black fur and open wounds of a dead animal. The blood and entrails had been pulled asunder; one eye was an empty gash that the crows danced and fought over.

She hurried downstairs and through the sleeping house. No-one was yet awake and the dawn was barely breaking. In the hall, she saw at once that the door to the library stood open. Here it was that she had meant to go, for the room being directly beneath her own looked directly out upon the place where the crows had gathered.

She had not thought to find another person there besides Mrs Curtis, yet here was a human shape wearing a black cloak that covered it from head to foot. It stood with its back to her, like death itself, peering over the couch where Mrs Curtis had lain. Going closer Fanny saw that the poor old woman had half-tumbled from the makeshift bed; her head was nearly touching the carpet and one arm was flung out as if to save herself. Fanny knew at once that she was dead for her mouth hung open and her eyes stared out at nothing.

Beyond this ghastly tableau, framed by the window, ravens and crows in greater numbers – for more had joined the feast by dint of sound or scent – hopped and fought and flapped their wings in bitter commotion.

'Do I dream?' Fanny seemed to hear the question as if it rose not from her waking consciousness but from some other far-off place. She gave a sort of strangled groan. The cloaked figure turned sharply. No skull's head was there, no grimacing death mask, but instead a girl's face that looked paler and gaunter under the black hood, but was yet instantly recognisable, for it was Rebecca.

The girl's expression was at first one of surprise, but then she shaded it into sorrow.

'The poor old thing is dead,' she whispered and the crows reached a fever pitch of agitation as a large herring gull joined them, its white head and grey wings, its fleshy pink feet no more a sign of purity and decorum than the crows' jagged mourning weeds.

Fanny screamed, her own blood turning cold at the sound. Her eyes closed tight to blot out the terrible sight.

It was answered by footfalls from above, quick steps, the pounding of feet upon floorboards, then a slammed door and a thudding down the stairs. And there was Matthew in his nightgown at the library door, his hair awry and eyes wide with alarm.

'Fanny!' he cried and, catching hold of her shoulder, shook her. 'What is it?'

If her scream had disturbed the birds outside the window, causing them to fly or hop away, they now returned, noisier and more agitated than before. There his gaze went, at first fearfully then, as if finally understanding everything, gaining its rational aspect.

'Ah, only birds,' he calmly said. 'They must have found some scraps of food.'

'No,' said Fanny.

She looked around the room, and glancing wildly about, she saw that the window was swinging open and Rebecca had escaped, her black cloak fluttering and fragmenting among the squabbling crows as if she had been transformed into a bird and flown away.

PART NINE

1967-1971

'If I cannot inspire love, I will cause fear!'

Mary Shelley, *Frankenstein*

MISERY

Helena looked up from the papers to face Jude. 'It's such a depressing story,' she said. 'All this misery and suicide and deception. And murder?'

Jude frowned. 'But that's what's so gripping. Besides, I'm hoping to find even more documents. I'm still searching. I thought I could lift some of the floorboards – whoever hid the papers was cunning – maybe the final part is hidden there. Perhaps we'll discover a happy ending.'

'Well, don't demolish the house in your search; you might rouse ghosts who won't go away,' Helena said. She'd meant to impart sarcasm, but her tone remained sweet so that her meaning seemed earnest.

'Oh, I'll be careful,' Jude said. 'I am always respectful of the dead. I found out that Fanny Imlay was buried in St Matthew's graveyard. I've already been there to commune with her. You know, just to feel her presence.'

'I thought she didn't die. Wasn't that the big secret? Didn't that poor drowned girl get buried in her place?'

Jude looked shocked. Confused by her own plot twists. 'Well, yes, of course! It would be Hannah buried there, poor thing.'

Helena wanted to confront her, to say, 'These are forgeries. Do you think I'm that much of a fool? That I was the only person who was mug enough for your scheme?' Yet she could not be so direct. Instead, she criticised the essence of the story itself. After all, according to Jude, she was not the author, therefore Jude couldn't be hurt by objective criticism. Whoever wrote this, according to the great pretence, was long dead – their feelings couldn't be injured.

There still remained a lingering doubt in Helena's mind as to the true author of the documents. While she knew that Jude had handwritten every single page, creating a very plausible forgery by using old paper, she still doubted Jude's ingenuity and skill in the language and storytelling. And this prompted an irresistible question; why, if Jude was capable of writing such a text, didn't she just write a novel? Some of the most popular and successful novelists of the age were women who wrote such books. There were Daphne du Maurier, Georgette Heyer and Mary Renault and probably a dozen more, so why not take them as role models? Why not make a success of her ability and transform her life? Why go to such elaborate and perplexing lengths for a mere hoax? Unless she meant to make money from it.

It seemed obvious to Helena that the text was either taken in its entirety from an unknown source – a book long out of circulation and forgotten – or it was done piecemeal - the whole created out of a patchwork of scraps, a paragraph from one work, a description from a second, conversations from a third. Names changed, places changed, events slightly altered. Then, to suggest that the story was actually real, Jude had introduced real characters like Mary Shelley and Fanny Imlay, adding some events and known facts about their lives in order to rewrite history. But why?

Yet still she could not bring herself to confront Jude and instead continued to pick away at the text in the hope it would provoke a reaction.

'It's so relentlessly grim,' Helena said. 'Quite horrid and cruel. Don't you think?'

'No. That is, yes, it's grim, but it's real.'

'What do you mean, "real"? As in life is like that? How do you know that any of it ever happened? It's absurd! Perverse! A woman – a *dying* woman – breast-feeding puppies!'

Jude was getting visibly upset, her expression fluctuating through rapidly changing emotions: disappointment, anger, confusion, wild arrogance, pain.

'Real as in real! It happened. It all happened!' she said, her voice rising.

'But how do you know that? You said you found these papers hidden away, but who wrote them? What if someone invented the whole thing? They might have fooled you, but they don't fool me,' Helena said, feeling smug. She imagined that Jude would confess, that it would be healing for both of them.

'You just don't get it, do you?' Jude yelled. She stood up and without another word she rushed out of the room and into the bathroom.

Helena stirred the papers around, picked up one and read the familiar words, 'she makes a luxury out of her melancholy.' She heard the toilet flush, then the taps running. After that there was a long silence. Jude was probably gazing at herself in the bathroom mirror, composing her face and a whole new set of lies.

Perhaps ten minutes had passed before Helena looked at her watch. Twenty-five past six. She got up and went into the hall, listening for sounds from the bathroom. She heard nothing.

'I'm going to put the kettle on,' she called. Then waited, listening. 'Jude? Would you like tea?'

A floorboard creaked and there was a very faint sound like that of a bracelet catching the side of the sink.

As the kettle began to boil, Helena looked at her watch again. Twenty to seven. She warmed the teapot, spooned in the fragrant Earl Grey that had surprised Jude the first time she'd given it to her. She set out cups and saucers on the tray, put milk in the jug, then as a treat – sugaring the nasty pill she'd just delivered – opened the new tin of biscuits and arranged the pink wafers, the lemon puffs and the iced biscuits on a pretty sandwich plate.

She looked at her arrangement, feeling there was some element missing. Later she would wonder at this rather strange concentration on such trifling details while a very upset, possibly insane and dangerous woman was locked in her bathroom, doing who knew what?

She stared at the mahogany tea tray; on it was the teapot, the cups, saucers and plates, the milk jug, sugar bowl and tea strainer. Reconsidering the biscuits, she decided she'd put out too many of the very sweet ones, so she added some plainer ones.

Her mind seemed to be straining after distant memories of the Girl Guides or domestic science classes at school. Something was missing. The Freudian obliqueness of this was astonishing. What was missing? Jude evidently, but no, it wasn't that. Helena worried about the tea tray – this symbol of domestic rectitude, the very altar of the good hostess. All the tray lacked was a cloth, for every altar must have one. She found one in a drawer. God knows where it had come from, but the white linen rectangle with its embroidered swags of flowers and curling stems, its lace edging, fitted the tray perfectly.

Now satisfied, Helena picked up the tray and, pausing outside the bathroom, called, 'Tea's ready!' in that bright reassuring way women who are mothers or wives use. It was the great panacea, the cure-all for every situation; plague, pestilence, war – all could be borne as long as there was a nice cup of tea.

'Jude. Come on, I'm sorry. Let's talk. Please.'

The only answer was silence and a sudden stir in the air. Not a breeze, but a definite draught whose source must be the open window in the bathroom. This window was larger than was normally found in bathrooms, the room having formerly served a different purpose. Ever since Helena had lived there, that window had never been opened due to the fact that it had been painted at some stage and then, evidently, closed before the gloss paint was properly dry. Christopher had said it was just as well because the window abutted the flat roof of an adjoining building and therefore, if left open, constituted an easy way in for burglars.

As if to further confirm this, another gust of wind caught and slammed the kitchen door, startling Helena so much that she nearly dropped the tray.

'Jude?' she called, then hurried to put the tea things in the sitting room before coming back. She knocked on the door sharply, called again.

'Jude? Are you okay? Jude!'

She tried the door, but it was locked.

She bent to peer into the keyhole but saw only the round silver end of the key in its nimbus of light and shade like some implacable and alien moon. She got on her hands and knees to see under the door but all she could see was a few inches of floorboard and the edge of the pink bathroom mat.

She stood up, knocked and called again. Went away and closed the bedroom window to prevent any more doors slamming. Looked at her watch. Ten past seven. Went back into the living room and saw, still hooked over the back of the chair where she'd been sitting, Jude's cream-coloured mackintosh and also one of those large cloth bags she always carried. If not for these she might have thought that Jude had left. Or that she had never been there at all.

There was nothing for it but to get into the bathroom. Helena knew the trick of this from a film she'd once seen. She'd never had cause to do it herself and wasn't even sure if it actually worked, but its physics seemed obvious enough. She got a newspaper from the wood box and a knitting needle from the drawer. She fed the open paper under the door, then with the needle pushed the key out of the lock. It fell on the other side; slowly she pulled out the paper and there was the key. She pushed it into the lock, called out 'I'm coming in', then unlocked the door to find nothing but an empty room and a window open to the darkening sky.

THE GHOST OF A FLEA

Helena had barely settled down after Jude's ridiculous flight through the bathroom window, when yet another mysterious disappearance occurred. This time it was less tangible yet more troubling. Something she could hardly even mourn or speak about even though her heart was breaking.

It began with a sharp and all too familiar pain low in her belly. She immediately went to see her GP, where after an hour sitting in the crowded waiting room, she was examined. She explained the missed periods, her certainty, as the doctor pressed the heel of his hand over her womb.

'I don't think so,' he said. 'The menstrual cycle can be irregular; it's not like a German train service, you know. Doesn't run like clockwork.'

She was silent. Tears ran down her face.

'Not like a German train,' she thought. 'Oh no, nothing like it.' Her only consolation was that, as yet, she'd told no-one. She'd been holding onto this secret and guarding it until she and Christopher had some time together, but he'd been so busy she'd hardly seen him.

She had rehearsed the words she'd use. Always beginning with 'Darling...' She'd imagined his reaction, his joy.

Now she imagined his disappointment. His irritation.

'You can hop down now,' the doctor said, as she was still lying on the examination table.

She reluctantly straightened her clothes and sat up, but didn't climb down.

He was sitting at his desk making notes.

'Is that it?' she said.

'Hmm?'

'Is there something wrong with me?'

Finally, he turned to look at her and saw that she had been crying.

'Is that what you're worried about?'

'I was sure I was pregnant. Someone else thought so too,' she said, thinking of Jude's words.

'Well, there's a possibility you were, briefly. Or it might have been what we call a phantom pregnancy. Famously, Bloody Mary, the daughter of Henry the Eighth, suffered two phantom pregnancies; she retired to her lying-in chamber with all her ladies, while her husband, Prince Philip of Spain and the court waited. And waited...' He paused for effect, '... and nothing.' He looked pleased with himself.

Helena continued to stare at him dumbly from her perch on the examination table.

'Very good,' he said, then stood up, opened the door and waited by it.

Helena climbed down, gathered her jacket and bag from the chair.

'Thank you,' she said, without looking at him.

On her walk home she turned it over in her mind: 'Why did I say thank you? I shouldn't have said thank you. I should have said I wasn't there for a history lesson and no, I'm not a German train. I'm not a Swiss clock. Why did I even thank him? Thank goodness I didn't tell Christopher. He would be furious. He already thinks I'm feeble. Thank God, I said nothing.'

Her thoughts took on the rhythm of her footsteps. The same thoughts over and over again. They pursued her. 'How dare he! I shouldn't have thanked him.' Walking briskly down Christina Street towards the Top Rank Suite. Turning left onto the Kingsway, she saw that 'Love Story' was showing at the Odeon.

'Stupid woman,' she thought. 'Stupid, stupid, stupid. Thank God I didn't tell anyone.' But Jude knew.

She had always half-dreaded seeing Jude. Of becoming

entangled, yet now she would have liked to see her, to ask her. She would say, 'Why did you say what you did? About me expecting a baby? How did you know?'

But Jude was nothing but snares and hooks. Lies and deception.

Helena sat on a bench in front of the multistorey carpark. Dug in her bag for a hankie, dabbed at her eyes and blew her nose.

She had made a mistake.

Why had she not even told Christopher? There must be something desperately wrong with their marriage. Something that could never be fixed. She suddenly saw how lonely she'd been. How timid and desperate for any scrap of attention. Jude must have seen that too.

Would Jude ever tell her the truth?

'Jude,' she thought, suddenly remembering a painting by William Blake, 'is the ghost of a flea.' It made sense for a second, then like a flea it leapt away.

She pulled herself together, crossed the road, went for a coffee in the Milkmaid and decided that for once she should stop being so timid.

THE OAK WASP

The conviction that Jude had forged the documents had grown from the moment Helena found the envelope. It seemed the answer to everything and so obvious that once revealed, Helena was astonished she had not seen it before. She thought about Jude's ink-stained fingers, her secrecy, her paranoia, the pencilled words on the scrap of envelope all written in varying styles. The very modern, very telling, typed name and address.

The idea that Jude would never return to the bookshop, that Helena would never get to the bottom of the mystery, nagged at her until at last she made up her mind to confront her. The only way of doing that was to find the address on the envelope, Ferryman's Cottage.

Perhaps the narrowness of her current life – the lonely rattling around the flat above the shop, the sometimes prolonged and aimless walks around the town, the endless waiting for Christopher to come home, the snatched phone calls with him which never seemed to last more than a few businesslike minutes – also spurred her into action, gave her a sense of purpose. Like someone in a fairytale, at last she had a quest.

The next day was a Friday and that seemed as good a time as any for an excursion. Edward would let himself into the shop at around nine-thirty, so she decided to set off before then. She wrote a note, 'Out for the day. H.', and stuck it to the kettle, locked up the shop and set off for the taxi office. She had to wait half an hour for a cab because, as the woman behind the glassed-in booth told her,

'They're all having their breakfast.' It had been on the tip of Helena's tongue to remark on the insanity of this, but she thought better of it and smiled instead.

On the wall of the tiny waiting area was a coffee-stained and heavily scribbled-on street map of Swansea. She ran her eye over it until she found Wind Street which seemed to her the centre of all things, then worked her gaze outward in broader circles. So many streets she'd never seen, so many areas and villages that were familiar as names but were as unknown as Kamchatka (which she only knew from the board game *Risk*). The radio in the woman's booth was tuned to a pop station. Helena listened as 'Ruby, Don't Take Your Love to Town' played. The words gruffly murmured from the tinny loudspeaker made her wonder at the threat the singer made: 'If I could move, I'd get my gun and put her in the ground.' Did anyone really listen to the words? she thought.

Then 'Suspicious Minds' came on and the volume was suddenly amped up. Elvis Presley's anguished wail, crackled and distorted, seemed to shake the glass, the floorboards, the thin partition walls. She turned towards the booth, meaning to issue a look of sharp reproach, but the woman was lost in some kind of ecstatic revelry, eyes closed, head swaying, shoulders lifting in tune to the beat. She was utterly oblivious to everything but the song.

Thankfully, as soon as the repeated chorus faded away and the over-excited disc jockey's voice blared out, the volume was immediately lowered.

'I loves Elvis, me,' the woman, possibly temporarily deafened, yelled at Helena who smiled sympathetically. 'I'd leave my husband for 'im, I would! Oops, speak of the devil, here's your ride, love.'

With this precious knowledge, Helena went to the cab pulled up outside. The driver, though a man of about fifty, had unnaturally blue-black hair that showed a much paler colour – possibly ginger – at the roots. It was styled, evidently to suit his wife's taste, in a sweeping greasy bouffant like Presley's.

Helena asked for Ferryman's Cottage in the Hafod and the driver, in a too-loud voice, said abruptly, 'Where?'

She repeated it and he suggested she give him directions.

'But I don't know where it is!'

'Well, that's a lot of good,' he replied. 'I'll drop you by the shops in the Hafod if you want.'

'Okay, let's do that, then.'

Helena had chosen to take a taxi rather than the bus with the foolish idea that the cabbie would know the address. As she was already seated in the moving car, she felt obliged to go along with him despite the cost. She stared at the back of his head as he raced erratically along, parping his horn at people he knew, accelerating rapidly to overtake slower cars, swearing constantly in a low mutter and, once, holding up two fingers to another driver in a threatening manner.

He swerved to a halt outside a row of small shops and asked if she wanted collecting later. She was very glad to say no, as she knew she could just as well get the bus back into town. Once he'd roared away, she stood for a moment taking stock of her surroundings. There was a laundrette, bakery, hairdresser, grocery, chip shop and newsagents. It was not yet ten o'clock, so it was still very quiet. Around five people stood waiting for the bus into town at the stop opposite. A middle-aged woman came waddling out of the bakers; she was very short and rather overweight. She smiled absently at Helena and taking this as an invitation, Helena called out, 'Lovely morning!' This caused the woman to alter her path until she had come right up to Helena.

'What's that?' she said. 'Couldn't hear you, dear.'

'Lovely morning!'

'Oh, yes, yes.'

'I wonder if you can help me?'

'Pardon, dear?'

'Can you help me?'

'Help you?'

'Where's Ferryman's Cottage?'

'What's that?'

Helena, nearly shouting, said, 'I'm looking for Ferryman's Cottage!'

The smile fell away instantly and the woman, who'd been leaning in toward Helena, all friendliness and open warmth, now shrank back, looked very hard at her and hurried away as if insulted.

Perhaps, being deaf, she misheard me, Helena surmised. She went into the newsagents and after a moment surveying the magazines and comics, noting amongst the usual – *Woman's Own*, *Radio Times*, *Beano*, *Bunty*, and the *New Musical Express* – that there were inordinate numbers of girlie mags. They seemed to leer garishly at her, as fleshy as the lumps of meat in the butcher's shop window. At the till she took a pack of Wrigley's Spearmint from the wire rack as she felt it would be unseemly to ask directions without buying anything.

'Thank you. Oh, while I'm here, I wonder if you could be so good as to help me? Do you know how I get to Ferryman's Cottage?'

The newsagent looked at her sharply, 'What, that witch's house?' he snarled. 'You in the coven, then?' This last was said lasciviously.

'No. I… oh, never mind.'

She approached someone else. A young man whose weekend clothes were evidently his grey school trousers and jumper but with the addition of a leather motorcycling jacket smiled shyly at her until she asked her question. Looking alarmed he said, 'Cowing 'ell, mun you don't wanna go there, missus. She'll 'ave you, she will. I seen that one in the woods collecting poison and that. She saw me and I nearly shit myself, I did.'

Helena tried in the bakers but was repelled. The laundrette was empty, though two of the machines churned and splashed and rattled, while the dryer spun and clanked as metal fastenings or loose coins crashed inside the giant drum. The chip shop wasn't open yet.

The bus came and Helena considered running across the road to catch it, but resisted. A sensible-looking man got off. He wore a tweed sports jacket with leather patches on the elbows and an Argyle pullover. He had the look of a teacher, intelligent but worn down.

'Excuse me,' she said.

'Yes?'

'I'm not sure if you're local, but do you know where I might find Ferryman's Cottage?'

He looked serious as he thought this over.

'Doesn't ring any bells, but at a guess it would have to be fairly close to the river. There's a few houses down there; I should think it's one of them.'

He then gave very precise directions and after following them, Helena found herself on a sort of muddy towpath that curved alongside the river.

There were indeed four houses that backed onto the river. Knowing which might have been Jude's seemed more of a challenge, except that the first three seemed in good states of repair: one had a very new-looking extension, and another had a swing set and various brightly coloured plastic toys in the garden, as well as an array of small dresses and tiny vests and socks on the washing line. The third had ruffled lace curtains in the windows, several rose bushes and a very ancient man tending them in the garden. The last house was set apart and hunkered like some bleak relic of another age at the edge of a wood. The foundations of what might have been a boat house lay under the piled-up timbers of its caved-in walls and roof, and Japanese knotweed grew tall and thick all around it. Beyond this were the last remains of an old jetty whose pilings ran into the river like a petrified forest of young saplings, the black arms pointing to the sky. A few planks of new timber had been laid over the first of these and nailed haphazardly in place. A small upturned rowing boat lay among the weeds, its hull like a wounded insect's shell.

The back of the house had been haphazardly extended using old window frames, doors and corrugated iron. Beside it there was a narrow path which led to the front of the building. Helena followed it in the hope that a house sign might confirm that this was indeed Ferryman's Cottage. On the dark stone surrounding the door, one block had some engraved words cut into it, but it had been painted over with tar-like black paint making it difficult to read. The first word was long and the 'F' was just legible, as was the 'C' of the second word.

There was little sign of life. The windows were greasy and speckled with dust and grime and cobwebs. Yellowing lace nets drooped sadly in front of curtains whose linings were shredded with rot. It was exactly as Helena might have imagined. Or possibly worse. And it was exactly the sort of house a child or other ignorant person might think belonged to a witch.

She took a deep breath and walked the three or four steps that brought her to its front door. There was no bell but a sturdy metal knocker that she used to rap out her presence.

No answer. No-one home.

Wordsworth's Ruined Cottage came to mind. Other lives, the ghosts Jude had spoken of, all lingered here in restless company with her and with one another.

She knocked on the door again. Thought about how peasants used to clatter on metal plates and pans to scare away birds. Remembered hearing that in southern Europe they threw up very fine nets to catch migrating birds – larks, blackcaps, song thrushes. How to trap a ghost was more difficult – perhaps they clung to Jude, invisible yet as wearying as the chains Jacob Marley dragged about him for eternity.

All that talk about witches must have turned her mind.

Helena stood for a while, thinking. It was possible that Jude had seen her arrive. Either by chance as she approached by the towpath or a moment ago on hearing the rat-a-tat of the knocker. It would be just like Jude to lurk hidden and silent in the gloom beyond the filthy curtain, watching Helena and ignoring her until such a time as she chose to come breezily into the bookshop again as if nothing had happened.

Helena rationalized – if Jude could invade her life with deviousness and stealth, then so could she.

She tried the door latch but while the mechanism lifted it would not open. The door had no letterbox, but on the wooden sill was an old square biscuit tin with the word 'HOPKINS' painted on it in crude block letters. Helena opened the lid and peered inside to see the heads of several nails that had been hammered into the bottom of the tin to keep it in place. It was odd; everything about the place was odd, dilapidated or makeshift. In a world where such eccentricities were increasingly dying out, it was easy to see how anything that deviated from the norm could be judged suspect. No wonder people thought Jude was a witch; simply living here would do that. And if the house had been passed down to her as she said then it was likely that the entire family going back countless generations had been outcasts. In a small community, who you were was inescapable in a sense – maybe that was why Jude changed how she looked so often, as if to prove that the surface of a person may tell one story, but that the surface, the trappings of certain clothes and styles of hair, really only gave a comforting illusion of conformity or the discomforting one of the outsider.

Helena walked back down to the river. This was no lovely beauty spot with clear lapping waters, jumping fish and rare water birds, but the abandoned and poisoned place of years of industrialisation. In a place like Devon, a property near the river and the woods would be prime real estate; here it was a worthless nowhere, damp and probably dangerous to health. She picked her way through the weeds and up what was left of a flagstone path. The rickety extension must have an entrance. Once she discovered it, she found the door was unlocked.

She entered a porch and found some piled-up wooden crates which contained grizzled-looking carrots, sprouting onions and a cauliflower whose white face was smutty with black marks of decay. It smelled earthy and vaguely stagnant. Hanging from hooks were dried bunches of herbs – lavender, thyme, sage and rosemary – and on the sill there were some branches of oak leaves and near them, a row of lumpy round brownish objects a little like nuts, each with a tiny hole bored into it.

Calling out Jude's name, as if that could excuse her trespass, Helena pushed on another door and it swung inward to reveal a space that seemed half kitchen, half laboratory. There was a 1950s table with metal legs and a Formica top, split and curled up at the edges. On this were several piles of old books, some leather and some cloth-bound. Beside these were several glass jars of different sizes. One held greenish-blue crystals, others a viscous black liquid. In an earthenware marmalade pot stood a quantity of large feathers. On the stove top there was a dented saucepan filled with a soup of brown liquid in which floated gritty particles of vegetation. Also on the stove top was a frying pan with a solid pool of cold white grease. A wooden draining board bore mismatched plates and cups in a haphazard pile.

There was no fridge in the kitchen, but a pantry door stood open to reveal a deep stone shelf that, in theory, kept foodstuffs cool. Here was a pair of white pudding basins. One held an open milk bottle in a few inches of water, the other a quantity of speckled dripping from which a spoonful had been scooped out. Greaseproof wrappings held sweaty cheese and slices of bacon. There was a cornflakes packet and an open tin of beans with half its contents gone and a noxious-looking fur of mould half-covering what was left. Elsewhere on a shelf were a few packets of dry soup and a Wonderloaf in its waxy paper.

One half of the kitchen table was empty, suggesting that the occupant of the house used this space to sit down and eat, or alternatively to read. Or, Helena suddenly understood, to write. There was no paper about but, lifting one of the feathers from the jar, Helena found it had been carefully cut to form the nib of a quill pen. Another was stained with brownish-black ink.

Looking more closely at the books, Helena saw that strips of paper had been used to mark different pages and on these were brief notes that read variously 'Food', 'Horses', 'Clothes', 'Books' and 'Language.' She picked up one, *Rural Rides* by William Cobbett, and opened it at one of the markers. Underlined very lightly in pencil she read:

'I gave them two quartern loaves, two pounds of cheese and eight pints of strong beer.'

One other word was circled: 'Breakfast.'

On another piece of paper was a recipe headed *Ink From the Oak Wasp Gall.*

So here it was, the alchemist's den, the forger's workshop – the tools of Jude's trade and her research materials.

If Jude had appeared at that moment, stepping out of the shadows after arriving home from some quite innocent shopping trip, then Helena might have accused her of creating the supposedly 'found' documents.

'What did you hope to gain by it?' she imagined herself asking in a scene like the unmasking of the murderer in an Agatha Christie novel. In those books, all the suspects are gathered together for the denouement, but in this mystery there were only two players: the criminal and the victim-turned-detective.

The problem lay chiefly with 'why?' rather than 'who?' and Helena desperately wanted to know that. The other part of the 'why?' question was why her? Of all the people Jude might have pursued with her cat-and-mouse game, Helena, besides being the wife of a rare-books dealer, had no influence, no knowledge, no access to the shop's money – or at least not the sort of sum that would allow for the purchase of a unique collection of documents. Did Jude think that Helena had any influence on her husband? That she could persuade him that the documents were genuine, then convince him to spend hundreds of pounds on them? She was sadly mistaken if that was the case. If she couldn't even persuade him to switch from sheets and blankets to a duvet, or force him to take her away to London or York or Edinburgh just once a year, then this last prospect was so far off the mark as to be comical.

She lingered a little while, resisted the temptation to explore the rest of the house, thought about leaving a note, but decided that would give the game away. Then she picked up one of the strange nuts and a single ink-stained quill pen, put them in her bag and slipped away.

LOVE IS STRANGE

Now and then, Jude put Olof's jacket on, wearing it like the ceremonial robe of a priest. She knew she looked ridiculous. Mostly she just buried her face in its coarse wool, breathing in his scent, savouring it like a sweet, musky perfume. But rapidly the aroma seemed to retreat, just as the faces of both Sigrid and Olof grew evasive. Their voices too, were retreating from her memory; each had a barely-there accent: a rocking, up-and-down Swedish, mixed with the Swansea rhythms they must have absorbed over the years.

How could it be that she had spent so much time with them and yet she had no photograph? No snapshot of herself with Olof standing on the cliff path between Caswell and Langland, even though Sigrid was there with her with her camera around her neck in its leather case. That day they had seen a peregrine falcon hanging high above them, barely moving its head while its wings fluttered to keep it in place. 'Look,' Olof had said, and they had all stopped to watch it. But Sigrid did not even open her camera case.

The falcon hovered. Olof named it. Saying '*Pilgrimsfalk*' as he pointed skyward, then as if she knew the word already, 'peregrine falcon'.

'*Pilgrimsfalk,*' she repeated, liking the sound of the strange word on her tongue.

'Oh!' Sigrid cried softly at the moment the bird swooped down like a dart and disappeared from view far behind the tangled gorse that loomed over the path.

They resumed their walk, going in single file in places, and stopping to let one or two other walkers pass. Jude held the word in her mind. The word, and also the sight of the falcon against the blue sky like a magic spell. Why, she wondered, 'pilgrim'? A word she knew already but whose meaning didn't seem to fit a bird of prey. It must be different in Swedish. Perhaps it meant something like a lone wanderer. She would ask them later. But as always one glittering thought or thing was swept away as more arrived. What was to Jude flotsam and jetsam moving too fast to be identified was to them familiar and known.

That day must have been before they adopted Nero as she couldn't recall him ranging ahead of them on his lead. Or perhaps they left him behind in the car. They had done that once or twice, believing it was better for the wildlife in certain places.

She kept Olof's tweed jacket on a hook in the kitchen, so that, glancing up, she could fool herself he was somewhere around. But the trick rarely worked and if it did, it lasted mere seconds.

'Please write,' Sigrid had said, but what did that even mean? Why couldn't they write to her? They knew where she was. And if the instruction was for her to write her stories, to encourage her, why had they not followed up?

Why had they abandoned her?

She went from sad to confused to angry in seconds.

She loved them.

She hated them.

Her view of them was like amoeba changing and mutating, impossible to hold still. She tried her best to be like them, often with the idea that when they returned, she would make them proud. She knew that they valued curiosity as much as learning – to them they were the same thing. But her resources were so limited.

She'd gone to Menzies on Oxford Street and descended the steep steps to the record department in the basement, where on the weekend, young people thronged, stoop-shouldered over rows of LPs. She wasn't in search of Sibelius but of Miles Davis. She didn't know whether to look under 'M' or 'D'. She had never even seen the cover of that album, nor those of any of the music they played.

Finding a place among the crowd around the record bins was

hard enough; finding what she only half-remembered was nearly impossible. Then someone close by moved and she stepped into their place and, copying the others, began to fan through the albums. She shuffled along the row as other people moved. Time, it seemed, stood still; she guessed that for all these people the point of the exercise was being there, of looking, not necessarily buying anything.

She studied each album cover briefly; such odd words: Captain Beefheart, Disraeli Gears, Frank Zappa, Soft Machine, Ummagumma. Such odd pictures: a smiling man whose face was gouged by a sharp-toothed rodent, a group of naked women half-reclining on the floor, a garish cartoon strip called 'Cheap Thrills', a distorted, close-up painting of a screaming man, many with alarming colours and swirling text, then another that was almost pure white. Looking at them, Jude felt like an early explorer in Egypt trying to decipher hieroglyphics.

Eventually she gave up.

Nothing worked to bring Sigi and Oli back. She had tried somewhat pathetically to replace them. Tried to recover the essence of them. If she could find the music they'd played, she might bathe in its sound, close her eyes, imagine…

She had tried to insert herself into Helena's world, had wanted to impress her with the wonderful and mysterious papers she'd found. Wanted to befriend her, but something had gone wrong from the start.

All the lies she'd told were crumbling away.

But the story she'd created – *that* should have had a life beyond herself. Yet Helena had found it ugly and cruel. *Relentlessly bleak*, she'd said. Even those parts which were true, she'd called absurd. The episode about Mary Wollstonecraft nursing puppies, she'd got that from William Godwin's book; it was real. She would never have invented such a gruesome thing – it passed the bounds of logic – but that had been an age when medicine was ill-formed and ignorant, when a doctor might leave one diseased patient to attend a birth, failing to wash his hands in between the two. Yet because of her story about where the papers came from and her own pretended innocence and wonder about them, she could not defend them without giving the game away.

Now it seemed that her invented tale was falling apart and poor Fanny Imlay would remain in her unmarked pauper's grave on the High Street. No second chance for her. No rebirth. No escape. No-one had come to unearth her, to scratch at her coffin. To set her back on her feet as she sank deeper and deeper into her laudanum dream.

She decided the only course of action was to write to Helena, to explain as best she could. Working on the papers she'd created now seemed useless, her ideas about the story polluted and decayed. When she had finished the letter, she signed her name, put the paper into an envelope and addressed it to Helena at the bookshop. She sat staring at it for a long time, wondering how Helena would react. How terrible would it be? Would she call the police? But why? What crime had she even committed?

She was sitting in the kitchen, wearing Olof's jacket and, as she often did, brushing the fabric of its collar gently over her lower lip as she considered her dilemma, when a sudden knock at the door startled her. She sat very still, listening, waiting, her breathing shallow.

People usually gave up and went away fairly quickly if she ignored them.

Not this person. They rattled the door knocker a second time.

Then, just when Jude thought they'd given up, she was astonished to hear a sharp rapping at the front room window. She had no doubt they'd next explore the path by the side of the house and come around the back to see her sitting frozen in place like a newborn deer.

The knocking sound came again, this time more determined, more deliberate. Not long now.

She leapt from her chair, stuffed the envelope in her pocket and fled to the garden, where she hid behind the old boat. The damp quickly soaked into the long skirt she was wearing. The skirt had once been Sigrid's; it was black taffeta, handmade by a seamstress, lined with baby-blue satin. Even Sigrid had said it was a ridiculous outfit, the weight and bulk of it a nuisance; she'd caught her heel in it, she said, nearly fallen head first down some grand stairs!

'I say it's a murderous frock, but please do have it if you like. You could make a bedspread or something from it. Curtains. I don't care.'

Now it was mud-smeared, filthy and wet. Ruined.

She heard footsteps approach and was astonished to see Helena. She considered crawling out from her hiding place and explaining all that she'd put in the letter in person, but she was fixated on the words she'd so carefully written, on the idea that she would not be there to see Helena's expression, to feel her anger and scorn. That might come, but later, not now, not today, not while she was garbed so absurdly in Sigi and Oli's mud-besmirched clothes.

Helena would knock at the back door. She might peer in through the windows. She'd wait a little longer, but then, surely, she'd give up?

Jude watched, shivering.

Helena did knock on the door, but then she put her face next to the window and cupped her hands over her eyes to see in more clearly. Knocked again. Stood back to look at the upstairs windows. Called, 'Jude! Jude, I know you're in there!'

Then she did something that truly astonished Jude – she tried the handle and pushed open the door. Distantly Jude heard her call, 'Hello-oo?' Then Helena stepped inside and shut the door behind her. Jude saw her moving slowly about in the kitchen, looking here and there, sometimes picking up objects to look at them more closely. Jude considered making a run for it across the yard and down the side passage, but Helena was sure to see her.

Just behind the upturned boat, the garden sloped down towards the river. Jude thought she could slowly tug the boat away from the house. As chance would have it, she'd moved the boat recently, chopping away the weeds that held it in their grip, rocking it free. She'd even got the old oar from the porch and used it to lever the stern from the mud. The oar was still there, as was the rope once used to moor it.

She began to wriggle and tug the boat free, looking up now and then to be certain she wasn't being watched. Helena was standing near the window to catch the light, reading a book. The next time Jude looked, Helena was touching a bundle of dried herbs that hung from the rafters.

Jude used the incline to flip the small boat over. It landed silently in the soft mud and rocked gently as if eager for its first taste of the river after years of deprivation. With a final heave, it glided smoothly into the water. Jude hoisted up her wet skirt in one hand and, using the oar for balance, climbed in. She checked the house one more time; Helena was holding Jude's favourite pen aloft like a dart. Cut from a crow's feather, it produced the most delicate of lines and strokes. It had taken Jude quite some time to cut it, then to master its use. In a passing thought, she imagined demonstrating its mysteries to Helena; impossible now.

She pushed off from the bank.

She had meant to guide the dinghy downstream twenty feet or so, staying close to the bank using the single oar as a makeshift punting pole, but the little boat had other ideas.

The river joined in with the fun, surging and eddying and sucking at the vessel as if it were a toy. The day darkened suddenly, a storm blowing in from nowhere, torrential rain pouring down her face. The wind threw her hair over her eyes and her feet struggled to find purchase. The skirt mutineered and tethered her ankles together.

By the time the downpour stopped, it was over.

THE BRIDGE OF SIGHS

Helena was in the kitchen stirring a pan of porridge and listening to a local radio station when she heard the news. An unidentified woman had drowned in the River Tawe. They reported how she'd taken a leaky old rowing boat out the day before. A witness said they saw her climbing into the boat around midday. It was raining heavily too. The witness said he'd called out to her but he didn't think she'd heard him.

Helena remembered the cloudburst of the day before; she'd just found a seat on the upper deck of the bus when a torrential storm began. Rain thundered on the metal roof and obscured the windows. The day darkened, cars put their headlights on and she saw them as fractured orange-yellow suns in the streaming rain. The bus slowed down. On the pavement people ran for cover, looking like blurs and streaks of glassy colour.

Then almost as quickly as it had started, the rain stopped and the sun came out to illuminate a sparkling, rinsed-clean world. While Helena had been congratulating herself for escaping the downpour, Jude (it had to be Jude, didn't it?) was struggling to control a leaky old boat.

What on earth had led her to even attempt to use the boat?

Helena remembered how, after leaving the cottage, the bus had come almost immediately. She'd climbed the twisting stairs to the upper deck and sat by the window gazing out, troubled but also pleased with herself. She had unearthed Jude's secret; she finally understood what had been going on.

That couldn't have been more than four or five minutes before the rain began.

She realised that Jude must have been in the house while she was there playing detective. Did Jude hide, then sneak out to the boat? Was it Helena's presence in the house that had made Jude try to escape the back way in the only way she could?

If so, had Helena caused her death?

Her heart sank as suddenly as the dilapidated dinghy must have.

She pictured Jude in one of her outlandish outfits: a long black skirt totally unsuitable for a boat excursion. A heavy tweed jacket with sleeves too long. Perfect clothes for drowning in.

But it mustn't be Jude. It just couldn't be.

The phone rang.

She hurried to answer it, thinking it might be Jude. Jude perhaps sneering at her, saying, 'Bet you thought that was me, didn't you? Poor old drowned-dead Jude. Stupid cow. Well, guess what?'

But Jude had never rung her. Not ever.

'Hello?' Helena said, a catch in her voice.

'Yes, hello, this is Police Constable Carl Powell. I'm ringing you with regard to an incident yesterday. We're trying to identify someone and a letter with your name and the address of a shop in Wind Street was found on her. I just wanted to confirm that this is you.'

'Yes. But the incident – do you mean the drowned woman? I heard something on the news just now. Was it Jude? Judith Hopkins?'

'I'm sorry, I can't confirm anything else at present. I'm going to send a WPC around for an informal chat. She should be with you in fifteen minutes or so.'

He hung up.

She stood there holding the phone and listening senselessly to the dead burr of an open line. A burning smell roused her. The porridge, thick and charred on the bottom, was bubbling and spitting explosively on the gas jet. She switched it off and opened the window. She had just managed to comb her hair and throw on yesterday's clothes before the doorbell went.

She hurried downstairs in time to hear the shop door opening and Edward's bemused voice saying, 'Yes, that's right. Come in, I'll call her for you.'

And a woman answering, 'Thank you.'

Edward looked at Helena oddly when she appeared. 'Police here to see you,' he said. 'Tell you what, I'll nip out and get some change from the bank, leave you to it.'

The Woman Police Constable had a sweet baby face under her official black hat with its checkered band and shiny badge. The uniform looked too big for her, or perhaps it was just that the severe skirt was demurely long, reaching her legs mid-shin.

'I understand my colleague has already spoken to you. Is there somewhere you can sit?'

Helena knew what that meant: she should sit while the terrible news came at her like a strong wind. What more did she need as confirmation of her suspicions?

'As you may have heard, a female was recovered from the river yesterday, following the heavy rainstorm. We believe you might help us to identify her.

'The only item on her person was a letter. I have it here,' she said, pulling a plastic evidence file from her WPC's leather shoulder bag. She laid it on the counter for Helena to see. The envelope and letter were yellowed and wrinkled, but they must have been written in biro (unusually for Jude) as they remained legible. 'We did our best to dry it out. However, we would like you to read it, see if it throws any light on matters. Some of her neighbours have said she was a rather disturbed young woman and the letter seems to confirm this. It's gibberish as far as we can tell. What do you think? Did you know her?'

'Yes. I knew her, but not awfully well.'

'She wasn't a relative?'

'Goodness, no.'

Helena looked at her own name written on the envelope. It was chilling to see it there, embalmed in clear plastic, as if the synthetic material separated this world from that of the dead.

How many times had she stood or sat reading Jude's words – not that they were construed as that – and now this, the last of them.

'I'll make you a cup of tea,' the WPC said, 'if you have a kettle and so on.'

'Yes, in there,' Helena said, bobbing her head in the direction of the kitchenette.

It was even more odd to read the cockled letter inside the evidence bag, like seeing something submerged in water. It was quite horrifying when she came to think of it. Jude must have written it not long before Helena showed up, then stuffed it in a pocket, meaning to post it later.

So, dear Helena, you've discovered my trick. Fanny Imlay died on the night of 9th October 1816 in a room at the Mackworth Inn on Wind Street, Swansea. No-one was there to save her or to offer her a second chance at life. She died. That is how the story ends. Your bookshop was built on the site of the old inn.

Do you believe in ghosts, Helena? I think I asked you that once and you said no. Or perhaps you said they were superstitious nonsense, I don't remember now. But I do remember your expression; you looked terrified.

You said the story I'd written was dark and depressing but I hadn't got to the good part yet. Imagine if you only read Jane Eyre up to the part where she is penniless and alone. She sleeps under trees and begs crusts of bread from strangers. What if it ended there? That would be tragic and probably true to life, but it doesn't end there, does it? No, reader, she married him.

I'm sorry I left the way I did, I just couldn't bear to hear you say those things. I'm not sure what I expected from you, maybe exactly that, but not by then, not once you had read so much of my story. I never expected you to like me, but I wanted you to like my creature.

Well, that's a laugh, isn't it? Does it remind you of anything? Think about it for a little time. Here's a clue – a certain young fellow takes the body parts of real people from the graveyard, he stitches them together to create a man, and brings him back to life. What does this strange creature want above all things? He wants human companionship or to put it another way: love.

Failing to get it he becomes murderous.

I've been awake all night. I sit and scratch away with my quill pen by candlelight. I conjure my ghosts by these means. The electric light frightens them away, or at least that is how it seems. But perhaps it's more personal than that. It probably is; there are no ghosts. There is only me and my imagination, which is the better part of my being.

You thought that the documents that I brought you had been copied from old 19th-century books, either whole or piecemeal. That's not true. I wrote it all, every word, every paragraph. If its only flaw was the darkness of the tale then I accept that gladly.

Maybe I've been fooling myself. Maybe it's a good thing that you hated the story, because as I said, it had become a monstrous child who was ever hungry for more and more ideas, more roads to go down, winding paths and dark avenues. I would pick around in history trying to find juicy gobbets to feed it. Did you know that the painter Richard Dadd was born on August 1st, 1817? He was an insane genius who murdered his father. What if, I said to myself, Fanny Imlay had been his mother? What if she conceived him sometime in November of 1816? What if the baby had been given to the Dadd family in Chatham, Kent? Wouldn't he have inherited Baxter's artistic skill along with his mother's melancholy?

But, Helena, think of the elaborate twists and turns of the plot to make that happen. How does the baby get from Swansea to Chatham? Overland would take days, possibly more than a week. What about by sea? Swansea had a large port and Chatham was the naval dockyard on the Medway in Kent. So there was that.

But why heap cruelty upon cruelty by taking Fanny's child from her? No, if my darling was to live I had to bestow her with happiness.

Suspend disbelief, Helena! To my mind the very idea that Fanny Imlay took the trouble to travel all the way to Swansea in order to die is somewhat beyond belief.

Perhaps that was what I was after; another version of truth. A truth which, because it came in the form of old documents – because it rewrote history – would become a new truth and, for Fanny, a second chance.

Don't we all deserve second chances?

Jude

EPILOGUE

1967-1971

Touch her not scornfully;
Think of her mournfully,
Gently and humanly;
Not of the stains of her,
All that remains of her
Now is pure womanly.

From 'Bridge of Sighs' by Thomas Hood

THE SCRIBE

One day, while Helena happened to be alone in the shop, a tall and elegant woman came in. She was dressed in navy slacks, canvas shoes and a navy roll-neck sweater; her hair was silvery blonde with a bright scarf worn like a headband. She was wearing tortoiseshell sunglasses, but took them off as she approached the counter.

'Good morning,' she said. 'My name is Sigrid Andersson.'

'How can I help you?' Helena asked, feeling certain that, unless this woman was searching for some rare first-edition book, she had probably wandered into the wrong shop. She certainly didn't look like their sort of customer.

'Are you Helena?' she asked.

'Yes.'

'I thought you must be, but in truth, it's someone else I've been looking for.'

Helena noticed the faint traces of an accent in the woman's voice.

'Oh,' Helena said, thinking that the woman looked a bit like Greta Garbo. Next her mind spun on the idea that this woman was one of Christopher's lovers. She was closer to his age for sure, and seemed beautiful, rich and educated.

'He's away. He won't be back for some time as he's gone to the States – to Boston.'

'No. You misunderstand me. I'm not sure who "he" is. It's a local woman I've been looking for. A very good friend. I'm afraid we somehow lost touch. Someone told me she spent time here, with you. Her name is…'

'Jude,' Helena said, interrupting.

The woman smiled warmly, 'Yes. So you do know her! I've been to her cottage several times, but I think she must have moved on. It looked in an even worse state than I remembered. Do you by chance have her current address? Or even better, her phone number?'

Helena just stared at the woman, unable to gather her thoughts, to arrange her words into any sensible pattern.

'You were friends?' she asked, stalling for time, but also disbelieving.

'Yes, she was like family to us. My husband, Olof, is particularly fond of her. He always says how very talented she is, especially with her stories – but you know that, I'm sure. Olof is unwell, so he has decided to stay at home, but I was hoping to bring Jude back to Sweden for a visit. I would be so grateful if you could help us to find her.'

'I...'

'Or perhaps you could give her my contact details, if it's a matter of confidentiality. I'm staying at the Dragon Hotel, room 16. Shall I give you the number or will you find it in the telephone directory?'

'I can find it.'

'So you don't have a number for her? She never used to have a phone. I'm not sure if it was a question of money or choice. She spent so much time at our house, the need for a phone hardly arose.' Sigrid stopped speaking abruptly and looked interrogatively at Helena. 'Is there something wrong?'

Helena shook her head mutely. Everything was wrong, but she couldn't speak. In her mind the memory of Jude, of all that had happened, was interwoven was sadness and guilt, with the loss of her expected child. Yet how can an imaginary child truly be lost? But Jude had known, Jude had seen. Yet her powers of prophesy had failed Jude at the end.

'Well, I'll leave you in peace. Do get in touch with me, or if you speak to her, please ask her to call the hotel.'

Helena nodded.

'Thank you for your time. Sorry to have disturbed you.' The woman replaced her sunglasses, raised one hand in a salute and walked briskly out of the shop.

Helena breathed out in relief. If she didn't know better, she'd have suspected Jude of creating this new development. Only a few weeks ago Helena had read *The Magus* by John Fowles and it had put her in mind of Jude's distortions and disguises, though in that book it was created on a much larger scale. Could it be possible that this very unlikely woman had been hired to show up and make such preposterous claims? Was Jude even really dead?

Her head swam with the thought, with the idea of such an unreality. She had to sit down as it seemed as if the floor might dissolve beneath her feet.

And she had thought the woman was one of Christopher's lovers!

All her stupid and irrational thoughts had been stirred up by the woman's arrival. If Jude had ever mentioned these friends of hers, she'd forgotten it. Even if she had, by then Helena was taking everything Jude said with a huge dose of salt. She'd been letting her spool out lie after lie in the hope of catching her out.

Who had caught who in the end, though?

She turned off the lights and locked up the shop. It was less than a ten-minute walk to the hotel. She entered under the large canopied entrance and before she'd even reached the reception desk, she saw Sigrid sitting at a low table, reading a newspaper. Almost immediately, as if sensing her arrival, Sigrid looked up. They locked eyes.

'We need to talk,' Helena said.

For months after her meeting with Sigrid, she had thought about Jude almost constantly.

There was so much she didn't understand.

Helena learned that, unwittingly perhaps, the Swedish couple had not only encouraged Jude to write, but had taught her at least some of a forger's skills. Their interest in home-made ink and quill pens and so forth was merely historical enquiry; Sigrid was shocked to learn what use Jude had put this to.

'Was it money she wanted?' Sigrid asked, a look of genuine concern on her lovely face.

'No. Never.'

'Poor Jude. Olof will be heartbroken.'

Helena made no mention of her own presence at Jude's cottage. Could not even confess her worry that it was she who had provoked Jude, and driven her to act rashly. She could not, would not carry that responsibility; Jude was irrational, possibly mentally ill. Yet the Jude Sigrid described was warm and loving; with the Anderssons she had flourished.

Helena had never told anyone that she had been there that day and no-one — not the people she'd asked for directions, not the cab driver, not the bus conductor — reported a strange woman searching for Ferryman's Cottage. But then, Jude herself had worn so many disguises that they might have thought she was Jude. Sneaking about, pretending not to know the way to her own house, play-acting as someone who'd lost their memory, probably meaning to scrounge money.

But that wasn't her style. It was an aspect of people's presumptions.

Poor Jude wore all those guises because she could not simply be herself.

Had it been suicide?

Helena thought not. For one thing, her story wasn't finished. Strands of plot still hung from it, as ragged and ripped as a butterfly's wings at the end of summer.

Helena knew she had let Jude down, had spoken harshly to her when she'd last seen her.

She said nothing of this to Sigrid but promised her she would let her see the story Jude had been working on.

'I would love to see what she wrote. Did she finish it?' Sigrid asked.

Helena shrugged noncommittally — when is anything truly finished?

Then she told Sigrid a little white lie — there would be some difficulty finding the papers; they were in storage, so it could take some time.

The other woman accepted this. In the circumstances it seemed completely reasonable. She decided to cut short her stay in Wales and return to Sweden the next day.

Yet Sigrid's visit unsettled her. She decided she should make some atonement for her part in Jude's demise at the very least, and, as the Swedish woman had said many times, Jude was a gifted writer, worthy of being published one day, therefore Helena was determined to share the manuscript with Sigrid and her husband.

She fetched the lacquered Chinese box from the bookshelf in the living room. It was inlaid with scenes in mother-of-pearl, strange landscapes of trees and rocks and busy little people: a man with a fish on a rod, a man with a lantern, and a child tending a water buffalo. She lifted the lid, and there, folded inside, were the handwritten documents Jude had brought her.

Perhaps as part of the deception, Jude had not presented them to her in chronological order. Helena decided that at the very least she should try to find a meaningful progression to the various parts.

Rereading them with hindsight, she found there was a shape of some sort; all that was lacking was a proper conclusion and a title.

She got a stack of paper from the drawer and Christopher's fountain pen. On the first sheet she wrote *The Forger's Ink* in large text. She blew gently on the page to dry it, then placed it face down beside the fresh paper. She took a deep breath, her heart beat a little faster, and she began to write.

After a moment or two she seemed to hear the soft rush of a distant river ceaselessly moving and knew she would let herself be carried by it as far as it would take her.

THE END

A NOTE ABOUT THE NOVEL

The Forger's Ink is a work of fiction; however many of the characters and events are drawn from real life. I have taken liberties with many of these historic characters, Thomas Baxter in particular. His Shakespeare Cup was on loan to the Glynn Vivian Gallery for many years and does indeed show a scene from Cymbeline, but the woman depicted as the supine Imogen is vague and generic, not a true portrait. Baxter moved to Swansea with his family in 1816 but it's unlikely he had time to do anything but work. His friend, Matthew, his housekeeper and all the other characters and events are pure invention.

1816 was known as the Year Without a Summer. The unusual weather was due to the 1815 volcanic eruption of Tambora (which was ten times more powerful than Krakatoa) which sent up a cloud of toxic materials that shrouded the atmosphere, causing crop failure, starvation, disease and death across the Northern Hemisphere.

Like the Lunar Society of Birmingham, Swansea had its groups of learned polymaths; among them, Lewis Weston Dillwyn (1778-1855) was an eminent botanist, Fellow of the Royal Society, founder member of the Royal Institution of South Wales and the owner of the Cambrian Pottery. His son, John Dillwyn Llewelyn, whose wife was a cousin of Henry Fox Talbot, was one of the pioneers of photography, recording day to day life at the Penllergare estate. John's sister, Mary Dillwyn, was the first female photographer in Wales and his daughter, Thereza, an astronomer and innovator in scientific photography.

It was in Swansea that The Cambrian, the first newspaper in Wales, was produced and it was this newspaper that announced the death of an unnamed woman who it emerged was Fanny Imlay. The importance of the sea to the development of Swansea and its industries should not be forgotten; I've often considered the idea that Fanny meant to continue her journey west by sailing to Ireland or even America, birthplace of her father Gilbert Imlay, but ran out of money.

Fanny Imlay is a mere footnote in the biographies of the group of writers, poets and thinkers who included Mary Wollstonecraft, William Godwin, Mary Shelley, Percy Bysshe Shelley and Lord Byron. Claire Clairmont (as Mary Shelley's partner in crime) was there at the Villa Diodati that infamous stormy night when a competition was held to write ghost stories. She was also the mother of Byron's ill-fated daughter, Allegra. A fictionalised version of Claire Clairmont is at the heart of Henry James' 1888 novella The Aspern Papers.

The 'Wind' in Wind Street in Swansea is always pronounced to rhyme with 'find' and can sometimes sound like Wine Street if the 'd' drops away. The second-hand bookshop there is an invention and not to be confused with either Ralph the Books or Dylan's Bookstore. Many places are otherwise real, and some still exist – in particular the Kardomah, which is little changed from the 1960s to this day. The mansion that once stood at Penllergare has gone but the beautiful, extensive grounds and lake remain thanks to the Penllergare Trust. The characters in the twentieth century part of this novel are not based on any person living or deceased.

ACKNOWLEDGEMENTS

I am extremely grateful to The Royal Literary Fund, the P D James Memorial Fund and The Society of Authors for their generous and practical support and unstinting encouragement over the years – many of my books would not exist without them.

I'd also like to thank Bronwen Price and the team at Seren, particularly Simon Hicks who nudged me into resurrecting the corpse of this book and suggested the title, as well as my editor Alison Layland.

For keeping me sane (just about) I would like to give love and thanks to my husband, Mark Matthews.

No book or author quite exists in a vacuum and I'm grateful to the family and friends who have supported me along the way in my slightly errant writing life; in no particular order they are: Rosa Truelove, Laurel Goss, John Lavin, Katy Train, John Goodby, Kathryn Gray, Gill Godfrey, Nico Jenkins, Meg Jenkins, Nigel Jarrett, Kevin Sinnott, Shani Rhys James, Gareth Southwell, Tim Pears, Richard Cooper and finally, Max Sommers who died suddenly in 2021.

ABOUT THE AUTHOR

Jo Mazelis is a novelist, poet, short story writer and photographer living in Swansea. Her first novel *Significance* (Seren Books, 2014) won the 2015 Jerwood Fiction Uncovered Prize. Her collection of stories, *Diving Girls*, was shortlisted for the Commonwealth 'Best First Book' and Wales Book of the Year. Her second book, *Circle Games*, was longlisted for Wales Book of the Year. Her stories have been broadcast on BBC Radio 4, published in various anthologies and magazines, and translated into Danish. Her third collection of stories *Ritual, 1969* (Seren Books, 2016) was shortlisted for Wales Book of the Year and longlisted for the Edge Hill Prize 2017. *Blister & other Stories* was shortlisted for the International Rubery Award.